all for show

Courtney Mariah

Copyright © 2020 Courtney Mariah

www.writingsonthewalls.com

All rights reserved.

This book is for my family, friends and everyone who said I could do it.

I did it y'all!

The Good News/Bad News

NIA

"What do you mean, you submitted me for a reality dating show?"

Stopping abruptly on the sidewalk, Nia Austin stared at her phone, making sure she was talking to the right person. Adjusting her phone so she could see the screen, Nia double checked that the name was in fact Lexie Whitmore, Nia's agent and supposed friend, who should definitely know how Nia felt about reality shows by this point in their relationship.

Around her, foot traffic adjusted, though tourists and locals grumbled as they dodged her still form on the sidewalk. An older woman didn't bother to stop, whacking her bag into Nia and breaking her balance. It was almost like being back in New York, except for the cool (well, Los Angeles cool) weather. Though it was nearing noon, outside was still a chilly sixty degrees with the threat of rain overhead. Contrary to the lyrics of a popular song, it did rain in southern California, but Nia loved it. It was the perfect time to stay home with a book or glass of wine and listen to some music or binge watch a show. She however, was on her way to meet her roommate Goldie at her shop on Melrose Avenue for lunch, and had decided to walk there instead of giving up her street parking space. It was a short walk, only about a half hour, but with the sudden hint of rain Nia made a mental note to catch a ride share back home. Calculating the cost quickly in her head, she figured it would be alright, and could maybe still order in for dinner. Maybe.

"You still there?" Lexie's voice came through the ear piece distantly.

Lifting the phone back to her ear, "Yeah, I had to make sure I was talking to the right person." It wasn't that Nia absolutely hated reality television; it was a passable form of entertainment with a group of friends and a large glass (or glasses) of wine. But to Nia, reality television was full of wanna be famous people and fabricated social drama that she could stomach only every now and then. And to work in it was something Nia had never wanted to stoop to do. Ever. She had principles, after all. "I'd rather repeat my middle school years than do a reality TV show."

"God, you're so dramatic."

"Thank goodness I'm in the right business then."

Lexie snorted over the line, drawing a reluctant smile out of Nia. She could practically see Lexie in her office, probably multi-tasking on at least three other things while she was on the phone in a badass outfit. Lexie was one of those annoyingly productive people, who had never met a goal she couldn't meet on or ahead of schedule. Nothing flustered her, and she was on a steady upward climb in her career, kicking ass and taking names. But she was also one of the most genuine people Nia had met in vain Los Angeles, and a karaoke fiend.

It was actually a stroke of good fortune when they'd met; Nia had been freshly back to Los Angeles trying to get some sort of representation and was failing miserably. Nia's little sister Yaya and Goldie had dragged her over to a karaoke bar in Culver City that had been more fun that she'd anticipated. When Nia was called up to sing "Mr. Brightside," she was surprised when some random woman in an amazing coral blazer started belting it out with her. The woman added her support to Nia, along with Goldie and Yaya, and the four of them had danced like crazy people, laughing and acting like they were in their own music video.

After, when Nia invited her over to their table, they'd all bonded and folded Lexie into their group. It wasn't long before Nia learned that Lexie was a growing talent agent. Lexie, hearing that Nia was still looking for an agent, took a chance and added Nia to her roster for representation, which she would be forever grateful for. Lexie had said to Nia that she would always give a fellow Black woman a chance, and Nia was determined to make them both some money. Opportunities had definitely opened up more since then, but it was still tough finding roles that didn't put Nia into a stereotypical category and would let her talent shine. That was one of the things Nia appreciated most about Lexie, was that she didn't just throw anything at Nia. She wanted to help shape her career in a meaningful way, and Nia had a lot of respect for her because of that. But that meant a lot of rejection, due to her constant applying to roles that didn't specifically ask for her race.

Seeing the pedestrian traffic light already counting down from five, Nia hustled to the intersection, where she was solidly in the middle of Fairfax Avenue when the light turned red. A car honked at her to hurry up and move, and Nia rewarded their patience with a flip of the bird. Maybe not the most mature, but definitely satisfying.

"Are you doing that thing where you cross the street like an asshole again?" Lexie's amusement came through the line, reminding Nia that she was still on a call.

"Not like an ass, just like an opportunistic individual."

"This isn't New York, you know. No one walks in LA, it's a driving city."

"Sure, but that's also why the air quality is so bad. I'm doing my part. However, you're not going to distract me from the issue at hand; why in the world would you submit me for a reality dating show?" Making it to the sidewalk, Nia ducked into a coffee shop, and smiled at the barista behind the counter. "Can I get two mocha lattes to go?"

"To clarify, it's to be the *host* of a reality dating show, not an actual participant." Lexie's holier than thou voice was a little smug. "The submission felt warranted."

"Ah, you found a loop hole." Swiping her card, Nia left a generous tip and went to the side of the counter to wait for her name to be called. She'd been a barista in college and had appreciated the good tip days. Now, she tried to pay it forward when she could.

"I'm good at that." Nia wasn't actually mad at Lexie, who was honestly amazing at her job. Lexie was trying to get Nia booked on something, anything really. Her last gig had been longer ago than Nia wanted to admit, and they both were getting antsy. Her bank account was barely in the positive, and she'd had to pick up extra shifts at her parents' restaurant to make her portion of rent. Even though Nia worked hard for her checks with her parents, it still felt like they were giving her an allowance at age almost thirty…and that was something Nia hated. She'd never wanted to be the kid that needed her parent's help this late in the game, even though she worked for her checks and wasn't just taking handouts.

For quite possibly the hundredth time Nia wondered if she was crazy for pursing this acting dream. Whoever said being an actress was easy work had clearly never tried to make a living doing it. Between constant classes to improve herself, endless networking and countless auditions, keeping her headshots up to date, it was like an endless stream of rejection that had taken over Nia's life. She tried not to be so pessimistic about it – this was not a business for people with thin skin. But it was getting tougher and tougher to not be at least a little jaded at this point.

Life as an aspiring actress in Los Angeles was hard enough, especially when it seemed like there were younger, hotter, more talented people moving into the city by the hour. Add on top the fact that Nia had more hips and butt than your average wannabe Kim Kardashian or Beyoncé, and coily hair that had a mind of its own, she had a harder time than most.

It wasn't that Nia was a bad actress – at least she didn't think so – it was that it was such a saturated market. And being a black actress, a lot of the parts that Nia fit the bill for were for sassy sidekicks or token roles that Nia was determined not to take. She wanted the good stuff, the leading lady material. Unfortunately, there was a dearth of people willing to take that risk on a relatively unknown actor. But Nia and Lexie had standards, and was determined to find roles that she could actually shine in. That sometimes meant that she went a while without work, but it was worth it. Nia was lucky enough to be able to pick up work in her family's restaurants around town if jobs were scarce, but she knew that not everyone was as lucky as she was. And if she couldn't make it work? Well, she didn't want to think about that.

But the reality show gig, much as Nia hated to admit, would be a godsend. It had been a bumpy ride in the four years since she'd graduated from the Tisch drama program at New York University and moved back to California. She'd gotten a few small parts here and there, mostly on student films, some as one or two-day shoots on television shows, but nothing really meaty. There was a national dental commercial that Nia landed, and those residuals always came in at just the right moment, but that was the last 'big' thing she'd done. Nia could feel the doubts about when, or if, she'd actually have a chance to prove herself getting louder in her mind. It was hard, trying to remain upbeat in the face of so much rejection, but Nia had turned over a new leaf after certain college events with He-Who-Is-Dead-To-Her and was not in the habit of admitting defeat so easily these days. The old Nia would have given up by now. Which is why she would probably consider this job…

"Alright Lex, tell me about this gig." Grabbing the coffees, Nia opened the door with her hip and continued down the sidewalk.

"It's a new Netflix dating show called With This Ring, and you'd be flown out to Oahu, all expenses paid, and stay at a resort off the beach for two months, March and April. The contestants are competing to become the bachelor's fiancé, and they have to do all kinds of crazy things to prove their love to this guy."

"March? That's next month." Nia walked into Let's Chakra Bout It, the reiki shop ran by her roommate Goldie Perez, who looked up at the chimes that sounded with the opening of the door. She waved from behind the counter, but kept her focus on a customer who was asking about a few crystals and their properties. Nia slid the mocha over where Goldie would see it, who gave a distracted wave while keeping the conversation open with the customer. Nia gave her some space, and wandered to the far side of the shop.

Goldie was one of those naturally attractive people who could literally never take a bad photo. She had gorgeous dark hair with golden tips that was a fantastic mane around her face, and long lashed almond shaped eyes in naturally tanned skin.

Her looks would be intimidating except for the welcoming personality that Goldie had. She never met a stranger, and was skilled at making people feel comfortable around her. Nia had known Goldie since their high school days, and they'd stayed in touch though they'd went to schools on different coasts. When Nia came back and mentioned she was looking for a roommate, Goldie had just gotten out of a bad relationship and was looking for someone else to move into her West Hollywood apartment. The two of them had been roomies since.

Nia looked out the window just as rain started falling outside. "Why so soon?"

"Get this - their initial host they had lined up broke both her legs, so they're scrambling to find a replacement."

"Ouch, that's got to sting." Nia winced, looking down at her own perfectly functioning legs and said a small thanks to the universe.

"Her pain is your gain." Lexie was unapologetic.

"Savage. What's the interview process like, when is it?" Goldie's eyes lit up at that, and she was doing all she could to not pepper Nia with questions. She hurriedly rang up her customer and waved her out the door before coming up behind Nia, obviously eavesdropping.

"About that - they're doing interviews today. Tight schedule and everything."

"Today? When and where?" Alarms were going off in Nia's head - she'd figure it would come soon, but not *today* soon. It wasn't enough time to prepare at all. She'd figured they'd interview her tomorrow or the day after, but today?

"Don't freak out, you've got a few hours. The interview isn't until three o'clock in Burbank, and it's just now noon."

"That's only three hours from now, not even enough time to prepare." Her mind whirled, judging how long it would take to get home, get ready, and get to Burbank from their West Hollywood apartment.

"Girl, you got this. I wouldn't have put you up for it if I didn't think you could nail this job. They just want someone with personality, and lord knows you have that by the boat load."

"I wasn't freaking, I was just expressing myself." Nia could see Goldie rolling her eyes at her, who knew that she was most definitely freaking. Nia would tap her thumb on the nearest surface or body part as her brain processed information – and she was doing it now.

"And it would be really great if you did book it – I'm getting pressure from the agency. It's been a while since your last gig and they're talking about trimming the fat."

The message was loud and clear – Nia needed to land this job or she risked losing Lexie as an agent. If that happened, it would make finding jobs that much harder in an already tough market. An icy wave washed over Nia as the seriousness of her situation really set in.

"Don't worry, I'm going to nail this audition. No more freaking out, I swear." At least, not out loud. Inside, Nia was a mess. She could feel the pressure ballooning up in her chest as she thought about how in the world she would book this job.

"Well…I haven't told you everything, so you might have cause to freak out a teeny tiny little bit."

Those alarms in Nia's head were at red alert now, blaring and demanding attention. Old Nia stood at attention, sniffing fear in the air. Lexie was always cool as a blast from a heavy-duty freezer, but there was something in her voice that made Nia's hairs stand up. For her to say there might be something worrisome about the job, however slight, was enough to make Nia nervous.

"Lay it on me."

There was a brief pause on the line. Goldie even leaned closer, waiting to hear. "The bachelor? It's Elijah James."

Well, hell.

Elijah James was not a name Nia wanted or expected to hear, at all. A successful actor, having had key roles in several blockbusters and indie films Elijah James was on the cusp of outright stardom. Attractive as sin, with dark hair, green eyes, and a face that was meant for the angels, Elijah had a perennial reputation as a womanizer, always with some pretty little thing on his arm. He also happened to be Nia's 'What If' guy; they'd gone to college together, Elijah having been a year ahead in the drama program.

"I thought you knew how to ice skate?" Nia threw the teasing words Elijah, who was barely managing to stay upright on his feet. It was another freezing day in New York, a fresh layer of snow having fallen the night before, thought it was now mixed in with whatever the disgusting street sludge consisted of, turning it inky black. They were at Bryant Park, having decided to make the most of a lovely day, and go skating. The sun glittered off the ice as Nia skated back to Elijah, showing off her limited skills as he clutched the wall beside him. "I should have known, with your tendency to exaggerate."

"Not everything." There was a glimmer of heat in his eyes, and Nia was reminded of how he'd woken her up that morning."

"Ok, not everything."

"Why don't you come over here and help me?" Elijah's rich, smooth voice was like a career to Nia's ears. She slid to a stop in front of him, and held out her hands.

"Take my hand."

HIs hands covered hers, warm even without gloves, their fingers lacing together as she slowly moved them around the ice. Elijah's balance was terrible, and he leaned his weight heavily onto her, but Nia liked it, liked the way they moved together and the necessary closeness it created. They made it around a full circle before Nia dared to let him go on his own. "Think you can do it on your own, Vanilla Ice?"

"You calling me a one hit wonder?" Suddenly Elijah was skating like a pro, doing laps and skating backwards with an ease that showed exactly how comfortable he was on the ice.

"You tricked me." Nia faked a pout before a laugh broke through.

"I just wanted to hold your hand." His smile, his dark hair that was burned red in the sun, his young beauty made Nia lose her breath for a moment, a small smile on her face. And then his lips caught hers, and she was the one who felt wobbly on the ice.

Nia and Elijah had been slightly more than regular hookup buddies, but never advanced to anything beyond than that. Elijah had always managed to avoid the conversation, and Nia was young and dumb enough to believe that if she stayed with him, he'd eventually come around. Instead, Elijah ended up ghosting her his senior year after landing what would be the breakout role that launched his career. She hadn't heard from him since, and only saw him when he popped up in movies and television shows when she least expected it. It was a mild heartbreak, really.

That was a Lie, and Nia knew it. It had broken her, the first time she'd really cared about anyone as much as she had with Elijah.

It only took Nia about two years to start dating again, and three to stop comparing him to everyone else she dated after that. Most people, when ghosted, weren't treated to images of their exes on fifty foot screens or in the comfort of their living room on the television, but Nia was obviously being tortured for past misdeeds of another life. She wasn't hung up about it though. At all. It hadn't devastated her and made her even more determined to be a successful actress in her own right, so she could rub it in his face. Nia had managed to move on with her life. But life had jokes. And it was on her, apparently.

"You still there?" Lexie's voice came through the line, while Nia wrapped her mind around the fact that she might be working with the guy who broke her heart. Goldie took the phone from Nia, and hit the speaker phone button.

"I'm tired of listening in the background. Lex? What did you say to her?"

"Just that she'd be auditioning for a dating show with Elijah James as the bachelor."

Goldie's jaw dropped. "Lexie!"

"I did not think she would take it this way." Lexie's concerned voice brought Nia back to the conversation.

"I'm fine you two." Nia shook off the mental fog and took the phone back from Goldie. "That was just very unexpected."

"I know, and I swear I didn't know before I submitted you for the show, or else I would have passed it over. But it's such a good opportunity, and if you do well, there's potential to come back as the host for future seasons and a steady paycheck."

"They can't change the bachelor?" Nia asked, not completely joking.

"Girl, no."

"Right." It wasn't how Nia wanted to see him again. She'd wanted to maybe accidentally run into him on a set, both of them powerful actors in their own right, and reject him when he tried to win her back...but it wasn't going to happen like that. She had bills to pay and was in no position to turn down work when it presented itself to her, and he was obviously doing well. "You can tell them I'll be there."

"Are you sure? I can find you something else-"

"I'll do it. It's just an audition, right? Anything could happen." But it wasn't just an audition. Nia needed to nail this, and bring in some more work or else she'd be out an agent, no matter how good a friend.

"This is why I love you. Ok great, I'll tell them to expect you and email you the details."

"Drinks are on you though. The next three rounds, actually."

"Every round is on me, you're a starving artist." That got a laugh out of Nia.

"It's the gesture that matters. I'll let you know how it goes."

Hanging up, Nia leaned against the counter, wanting to press her face against the cool glass, but didn't want to make Goldie wipe up her face smudges.

"You good girl? Do you want to do this?" Goldie picked up her phone, opening up an astrology app. "I wonder what your horoscope says for today because that is some crazy coincidences right there."

"I don't want to do this, but what choice do I have? I need the work."

"Maybe you don't get the job, it's not set in stone."

"But I need it. Lexie basically said that the agency is thinking about dropping me if I don't start booking more work."

"Damn girl. But nothing happens without reason, the good, the bad, the ugly. And if the universe is bringing Elijah James back into your life, then you better be ready to knock his socks off and show him what he's missing."

"Like he's really missing out on ramen noodle and Korean Drama nights with me."

"Don't talk down on K-Drama days. Those are sacred." Nia laughed at the seriousness on Goldie's face.

"I'm serious. Go out there and show him and those producers and casting director what they're missing. You're amazing girl, and don't let anyone tell you otherwise."

Pushing off the counter, Nia grabbed her purse. "Have I ever mentioned how much I love your pep talks?"

"You could stand to do it more often."

"As you wish. Are you ok if I do a rain check on lunch? I want to get home and change before heading over to Burbank."

"Go ahead – but I want to hear all the details tonight when you get back."

"Of course." Nia pulled out her phone to call for a ride. She wondered if she would see Elijah today, and then immediately chucked that thought out the window. What did she care if she saw him today? But still, some little feeling tickled her heart, whispering to her that she wanted to see Elijah again. That was something Nia would worry about later. Right now, she had to nail this audition, and worrying about Elijah was not part of the plan. And now, Nia had to track down her Uber driver, who was not where he should be. Ducking across the street, Nia let thoughts of Elijah James fall away. She had work to do.

The Audition

ELIJAH

Elijah James, slouched in his uncomfortable chair, was wondering what would happen if he just closed his eyes and nodded anytime someone asked him a question. Testing the theory, he closed his eyes and slumped even further down in his chair.

They kept talking.

Elijah sighed mentally, wishing he were anywhere but here. It wasn't like they were really asking his opinion about the women they were casting – Warren Alexander II and his fellow producers were determined to pick the most dramatic, television worthy individuals in order to make sure that the show was as energetic as possible. Elijah was purely ornamental at this point, a prop to see how the women reacted in his presence.

"Remind me why I agreed to do this again? It feels like a step backwards." Elijah slumped ungracefully back into his seat in the sterile casting room as Warren paced the room, somehow still grossly energetic despite having just scarfed down an obscene number of tacos for lunch just a half hour before. Elijah had been impressed with how much Warren had tucked away, especially given how thin he was. The burrito, chips and guacamole and churros that Elijah had eaten had filled him up, and all he wanted to do was go home to his couch and turn on the NBA playoffs, maybe take a nap. Dim overhead lights and grey walls didn't help the situation either.

"You're doing this as a favor to get in the good graces of Chris Parker and his wonderful production company, so you actually have a shot at playing Commander Hex in this life time." Warren wasn't even slightly put off by Elijah's acerbic nature.

Right. Elijah had gotten caught up in a massive scandal when he'd supposedly started a raging affair with his ex-girlfriend Emma Jones, a pretty starlet that was now married to some hot shot producer. In actuality, Elijah had simply been photographed in the wrong place at the wrong time and the press ran with the story. It didn't help that Emma didn't even try to come to his defense, making it sound like Elijah wanted her back and was trying to encourage her to leave her husband. Any time Elijah had tried to deny it, Emma would negate what he said, gossip blogs would run with it, and it was another round of he said she said. Elijah had just stopped talking about it and laid low, hoping it would stop soon.

It had actually blown over for the most part, but Chris Parker was family man, and as such, was not entirely certain that Elijah would have the mass appeal that he was looking for. Elijah had learned from Carter Graham, his best friend who worked at

Parker's production company, that he was not thrilled with the idea of someone with a 'reputation' going into a movie that was supposed to have mass appeal to families.

That had been an unexpected blow in Elijah's career plans.

Which was why when Warren sent this job to Elijah's agent, his manager encouraged Elijah to take it. It would fill the gap in his schedule and put him back on Parker's short list, in a roundabout way. It was one of the things Elijah hated about Hollywood life, the amount of brown nosing he had to do to make himself likable enough to be remembered in the right rooms. Hollywood was all about relationships, who you knew, and more importantly, who knew you. Elijah was tired of playing the game, of balancing on the cusp of almost hitting his goal, only to miss it at the last minute. He'd always wanted to be able to have parts that spoke to audiences, and was ready to upgrade to the big leagues. Playing a superhero felt like a defining way to reach that goal. But this felt like a major backwards step.

"This better work. I can only imagine what people will have to say about this."

"They'll say it's about time you settled down and start thinking about a family. Besides, you should be stoked to spend some of the coldest months of LA on a frigging island surrounded by hotties fighting for your attention." Warren sighed, looking over some of the headshots.

"You sure you don't want this gig?" Elijah was concerned with the look Warren was making at the photos.

"I wish. They wouldn't know what to do with me. But I'll have my fun." Warren licked his lips as he looked at another photo.

Elijah, now very uncomfortable, changed the subject. "How many more interviews do I have left to sit through?

Warren shuffled through the remaining photos. "There's eight women left, and then we'll narrow it down to the finalists."

Elijah sighed, mentally preparing to turn on the charm. He could make it through this, and if he was being completely honest with himself, he did want a shot at playing in the next cinematic comic universe.

"Oh, and we're also holding a couple last minute interviews for the host position after Willow, the initial host we had broke both her legs up at Big Bear a week ago."

"Ouch."

"She should have stuck with the bunny slopes." Warren shrugged, unconcerned.

"She was on the bunny slopes, apparently." They both looked up as Kerry Trent entered, having caught the tail end of their conversation. She was with Isaac Union, another producer, and Linda, the casting director, each holding fresh cups of coffee. They found seats at the table, Kerry taking the seat next to Elijah and rolled her eyes. "It was her first time skiing as well."

Elijah shook his head. "Bad idea, right before a shoot."

"But that coffee looks like a good idea." Warren moved toward the door. "I'll be back in second and we'll get started. Oh, and Eli - the host headshots are in there, a Nia and a Melanie. You're welcome to stick around for those interviews as well, for some eye candy. The first one is my favorite." With a salacious wink, Warren darted out the door.

Kerry looked over at Elijah, and rolled her eyes. "It's almost like he's picking women that interest him, and not you, the bachelor."

"What gave you that impression?" Elijah touched his chest dramatically, a faux look of shock on his face.

Kerry and Isaac both laughed, knowing that Warren was one of the tamer examples of higher ups willing to abuse their power for a pretty thing to look at. There were worse people out there for sure, and for the most part, Warren was harmless.

The name Nia stuck with Elijah. He wondered…no, it couldn't be *her*. There were probably a million other Nia's out there. What would be the odds of that ever happening?

Elijah's curiosity wasn't settled with that thought though. It was probably a long shot - he hadn't seen or heard from Nia Austin in years, since he left in college like the asshole he'd been back then. As casually as he could manage, Elijah picked up the pile of headshots left and started going through them. A few pictures later and he found himself staring into Nia's memorable almond brown eyes.

The breath left his chest. It was her. Nia Austin, the woman who'd been so good to him and he'd screwed it up. The years had been more than kind to her. Rich, smooth brown skin with golden undertones and a tapered halo of curls that refused to be tamed, Nia's smile touched a cold spot on his heart that hadn't been reached in a long time. And she was coming here, today. That thought caused his heart to pound like it did whenever he was heading in to an audition, his nerves ratcheting all the way up.

Back in college, she'd been quiet and studious. He'd noticed her back at NYU when she moved into the same dorm as him his junior year, and had seen her around campus pretty often when she had later transferred from her marketing major to the dramatic arts program. Elijah hadn't understood what made her switch in the first place, and was curious when she showed up in one of the same film theory lectures that he was taking. They'd actually ended up working on a short film together at one point – the initial actress had gotten sick and Elijah had suggested to Nia's roommate Sarah, who was directing the project, that Nia fill in. That was when he'd officially met and had a conversation with Nia for the first time.

Elijah had found himself enjoying shooting their scenes together. She'd surprised him with her wit and humor, opening up and revealing a vivacious personality as she got to know him better. After they were done filming for the day, he'd asked her out for a slice of pizza (from one of those dollar slice places, because he was broke back then, but they were also so greasy and delicious) and that's where their pseudo relationship blossomed. They'd become something more than hookup buddies, though he had pumped the breaks anytime she mentioned them putting a label on it. Because he'd been scared, he could admit that now. He hadn't wanted anyone else to have her, but he was also terrified of the depth of emotion that he was developing for her. It had scared him then, and he'd been too immature to handle it properly.

That was something he still regretted to this day. Nia had been one of his favorite parts of college and he threw it away without any explanation to her, falling into the typical 'real men don't talk about their feelings' trap. But for him to run into her now, after all this time? He wondered if it was a sign or some astrological shit his buddy Carter was always spouting.

Warren came back in, holding his cup of coffee and pep in his step. Elijah pushed the photos aside, and tried not to look like he was paying any one photo a lot of attention.

"Ready to get part two started?" Warren asked the room, no doubt expecting them to break out in cheers. Everyone just nodded, and Kerry sent Logan, her assistant, to bring in the next girl.

Time to put on his game face. He'd see Nia soon enough. Elijah leaned back into his seat, ready to start, a little more excitement in his demeanor now that he knew he'd see her. The first woman that came in immediately burst into tears when she saw Elijah in the room.

"You're Elijah James!" Another round of tears.

"Last time that I checked." Elijah smiled at her and her knees buckled.

"Yes, he's here to start meeting some of you." Kerry looked at Elijah, a sympathetic wince in her expression.

"Are you going to marry me?" The woman looked at Elijah with huge, watery eyes. He didn't know how to answer to that without more tears.

"Um, maybe?"

She started sobbing even harder. Elijah awkwardly gave her a hug before Logan escorted her out. Logan's dark lined eyes definitely had things to say, but professionally, he held them in. The next woman, Erin, was only slightly better. She thought she was God's gift to men, apparently, and was so sure Elijah would fall for her overly pouty lips and not so subtle words.

"Why do you think you'd be a good fit for the show?" Kerry asked, tapping a pen to her lips.

"I've been told I fit perfectly," Erin threw a wink at Elijah, "and I know that I'd make a good, dedicated little wife."

Isaac shared a look with Kerry before looking at Elijah and Warren. They ended that interview relatively quickly after that. The following women were a bit better, and they managed to have normal, civilized conversations. After the last woman left, Isaac turned to Elijah, stretching a little.

"If you want, you can head out now. We've just got these two interviews left and then that's it for the day."

"I can stay. For moral support." Elijah was calm on the outside, but his heart beat a little bit faster at the thought that Nia would be there, soon. Logan brought in Melanie first, who was perfectly charming, if a little predictable. But Warren liked her, and kept the interview going a little longer than necessary. Elijah had to reign in his impatience. He was so close to seeing Nia, and Warren was definitely dragging this along for his own sick pleasure. Finally, the woman left, and Logan went out to bring in Nia.

Elijah felt his palms get sweaty, and rubbed them on his jeans underneath the table. He hadn't been this nervous in a while, which made no sense. He was just running into the woman he'd compared all other women to after all this time. Piece of cake.

The door opened, and Elijah got his first look at Nia in four years. She looked even better in person, and their eyes connected immediately. Her eyes widened slightly, as she took him in at the table before shuttering closed with a professional smile. Elijah couldn't help noting the lush curves that begged to have a hand caress over them, but also her more open personality than she'd had a few years ago. Nia seemed to have come into her own, and Elijah smiled at that. Her smile was still just as he remembered, at least the one she aimed at others. The smile Nia gave him was not the one he wanted, just a little tight around the edges, but Elijah knew he didn't deserve it. As Warren started asking questions, Elijah leaned in, ready to hear what Nia had to say.

NIA

Nia tried to keep as much confidence in her walk as possible as she stepped to the middle of the casting room, facing the table filled with producers, and of course, Elijah. She was glad that Lexie had given her a heads up; Nia had a feeling that if she didn't, she might have done something regretfully embarrassing, like trip or make a fool of herself. The mantra that she'd stuck to played in her head – *I am in charge of how I feel. I am successful. I am more than enough.*

Straightening her shoulders, Nia addressed the table. "Hi, I'm Nia. Thanks for having me here today."

A soft brown skinned woman smiled warmly at Nia. "Hi, I'm Kerry. Thanks for coming out at such a short notice, Nia. I know it probably wasn't easy."

"A little spontaneity never hurt anyone." Nia smiled, determined to not let them know she was even a teensy bit flustered. She could feel Elijah staring at her, and pointedly ignored those green eyes of his tracking up and down her body.

Kerry pointed at the people around her. "This is Isaac, Warren, Linda. You probably recognized Elijah James already."

"Hard to miss him." Nia could do this. As long as she didn't look at Elijah.

"Well let's get this started, yeah?" Warren took control of the conversation, and Nia directed her attention to him. "We're just going to ask you a few questions, answer how you would. All we're looking for is what your sparkling personality has to say." Did he just wink at her? No, she was making that up. But then he winked again, and Nia sighed internally. It wasn't that she had never been hit on in a casting room; she had been. But it always made her want to double down and be a bitch. Unfortunately, she needed this job and was running out of options.

Smiling, she easily made her way through the first volley of questions, where she was from, her favorite spot for tacos, telling an embarrassing childhood memory. It was simple enough, playing part, and Nia hoped she was charming them with her answers. But then, Elijah had to open his mouth. "Have you ever hooked up with a random stranger?"

Nia paused, off track. "Why, are you volunteering?" She did not mean to say that, but it got a laugh from the rest of the room. She might as well roll with it. "I don't kiss and tell, I'm a lady. Unless there was something worth sharing, of course." She added a wink at the producers, and watched as Warren ate it up. Elijah had a tiny smirk on his face that Nia remembered - it usually meant trouble.

"That's respectable. I live by the same principle." Elijah looked thoughtful.

"That's hard to believe with your reputation." Nia knew all about him and his womanizing tendencies. Everyone did.

"Do you always believe the tabloids?

"Only when I have yet to see any evidence to the contrary."

"Don't believe everything you read." There was a subtle tensing of his jaw that Nia noticed immediately. It was always his tell, that he was agitated about something. *Good*, Nia thought. *He should be just as worked up as I am.*

Elijah settled into his chair, watching her. "How was your last date?"

That was unexpected. "Disappointing."

"Ah. That's…predictable."

Nia's jaw dropped. Did he really just…?

"Excuse me?"

"You seem like the type to ask a lot of a partner." He was definitely pushing buttons now.

"The sex was great, he just had commitment issues like most LA men." With a deliberate pause, Nia looked Elijah up and down. "Present company excluded, of course."

She watched as her words hit the intended mark. Elijah's eyes narrowed, and he shifted in his seat. "You wound us, Ms. Austin."

"I speak from experience, unfortunately."

Their eyes collided, and Nia saw the questions, and a hint of apology in Elijah's expression. For a moment, it was just the two of them in the room and Nia was hyper aware of the heat flooding her face as their eyes searched each other's. She could feel the swelling of emotion in her chest, and struggled to break free of Elijah's gaze.

Blinking, Nia tried to steer the conversation back to Kerry and Warren, who were watching her back and forth with Elijah with amusement. "I'm so sorry, I feel like we got off track…"

"Experience, huh? What's the most risqué thing you've ever done?" Elijah threw out the question, which made Nia's head whip back over to him. She immediately thought of the time they'd gone to Rockaway beach one summer and done dirty things in the water, under full view of anyone else who bothered to look closely. It had been one of the hottest moments of Nia's life, and if she needed to get off fast, that's what usually came to mind. But Elijah didn't need to know that he was still the best sex of her life, and that made her mad. Nia hated that he had set the bar so high, and had prayed fervently for someone who could make her forget him. But that person hadn't come along yet, and so she was left with a mixed bag of emotions.

Looking him up and down, she let a smirk play over her lips. "You wouldn't even believe it."

"Try me." Their eyes locked, Elijah's challenging hers and letting heat fill them up. God, the chemistry was still there, much as Nia hated to admit it. She wanted to know more about adult Elijah, what he liked now, what they'd be like together. Which was crazy talk. She wasn't here to date him. She was here to get a job, which reminded her that there were other people in the room. And they were all waiting for her to say something.

Nia's mouth opened before she shut it quickly. Allowing a smirk on her face, she looked him up and down. "That's private information, unfortunately."

And swear to God, Nia watched as Elijah flushed, clearly remembering something about the two of them.

Warren jumped in, very interested. "I definitely want to hear that story sometime." He was practically salivating over the words.

Isaac and Kerry nodded in agreement, looking more interested in Nia than they had a few moments ago. Thankfully, conversation went back to a more neutral topic, before Warren asked one last question.

"Why do you want to be on this show?"

Nia thought about that for a moment. "Reality television was never my career goal. But I'm always open to trying new things, and seeing where it takes me. This seems like the perfect opportunity."

Kerry jumped in, curious. "Do you watch reality shows?"

Nia hedged, before answering honestly. "No…not super often. Occasionally I will, with my friends."

They looked at each other, and Nia just knew that was the wrong thing to say. She'd screwed up. It was like an icy wave crashing over her and she had to fight to keep from beating herself up over it. Kerry smiled at Nia, and thanked her for her time, effectively dismissing Nia from the room. She gathered her bag and jacket, and left the grey room, making it down the hallway and outside into the cold air, the light rain having stopped a while ago. She had no one else to be mad at except herself. Nia unlocked her car and sat in it, not turning it on just yet. Her head fell to the steering wheel, and she focused on her mantra. *I am in charge of how I feel.*

Realistically, Nia knew that the interview went mostly well, up until the last part. She was trying not to let that little moment throw her off, but it was hard. Annoyingly, Nia could feel the prickle of tears at her eyes. All she'd had to do was go in and nail this audition, book the job, and she'd be set. But now, it was hard, knowing that she could have hurt her chances.

Much as she wanted to blame it on seeing Elijah, Nia wondered for what felt like the millionth time, *Should I give up on acting?* It was a thought that had been plaguing her for a while now. Nia was struggling to justify the continued journey. Her parents were constantly worried about her ability to care for herself, Nia was never the one able to treat her friends to dinner or drinks, and she didn't know how much more rejection she could take.

The pinging of her phone pierced her melancholy, and she saw a message from Lexie, no doubt wanting to know how the audition went. Later, she'd tell Lexie about it. But right now, she wanted a milk shake. After seeing her not quite an ex after four years, and possibly bombing an audition, she figured she could use the treat.

A knock on the window scared the breath out of her. Looking up, Nia saw Elijah at her window, gesturing for her to roll it down. Of course he was here. Nia sighed. *My milkshake,* she thought glumly. The milkshake would have to wait.

The Car Ride

NIA

Elijah waved again, gesturing for her to roll the window down. Did he follow her out here? *What could he possibly want?* Nia wondered if she ignored him long enough, maybe he'd just go away? She closed her eyes and started counting to ten.

"I'm not going anywhere Nia. Roll down the window. Please?"

Sighing, she cracked it open. "What do you want?"

"Can I have a ride?"

Nia's eyebrows rose high in confusion. That was not what she was expecting. "Can you have a ride?"

"My car is in the shop, so I Ubered here."

"And what, I look like I drive for Uber?" Elijah didn't have to know that she did, in fact drive for Uber some weekends. "You can Uber home." Nia started to roll up her window, but his hand came up as if to grab it before he checked himself.

"Please? I really want to talk to you."

"But I really don't want to talk to you." Ok, that was a Lie. Nia had a range of questions ranging from "Why the hell did he ghost me?" to "Why the hell do I still compare everyone else to you?" but those weren't likely to have answers she'd be happy with. And he looked good. Better than good. Nia had thought that she'd be used to his face, considering the amount of times he'd popped up on her screens, but the magnetism Elijah radiated was much, much stronger in person. That was half the problem: this man ghosted her and she was still attracted to him? She needed to keep the distance between the two of them. Preferably a few states.

Somewhere nearby, a door opened and Nia could hear voices approaching. Elijah turned begging eyes on her.

"Please Nia? Just this once?"

She knew she would regret this, but found herself unlocking her car anyway. "Get in."

Elijah ran around to the passenger side and slid into the seat, buckling his seatbelt as if he anticipated her throwing him out of her car…which was still a possibility.

"Thank you for this. I live out in Santa Monica."

Nia almost kicked him out right there. "Excuse me?" She thought about the traffic going from Burbank to Santa Monica in rush hour and cried a little inside. That milk shake was looking more and more like a dream. If she did get it, there had to be liquor added to it. Maybe Kahlua?

Elijah broke out in laughter, jerking Nia's attention back to him. "I'm joking! I just wanted to see what you would do if I did live there. My place is in Los Feliz." Grabbing her phone, he put his address into her GPS system and leaned back into his seat. Interestingly, Elijah lived about ten minutes away from her, without traffic. She tucked that information away for when she could think about it more.

Nia let a tiny smile crack. "I was about to drop you at the nearest bus stop."

Elijah fell dramatically back against the seat. "You would leave me like that?"

"My bad, I clearly had the roles reversed." Nia couldn't help saying, and watched as Elijah went quiet. She could feel him looking at her as she drove and wondered what he was thinking. *Did I make it awkward?*

Nia brushed that off. So what if she'd made things awkward. One of the things Nia had learned after Elijah unceremoniously dumped her was to say what was on her mind. It helped her avoid disappointment in the future, and made her feel like she had some control in her life. But right now, she was waiting for Elijah to say something.

"I definitely owe you an apology for that. It was not the most mature way to end a relationship."

"We were never in a relationship, Elijah. You made that clear several times." Another awkward silence as a car honked at someone nearby. A memory suddenly made its way to the front of Nia's mind.

"Are you seeing anyone these days Nia?" The question came from Lake, a pretty

brunette that was the same year as Nia. They were at a party held by one of the drama students in Brooklyn, celebrating midterms being done.

"Still Elijah, at the moment." Nia took a sip from her cup and looked around for him. He'd disappeared to get them some more drinks a while ago and she hadn't seen him since.

"No, I mean actually seeing someone." One of Lake's friends snickered behind her red solo cup.

"What's that supposed to mean?" Nia finally found him, talking about something, his hands gesturing to make his point as usual. She'd be surprised if there was anything left in their cups by the time he made it back to her.

"Oh, you know. Just that you and Elijah aren't a 'real' thing. I was just wondering if anyone had made it official with you yet."

"Probably not, who'd want to?" Lake and her friend giggled together, and that thing happened to Nia where she badly wanted to say something, but she froze.

Lake rubbed Nia's shoulder condescendingly. "Don't feel bad, especially if you two are just having fun. That boy is going to be forever wild until the right woman can reel him in."

Nia frowned. "The right woman?"

Her friend nodded. "Someone to bring home to mom. He's going places though, that's for sure. I totally get you trying to hitch your wagon to his."

The unspoken words were clear - Nia was not enough for Elijah. She'd excused herself and left as subtly as she could, needing some fresh air. And she'd been out here ever since, crouched on the cold brownstone steps, debating if she'd even go back inside.

Her breath frosted in the air, though it wasn't cold enough for snow yet. Around her, the normal New York sounds filled the air, the faint thump of heavy bass could be heard from outside, a few rowdy cheers accenting the noise.

"What are you doing out here? The party's inside." Nia felt a warm jacket drop over her shoulders, and looked up as Elijah sat down next to her.

"Not a party I want to be at."

"Did something happen?" Elijah's arm wrapped around her, bringing her body to his.

"Just some girls talking."

"About?"

"Us. Or the lack thereof." Nia met his eyes, that were shadowed by the street lights. "Are we ever going to be an actual thing?"

"We are a thing."

"You know what I mean. What are we doing?" She watched as Elijah stood, and paced under the streetlights.

"I already told you how I feel about relationships. We can be committed without having a label on things. It's more than most married people do together."

"That works for you, not me."

"What do you expect me to say Ni? Let's slap a label on this and then watch it eventually implode on itself?"

"No, but you know what I mean."

He stopped in front of her, and knelt. "I think we're great where we are, and don't want to mess up a good thing. Because we go together." Elijah met her eyes. "What does it matter what anyone else thinks?"

Nia had nodded along with him back then, even though to her, it had mattered. Shortly after that, he'd left without a word of explanation.

Elijah sighed, bringing her back to the present. "I was a piece of shit back then, and should have treated you better. Or not strung you along as long as I did without giving something in return. And I'm sorry for that."

Ok, Nia was not expecting an actual real apology from Elijah. At all. She had been fully prepared to ice him out, give him the cold shoulder, show him what he was missing.

"You never told me why you ghosted. You left two years of us like it was so easy. What happened?"

ELIJAH

Elijah thought about how to answer that. He'd unexpectedly gotten a call from his family back in California that he'd needed to catch the soonest flight home. Rebecca, his mom, had been in the hospital. Elijah dropped everything and flew back, where she was recovering from a few injuries from an incident with her dick wad boyfriend at the time. It had turned out that he'd been hitting her for a while, but this time she fought back. Elijah remembered how angry he had been and was determined to find the man and put him in his place. But his mother had convinced him to let it be, and wanted to focus on her recovery.

He hadn't told anyone about it only because his mom had asked him not to. She was embarrassed to have found herself in a situation like that, and wanted to keep her chin up and move on as if nothing else had happened. And he'd wanted to keep her as comfortable as possible, so he hadn't said a word. And later, when she'd been getting better, Elijah had run into Vince Brandon, a casting director, who had stopped him in the middle of a pharmacy to see if Elijah had any acting skills. Thinking it was a joke at first, Elijah almost threw out his business card, until he'd gotten home, did some searching, and realized that the guy was legit.

Rebecca had twisted Elijah's arm to keep the appointment, which is how he found himself cast in a film that would ultimately raise his star. His career had taken off from that point, and he'd barely managed to finish his degree in between meetings, rehearsals and his mother's doctors' appointments. As to why he didn't tell Nia what was going on – he was so angry for a while about his mother's abuse, he didn't know what to say. And by the time he'd figured out what to say, it had been too awkward to try and come crawling back. So, he'd let it die, figuring that was easier. But he'd later realized that easier wasn't always better, especially as he saw how much he missed Nia in his life.

Nia was still waiting for an answer, however, and Elijah sighed. "I was asked not to, by my mom. She'd gotten into a…situation, with her boyfriend at the time. Abuse. And I was angry. All I wanted to do was find the guy and beat his ass, but she'd told me not to do or say anything. To anyone"

He could see the careful, but curious expression on Nia's face. "I didn't know that."

"You wouldn't know. I should have said something to you, but I was too caught up in my own head that I ignored, or reasoned away me not communicating. And for that, I'm sorry."

It was Nia's turn to be silent for a long while. She turned down his street, and Elijah pointed out which house was his. Pulling into the driveway, Nia put the car in park but still hadn't said anything. Elijah turned to her, a questioning look on his face.

"Did I shock you? I'm surprised this new and improved Nia doesn't have anything she wants to say. You're a lot more direct now than you were back in college." Elijah let a small smile play on his lips.

"I'm trying not to be so direct that I'm rude."

"It's alright. It was a long time ago, and she's better now. And it helps that I eventually sued the shit out of his ass as well."

Nia nodded, understanding. "This is all very weird. When I saw you, I was not expecting, you know, an actual apology like a reasonable adult."

"Men are capable of showing maturity as well."

"Could've fooled me." Nia let a smile out. "Thank you for your apology."

"Of course."

Elijah could see Nia was still processing everything, so much as he wanted to stay and talk more, he knew he'd taken enough of her time already. Unbuckling his seatbelt, Elijah moved to get out of her car. "I'm glad I ran into you today, however awkward it was. I would have said I knew you, but I didn't want to risk jeopardizing your chances of getting the job. But I think you killed it anyway."

"You think so?" Nia had a sweet hint of uncertainty in her voice, her big brown eyes landing on his.

"I know so. If they don't book you, it's their loss." Nia had a radiance that shone in her acting, and he was surprised she hadn't done more by now.

"Well, we'll see what happens."

"Thanks for the ride. I appreciate it." He stopped, before ducking his head back in the passenger seat. "Can I have your number?"

He enjoyed the look of surprise that came on her face.

"My number? Why?"

"To keep in touch? Maybe grab a drink sometime?" It was a lot to ask, but he could see the decision warring on her face.

"I don't know, Eli. Is that a good idea?"

Headlights appeared, and Elijah saw it was his best friend Carter, here to watch the basketball game, parking his car on the street. Of course he was early, Carter was never later to a function. Elijah could see him getting out the car, obviously curious, so Elijah pulled his keys from his pocket and took a business card out his pocket and passed it to her. "If you change your mind, here's my number. It was great seeing you again."

"You too. Take care." He shut the door, and waved as Nia backed out his driveway, her tail lights glowing in the now night. Carter came walking up, a pack of beer in his hands.

"Who was that?"

"An old friend." Elijah turned and went to his door, Carter close on his heels.

"She was hot, not old."

Unlocking the door, Elijah stepped in, flicking on the lights and kicking off his shoes.

"Also, why was she dropping you off? What happened to your car?"

"I left it at the stage. I'll go back and get it tomorrow."

Carter opened his mouth to as another question, but Elijah stopped him. "If you ask me another question, I'm not getting guacamole with the tacos tonight."

"Dude, that's ridiculous. You have to have guacamole on Taco Tuesday." But Carter got the hint and stopped asking questions, at least about Nia. He wanted to know if any of the women they'd interviewed weren't picked, and if he could get their number, for consolation purposes. Elijah laughed at that. Inside he was glad Nia had let him say his piece. He hadn't known if she would still talk to him after all this time, but he was glad she did. Even if that meant he had to wake up and catch a ride to Burbank to get his car. Being able to talk to her had been worth it.

But now, he realized that niggling feeling that none of these women were right for him, was back full force. Adult Nia was a revelation. And he wanted to know more. He hoped to God Warren did the right thing and booked her for this show. Life had brought Nia back in his world. And for whatever reason, he wanted to keep her in it.

The Phone Call

NIA

"He did what now?" Goldie almost spit out a load of rice, as they sat crowded around their living room table. Nia had made it back home where Goldie had called over Lexie and Nia's little sister Yaya. They'd crowded around the coffee table and dug into containers of Thai food as Nia told them all about the audition. There were several pointed exclamations, but minor interruptions for the most part. Nia didn't give them every detail, feeling the need to keep what had happened to Elijah's mother between the two of them. She didn't feel right sharing that to everyone. When Nia had gotten to the part where Elijah apologized, Goldie couldn't help herself.

"You're telling us that this man actively sought you out to give you an apology that's what, four years past due?"

"And was able to talk about it in a mature and adult way?" Lexie shook her head. "I can't believe it."

"I know, right? I didn't know what to say when he was being all mature and shit." Nia shook her head, still replaying their conversation over in her head. What she had expected to happen was he'd play the charmer and try to talk his way out of what he'd done. Instead, she'd gotten the complete opposite.

Yaya interrupted, waving that off. "Ok, enough about how Elijah is now an emotionally stable adult – how hot is he actually in real life now? Like, are the muscles real or courtesy of Photoshop?"

Nia rolled her eyes at her little sister's priorities. "You'd think you hadn't met him before."

"Yeah, but I met the theater kid version of Elijah, not sexy as hell, can afford a celebrity personal trainer version of Elijah." These were two very different distinctions in Yaya's mind, and Nia knew she wouldn't let up on her until she got her answer.

"He's hot. Like, he rescues kittens, fights for Black Lives Matter and can manage his way around a bedroom hot."

There was a brief moment of silence as the women digested that.

"Damn girl." This came from Goldie, who poured herself more wine. "I guess this was good that you went. You got some closure."

"True." But Nia also had so many more questions. Who was this new Elijah? And why had she been tempted to take him up on his offer of grabbing a drink. "He also asked me for my number?"

"Is that a question or a statement?" Lexie asked, smirking behind her own wine glass.

Nia rolled her eyes, but smiled a little. "He asked for my number, and wanted to meet for a drink sometime."

"And you said yes, took his number and saved it in your phone immediately. Right?" Yaya poked Nia with a chopstick.

"I said it probably wasn't a good idea." Nia poked around for another piece of curry chicken.

Goldie and Yaya shared a look with each other while Lexie studied Nia before commenting. "I think you're probably right about that."

"Are you serious? This is Elijah James we're talking about!" Goldie shook her head. "I'd have been all over him."

"That's you, not me. And it's not like it could go anywhere anyway. Remember this whole little dating show I just auditioned for? He's the bachelor, if you've forgotten."

"Oh yeah. I'm still confused as to how you ended up giving him a ride after. Like, did he not have a car or anything?" Yaya stood, heading into the kitchen.

"He'd said it was in the shop." That had been strange to Nia as well. Too bad she didn't know enough about him now to know what kind of car he drives.

"I bet forty bucks that he left his car there intentionally, just to talk to you." Coming back with a fresh bottle of wine, Yaya refilled all their glasses.

"He wouldn't do that, it reeks of desperation." But the more she thought about it, the more the idea had some merit.

"I'll take that bet," Goldie reached out and shook Yaya's hand.

"He wouldn't do that though." Nia wondered aloud, but Lexie shook her head doubtfully.

"Are you sure about that? You don't really know him that well anymore."

Nia sighed, now wondering if she'd gotten a glimpse of car keys on his key chain.

"It doesn't matter though. It's not like I've got the part, and even if I do, Elijah James is no longer a part of my life."

"Do you want him to be though?" Yaya asked the question that had been tickling the back of Nia's mind. Did she want Elijah James back in her life? Her logical side said hell to the no, but her emotional side was…curious.

"Don't answer that if you don't want to, Nia." She could always trust Lexie to know when to change the subject to safer waters. "I want to know about the sub shop bae, Goldie. What's he been up to?"

As Goldie launched into the latest dealings with the supposed prince she'd met in a sandwich shop, Nia knew thinking too much about Elijah would just lead her to ideas and problems she didn't need in her life right now. Decided, Nia pushed him back to the corner of her mind where all things Elijah James went to rest. She had moved on once. She could do it again.

Two days later Nia was regretting telling her parents about the audition. It was a rare day, the four of them all working at the restaurant at the same time. Nigel, her father, was back in the kitchen, cooking up a storm while her mother Yolanda, bustled around, greeting people and making sure they were comfortable. Yolanda had been constantly pestering Nia about following up, and sending thank you notes and generally ramping up Nia's anxiety even more.

Nia was in the kitchen of Dinner at Nigel's, a chain of successful cajun style restaurants owned by her mother and father, waiting for her orders to come up. She was filling in for a sick waitress, and it was a particularly busy day, the dinner crowd starting earlier than usual. Already planning a nice long foot soak when she got home, she was stopped by her mother as she carried a hot tray of shrimp étouffée and seafood gumbo. "Have you heard anything back yet from them?"

Nia faced her mother, trying not to drop the tray. "Not yet. You guys will be the first to know either way." She disappeared out, dropping off the food before circling back to the kitchen where her parents worked.

"If they don't pick you, they're the biggest idiots I've seen." Yolanda might have been on the smaller side at five feet four, compared to Nia's five foot nine, but she was a scary sight when angry. Nia remembered once when she and Yaya were younger, their mom had found out about a boy that had been bullying them on the bus. Yolanda went with them to their stop and rode the bus to school, staring daggers at the boy and silently daring him to do anything to her girls. It was significantly embarrassing, but he, nor anyone else, messed with them again.

"I'm not going to say I don't agree with you mom." Nia laughed, and rolled her eyes at Julio, their sous chef who was the most soft-spoken man – outside of the kitchen.

"I'm sure you'll get the part, honey. You should've been the next Regina King by now." Julio was adamant that Nia would make it. He swore up and down that Hollywood would recognize it soon.

"You can always stay here and work in the business." Nigel stood over the stove, stirring a new batch of roux with skill borne of years of practice. "There's always a place for you here."

"Not this again, dad." It was a sore spot, her not wanting to stay in the business. Much as Nia loved her family and working with them, she had other dreams that she wanted to chase. Unfortunately, it upset her father, who had always wanted to see his family working together one day. He'd wanted to pass the reigns to Nia, and had been displeased when she'd decided to switch from a marketing major to a drama one. Needless to say, the fact that her acting career hadn't taken off like Nia had hoped had only made Nigel more determined to have Nia stay in the business.

Rolling her eyes, Nia took the plate Julio offered and went to take it to its table, before checking in on her other one. It was a young Instagram model wannabe and her group of girlfriends. Nia smiled, checking in with them. "How's the food? Is there anything else I can get you?"

"My food was cold." This came from another model wannabe. "Can I get a fresh one?"

The girl had eaten more than half the plate of food and was asking for a fresh plate? Nia barely managed to keep from rolling her eyes. "I'm so sorry, we'll get that taken care of for you."

"Good." The girl barely even looked at Nia, going back to the conversation with her friends. Before Nia had gotten completely away, she heard them giggling, and knew that they'd probably planned it. She did not have high hopes that her tip would be decent today.

Taking the plate back into the kitchen, Nia met Yolanda and Julio's questioning faces. "A customer at table eleven said her food was cold. Wants a new plate."

Yolanda rolled her eyes, but Julio's calm was shattered. "She's accusing me of sending out cold food? The audacity, let me fix her plate again right now."

"None of that, we don't need any negative reviews. We'll fix it and get it back out to her." Yolanda was well aware of the ways customers tried to get as much out of a restaurant as they could, and had been able to accept it as part of the business. Nia hated it; it was one of the reasons she didn't like waitressing. Her mouth usually got her in trouble.

Out front, there was a small commotion, louder than the usual din of night time eating. "What's going on out there?" Nia peeked through the small window though she couldn't see much of anything. And then Yaya burst through the kitchen door, excitement written all on her face and knocking Nia to the ground. "Nia. NIA."

Nia stood, trying not to be frustrated with her sister's exuberance. "Thank you for knocking me over."

"He's here." Yaya eyes were big, and she whipped out a tube of lipstick, trying to smear some of the stuff on Nia's lips.

Avoiding her, Nia put their mother in between her and Yaya. "That fake food reviewer?"

"Not him. *Elijah*." Yaya practically bounced on her toes. "Elijah James."

Of course he's here. Nia tried to hold Yaya away from her as Yolanda stood on tiptoe, trying to peer out the window of the kitchen door. "Why?"

"Yeah, why is he here?" After not hearing from Elijah for over four years, she was seeing him twice in a week? It was too much.

"I don't know, but he's in your section." Yaya tried to attack with the lipstick yet again.

"Hold up, I have to deal with him? No, you can do it Yaya," Nia started, but

Yolanda shook her head.

"Yaya's here to help with some marketing strategies with me. It's on you today." She could have been imagining it, but her mother did look a little too eager to have her oldest daughter interact with a celebrity, even if said celebrity had broken her daughters heart.

"Why is it on me? I just wanted to get this girl her plate and go home."

"Because I want to know if he's here for you, or if it's just a coincidence." Yolanda said, pushing Nia out the door. "Now go."

Sighing, Nia passed her hand over her hair, smoothing down fly aways, and made her way over to Elijah's table. He was seated with a friend, (who was quite cute as well, Nia noted) in an animated conversation. As she got closer, she didn't know if he'd heard her approach or just felt her, but Elijah looked up and directly at her. And smiled as she came to a stop in front of his table.

Pasting on her most courteous smile, Nia addressed the two of them. "Welcome to Dinner at Nigel's, can I get you guy started with some drinks?"

"Nia, what are you doing here?" Elijah looked surprised to see her here.

"It's my family's restaurant, I help out sometimes. Can I get you something to drink?" She looked over at Elijah's friend, who was bouncing back and forth between them. He seemed a little familiar.

"Hi, I'm Carter, because Elijah obviously isn't going to introduce me." Carter looked like a mix between Steven Yuen and Penn Badgley, and made it model.

"Hi Carter, I'm Nia. Can I get you something to drink? Maybe an appetizer?"

"I really want to know more about you and my best friend Elijah, who hasn't stopped looking at you yet." Carter's smile was almost as charming as Elijah's.

Elijah rolled his eyes at his friend. "I was just surprised is all, I remembered your restaurant from school. I'd figured you'd be packing by now."

Nia frowned, confused. "Why would I be packing? You haven't run me out of Hollywood yet."

"For Hawaii, of course."

What was he saying? Could he mean… "Are you telling me that they picked me?" Nia felt her knees give a little and took an open seat at the table. "I'm on the show?" Elijah immediately looked guilty for spoiling her phone call notification.

"You didn't know yet? I'm so sorry, I thought they'd told you yesterday."

Nia shook her head, still letting it soak in. "No, I haven't checked my phone in a minute." Nia usually had her phone on her, but had left it in her locker in a rush to get out to the floor today. She stood on shaky legs, and decided to go check her phone. A wave of excitement flooded her stomach, but she tamped it down. He could be pulling her leg, but she had to know. "I'll be back with some waters while you two look over the menu."

Nia managed to make her way to the back of the restaurant, where Yolanda and Yaya were waiting excitedly for her.

"What did he want?" Yaya asked, peering out the window to their table.

Yolanda was more concerned with the look on Nia's face. "Is everything alright Nima?" She reverted to Nia's old nickname from childhood.

Nia nodded, but opened her locker and dug through her bag for her phone. "I think so." He had a few missed calls and a message from Lexie, and her heart immediately started pounding. Maybe he wasn't lying. Maybe she could really believe it. A quick listen to her voicemail confirmed it: she had gotten the part. Nia let out a squeal before jumping up and down, shocking her mother and sister.

"Nima, what's going on?" Nigel asked, coming in and seeing the commotion.

"I got the spot! I'm going to Oahu!" Nia threw her arms around her family as they celebrated with her. Julio stuck his head out from the back, alerted to the chaos, holding a knife in his capable hand.

"What is going on out there?" He looked at the trio of women celebrating together.

"Nia's going to Hawaii!" Yaya let Nia go finally. "I wonder if I can fit in your suitcase?"

"That's amazing, I knew you'd get it." Julio smiled at Nia before ducking back and yelling something at his sous chef.

"Elijah accidentally told me out there, that's why I was in shock."

"He must have been excited for you." Yolanda smiled, squeezing Nia a little tighter. "I am proud. We will celebrate this weekend; your dad will cook you something."

Nigel smiled, "Of course I will."

"Thank you." Nia smiled, and a million thought ran through her head at once. "I should probably get back to my tables."

Nia made her way back, checking on her tables with a huge grin on her face. No matter how many people asked for ketchup or refills, nothing could shake her happiness. She even shared that smile with Elijah, who looked relieved at her happiness. "You were right, Lexie called me. I'm going to Oahu."

Elijah's green eyes smiled up at her. "I'm glad you'll be there to witness the madness."

Nia was too. She felt like things were starting to change for her, and couldn't wait to see what else the future had in store for her.

The Flight

NIA

After what felt like a week of rushed primping, packing, and preparations, it was finally time for Nia to catch her flight to Oahu. It felt like she got wave after wave of information from the producers and coordinators with shooting schedules, itineraries, and cast lists so she could start familiarizing herself with the contestants. Nia tried not to pay too much attention to Elijah's bio, but who was she kidding? Nia drank in information about him under the cover of night when she was alone in her room.

On top of getting details about the show, Nia and Goldie had gone bikini shopping, since Goldie had sworn up and down that Nia would need options to look sexy. And it was also just a good excuse to go shopping, which was always fine in Nia's book. Yaya had gone with Nia to their usual salon, having her hair freshly cut and adding in some caramel highlights that really set off her skin tone. Lexie had been calling on and off, giving Nia last minute details production wanted her to know.

She'd tried to keep herself busy, too busy to think about Elijah. She was waffling between obsessing over the fact that she'd be on an island with him for almost two months, and pretend nonchalance. It'd gotten to the point where Yaya had staged a mini 'intervention' the night before she was to go to the airport. Nia had gotten back in from the gym, and found the whole group there with a pitcher of frozen margaritas and salads. Setting her bag down by the door, she looked at her friends who looked at her with knowing expressions.

"What's going on? What kind of farewell dinner is this?" Nia took the seat Lexie patted next to her on the couch. "It's got to be serious if Goldie actually put in the time to make frozen margaritas."

"We just wanted to check in with you, and make sure your head is in the right place before you go to a crazy romantic island with your 'What If' guy who's suddenly made some major personality changes." Lexie poured Nia a glass.

"You guy's solution is to ply me with alcohol the night before a flight?" She looked at her friends with a fake stern expression. "At least you could've gotten some burgers to soak up this liquor."

Yaya popped up, and scurried into the kitchen. "We have them, I just had to make sure your head was on right." She came back out with a few bags of In-N-Out and set them on the table.

Nia grabbed a carton of fries and settled into the cushions. "Ok, let me have it. You all clearly think I've gone off the deep end or something."

"Not true. We just know you and how good a heart you have." Goldie bit into a burger. "All we wanted to do was remind you that this man did break your heart, however long ago, and even though he did apologize, please don't go to Oahu and fall in love with him."

"Again." Yaya poked Nia in the side. "We know you, and are just trying to keep from having to beat Elijah James' ass. Dad would not be happy if that made the six o'clock news."

Nia laughed, shaking her head. "I'm not going to fall in love with Elijah. That part of my life is over with. Did you ladies forget he's literally there to date other women?"

"Nope." Lexie downed a gulp of her margarita. "We didn't forget. You shouldn't either."

Nia rolled her eyes, though she knew her friends were just looking out for her. She had been a mess for a while after the breakup, and even though Lexie didn't know Nia back in college, she'd still been subject to one or more drunken rants about how the perfect one got away. "The thought did cross my mind, but don't worry. I don't want to fall for him again. He had his chance, and it's done now. So, I'm going to go to Oahu, soak up some sun, and maybe find a local hottie to spend some time with."

"Aye, that's my big sis!" Yaya clapped her hands. "Ok good, now that that's out the way, a toast!"

Goldie rolled her eyes. "Girl, this is not a wedding. We don't need a toast."

Yaya hushed her. "I'm toasting here! Nia. Here's to life changing experiences and new beginnings – this is your year. To Nia!"

"To new doors opening." Lexie raised her glass.

"And to finding hot island men." Goldie added, lifting her glass.

Nia raised her glass to her friends. "To me! And my bad ass friends." They clinked their glasses and she smiled, glad to have a tribe of friends who were always looking out for her. She knew going in that working with Elijah might be difficult, but she was determined to keep things professional. There was no room for him in her life again. Nia just had to keep telling herself that until she remembered it.

The next morning, Nia strolled through LAX with a pair of huge sunglasses on her face to help block out excessive light. They may have had a few drinks too many, and now Nia had a hangover to deal with, on top of her fear of heights. Goldie dropped her off, barely functional, for her eleven thirty flight. "I know you're an adult and everything, so take what we said last night with a dash of chili oil."

"Chili oil?"

"Yeah – it's either really good for you and adds the perfect kick for your life, or it doesn't do anything beyond adding misery and pain."

Laughing, Nia pulled Goldie into a hug. "I wish I could bring all of you with me."

"We'll do a girl's trip soon enough, momma needs a vacation. But right now this is your chance. I know you're going to kill it, and you'd better call us with any and all details!"

Nia waved goodbye, and carted her luggage to bag check. Once she was through the security check point (after being stopped for them to feel up her hair, as usual) she made her way to a travel shop and got a few flight snacks – Toblerone bar, flaming hot Cheetos, and the biggest thing of water she could find. Nia knew she didn't need the junk, but felt it might help her nerves on the flight. Though she was glad to be flying out a day before the women were to arrive, it would have been nice to have someone Nia knew on the flight with her. There was one time Nia had gotten so freaked out during a particularly turbulent flight that she'd passed out, and had to be tended by another passenger on board. She'd thought she'd been lucky there was a doctor on the flight, but the older gentleman had told her he was actually a veterinarian. Now, Nia usually took a Tylenol and knocked out for the majority of a flight.

As she gathered her bag and began walking to her terminal, Nia swore she saw someone who looked a lot like Elijah ducking into the men's restroom. He was well built, with a baseball cap situated low over his forehead and a dark jean jacket. It was more of a passing sense, and Nia didn't get a good look at him before he'd disappeared into the bathroom. Then she shook her head at her imagination, because there was no way Elijah would be flying on the same flight as her. He probably flew private now, so he didn't have to deal with regular people anymore.

Finding her gate, Nia took a seat by the window and watched planes coming and going. The weather was nice, some grey skies, but it was pretty early still in the morning. Before she knew it, the flight attendant was calling for boarding, and Nia sprung up, glad the show had gotten her a first class ticket. She found her aisle seat with ease, and got all her necessary things ready for the flight – neck pillow, Tylenol, water and headphones. Nia was debating closing the window next to her when a passenger stopped next to her and spoke in an all too familiar voice. "Excuse me, I think that's my seat over there."

Elijah smiled down at her before shoving his carryon bag in the overhead storage, his shirt lifting with the movement and giving Nia a glimpse of rock hard abs before it slid back into place. Her eyes made their way back up to his, and saw the smirk in them before he moved across her to and settled into the window seat next to her.

"What are you doing here?" Nia blurted, as he stretched his legs out, testing the amount of leg room he had. Elijah's big frame took up more space than should be allowed, making Nia vividly aware of how close he was to her and how her body was responding to said closeness. *Tap that shit down, girl.*

"It's actually really cool, I'm flying to Hawaii for work on a new show. How about you?" Elijah's arm went to the divider between them, and Nia moved hers away from his.

"You know that's not what I'm asking." She looked around at the other passengers loading on the plane. "Why are you flying with me?"

"I asked them to." Elijah settled deeper in his seat, doing that annoying man spreading thing that caused his knee to touch hers. There was absolutely no reason for her whole body to tingle at the small contact but it did, and the awareness of where their knees met drew Nia's attention.

"Why?" That made no sense, and was the last thing Nia was expecting.

"Why not? We're friends now, right?" She watched as he shut the window next to him, and breathed a little sigh of relief. He probably didn't remember her fear of heights. Probably.

"Are we? I thought it was more like acquaintances." Around them, more and more passengers began loading into the plane. Nia had to dodge a few bags that came a little too close, trying to focus on Elijah, who was looking at her with earnest green eyes.

"Look, Nia. It's not that big a deal." Elijah leaned his head back on the head rest. "Can we just…start over? We're about to be trapped on an island for two months. It'd be nice to go in with a friend."

He wanted to start over? Nia dodged another bag as she took that in. "Do you even know what that would look like?"

"Two adults being cordial and I don't know, friendly?" And while Nia knew it would be dangerous to be too close to Elijah, she knew it would make more sense for them to act civil towards each other. Openly disliking Elijah would only bring more attention to them when she didn't want anyone to know of their failed history. For the time being, Nia could try to put aside her feelings and be civil.

As she opened her mouth to respond, another bag hit her, this time in the head. It didn't hurt, and Nia was more surprised than anything, but she was more surprised when Elijah stood abruptly.

"Switch seats with me."

"What?" Nia waved off the apology the bag owner offered.

He practically lifted her from the seat and did a little tango, setting her back down in his chair and taking her aisle seat. "So you can stop getting hit by all these bags." The move was surprisingly sweet, causing a little tingle in her insides.

"Thank you." She paused thinking. Maybe it would be good to start as friends with Elijah. "We can be friends." Elijah did a little fist pump at that. "But only friends," Nia smiled, rolling her eyes. Overhead a flight attendant's voice asked them to fasten their seat belts and prepare for departure.

"Thank God. I thought I'd have to beg you." Elijah winked at her and Nia's insides melted a little more.

"You, begging? I can't imagine." The plane began to move and Nia clutched the arm rest unconsciously.

"I'm not very good at it." With a wink, Elijah made himself comfortable in his seat as they taxied down the runway while Nia's attention was on the plan lifting into the air. Some part of her brain recognized Elijah's strong arm pressing against hers, his hand within reach should she want to grab it. She didn't, of course, but the warmth of his hand was nicely reassuring. Once they were safely up, Nia let out a tight breath of air. The second worst part was over, the worst part being landing and knowing the ground was rushing to meet you at thousands of miles per hour. But she had about five hours before she needed to deal with that. Idly, she wondered where her Tylenol was.

Elijah's soft voice drifted over to her. "Still not a fan of heights I see."

"I didn't think you remembered that."

"I remember a lot of things."

Though there wasn't any intentional heat in his voice, Nia automatically thought of some of their time together. And was glad for the shut window and dimmed overhead lights, because had it been brighter in the cabin, he'd definitely see her blush.

"It's fine, I know how to manage it now." She picked up her bag and dug through it, unearthing her Tylenol. "I've got drugs to help me."

"Remember that time we had to dodge the RAs in Hayden?" Elijah chuckled.

"When Trevor and Malcolm had that huge party and like twenty kids got busted?" Nia smiled, the memory rushing back to her. It had been a high strung party, with weed and alcohol and plenty of loose inhibitions. The resident assistants had heard the music and knocked on the door, causing everyone to panic. It had been a crush of a party, and when the door opened, Elijah had grabbed Nia and hauled them out of there and into the stairwell, where they'd escaped out a side door. It had been wild and fun, the two of them hiding out in Mamoun's off of MacDougal Street until the coast was clear.

"We barely made it out without getting caught. Thank god I got us out of there." Elijah's smile flashed in the dim cabin interior.

Nia burst out laughing. "You were the reason we were there in the first place."

"You told me you wanted to do something fun that night. I simply provided the opportunity." She felt his big hand cover hers, and though it was a brief touch, she silently cursed the zings running throughout her body.

"You definitely did." Nia smiled at that. "You were always ready for a good time."

"I was wild back then." Elijah had the grace to look…disgraced.

"And you're not now?" Nia questioned, eyebrow raised.

Elijah huffed. "Only when the occasion calls for it." His knee pressed hers again, and Nia just knew that it was deliberate. But not entirely unwanted.

Feeling off balance with all the emotions parading through her, Nia looked for a way to go back to more neutral topics.

"Why are you doing this show anyway? I thought you were mister super star now."

Elijah's mouth twisted. "Not a super star. And there was a hole in my schedule that my agent wanted me to fill."

"And a reality dating show fit the bill?" Nia eyed Elijah, noticing the tensing of his jaw and wondered why it was such a touchy subject . "That doesn't add up."

Nia wouldn't have believed his jaw able to get more tense than it already was if she hadn't seen it for herself. "It doesn't have to add up." Elijah's mouth shut tight after that, clearly not wanting to delve further into that topic.

"Grouchy. Sorry I asked." Nia settled into her seat, wanting to be annoyed by his sudden change in mood but knew that she had been prying into his personal life. She was used to getting honest answers from him, but it had been a while since they'd been actual friends. Right now, Nia didn't know exactly what type of 'friends' they were going to be at this point - maybe they would just be casual acquaintances. Shrugging it off, Nia bent down and rummaged in her bag until she found her Tylenol. She popped a few and settled back into her chair to wait for them to kick in.

ELIJAH

Elijah let out a huff of air as his head connected with the cushion on the back of his seat. He knew he'd been short with Nia, especially as he watched her pop a few Tylenol to sleep through the flight. Her body language was closed off to him, her knees pointed away from his and her face angled toward the window, even though it was shut tight.

A flight attendant passed by, asking about drink orders. Nia shook her head no in response to the question before turning back to the window, eyes skipping over Elijah which made him feel even worse. He just didn't know where to begin with explaining that whole mess that brought him to this dating show. It was one thing to talk about it with various producers and agents who were actively trying to help him get his career back on track. It was another thing to talk to someone he actually respected and portray himself in what could be seen a negative light.

"I'm sorry." His voice was low in the cabin, wary that ears might be listening in. "I didn't mean to snap. I just don't like talking about that situation." He waited, looking at her face that was still angled away from him. She turned a little, watching him out the side of her eye. Eventually, Nia let out a soft sigh.

"It's fine, I was definitely prying. You don't have to talk about it."

Elijah smiled a little. "We can, just probably not while we're on a crowded airplane."

"Good point." She was smiling fully at him now, her body slightly angled toward him. The pilot came over the intercom, mentioning turbulence, right before the plane bounced a little. He saw Nia's hands grasp the arm rests and his own came and covered hers. To his surprise, Nia took the comfort he offered, turning the palm of her hand up into his, and their fingers laced together. A wave of protectiveness passed over him as he watched her breathe carefully. It touched a part of him, that despite their past, she was still able to trust him to care for her, even in this small way. Their hands were joined until the plane went back to a smooth cruise, when Nia bashfully smiled at him before pulling away.

"Thanks. I always think it'll get easier the next time I get on a plane but it never does."

"I'm still trying to figure out how you made it all the way to New York and back during holidays."

"Lots and lots of Tylenol."

They shared a smile, and Nia let out a yawn.

He laughed as she popped a few and waited for them to kick in. "Do we do the same drugs these days?"

Nia laughed, shocked. "Is that a Chance the Rapper reference?"

"You were such a big fan, I finally listened to him."

"And? Isn't he amazing?"

"I'm over here quoting his lyrics, right?"

Nia laughed quietly, shaking her head. Elijah just kept surprising her. They both fell silent, and eventually, the Tylenol kicked in and Nia fell fast asleep.

The rest of the flight was uneventful, as Nia was sleep for the majority of the trip. Her head did fall to Elijah's shoulder, and he held himself still, not wanting to wake her up. She woke right before their descent, groggy, while Elijah had his own eyes closed. He heard a little gasp from her right before she shifted away from him. For a moment, Elijah debated telling her she could have stayed there, but knew that would probably be unwelcome. He'd liked the weight of her head on his shoulder, and that even in sleep, Nia couldn't help but be drawn to him.

Hearing the ping of the seat belt sign coming on, Elijah stretched and looked over at Nia, who was back to ignoring him. Mentally he sighed. Elijah wasn't sure what these next months would look like, but he hoped that the could work something out. Overhead the flight attendant made an announcement: "Ladies and gentlemen, we're making our descent into Honolulu, where the local temperature is seventy-four degrees and sunny. Welcome to Hawaii."

The House

NIA

After making a safe landing, a groggy Nia and annoyingly peppy Elijah deplaned and made their way to baggage claim, where Nia slowly realized her bags had been misplaced. She'd waited until the next flights bags started rolling down before she realized something was wrong. Though the airline apologized profusely and promised to reimburse Nia for anything she had to buy while they tracked down her bags, Nia was left with the few items she had in her carry on. It was the perfect way to start this Hawaii trip.

Once she was done filing her claim, Nia made her way out the terminal and into the bright Hawaii sunshine. Squinting, Nia scanned the cars lined up on the curb until she saw a town car with a ring decal in the back window that proclaimed it part of the show. Elijah had volunteered to come with her, but Nia reasoned that he'd be less likely to be recognized if he waited at the car. He hadn't liked that much, but had grumbled on his way outside to track down the car production had sent. As her eyes adjusted to the bright sun, Nia caught a good look at Elijah as he waited for her by the car in the distance. She was struck again by how much he'd really changed since college. Elijah was really settling into himself, and she could see the confidence that radiated from him that hadn't been there when she'd first known him. He lifted the cap from his head and ran strong fingers through his dark hair before replacing it back. Nia clenched the hand that was tempted to run her fingers through the silky locks, and she reminded herself that he was not for her. Even if the wild Nia she kept chained in the back of her head was screaming for her to be reckless for a change. Nia couldn't afford to be wild. Not when this job represented so much to her.

As she got closer, Nia could feel Elijah's eyes lock onto hers. Did it just get hotter outside? She didn't want to look up, though and give herself away. *Go ahead and give it all away, it was already his,* the little voice in her head whispered. Nia slammed the door on her harder, and gave a friendly, non-romantic smile to Elijah. He pushed off the side of the black sedan, his eyes travelling her up and down. "What's the word?"

"Nothing yet, but they'll call me as soon as they figure it out." Elijah took her carry on, shrugging off the help offered by the driver and placed it in the trunk himself before shutting the trunk. Elijah had just opened the door for Nia when they heard a piece of gum snap.

"Omg, you're Elijah James." Turning, Nia saw a young, dark haired teen who had Elijah locked in her sight. "Omg! You're ELIJAH JAMES."

Nia smiled as Elijah took a quick selfie with the girl, who fan girl-ed for a moment. After saying good bye to her, he hopped in the car, taking the back seat next to Nia. "Does that happen a lot?" Nia wondered as the car pulled away from the curb.

"More and more frequently. It's weird." Elijah ran a hand over the back of his neck. "I kind of miss anonymity."

Nia smile at that. "What, you miss going out in sweats and ratty band t-shirts?" It had been one of his usual outfits back in college.

"I've got some sweats that would look great on you if you want." His eyebrows bounced up and down lecherously, causing a laugh from Nia.

"While that's tempting, I did manage to pack a few essentials in my day bag, so that was a bit of luck I think. But I'll probably have to go shopping for a few outfits just in case."

Nia's next comment faded away as she caught her first look at their gorgeous surroundings. She'd always meant to get to Hawaii at some point, and it did not disappoint. Overhead, the sky was pure blue with fluffy clouds icing it, and the sketch of mountains on the horizon. Their trip was surprisingly short, and within a half hour Nia and Elijah stepped out of the car and took in their home for the next few weeks.

Banyan Beach resort was a tropical paradise. Lush foliage accented the tan stone of the archway leading to the house (which was more like a mansion) with sweet scents drifting on a breeze. Their car pulled into the rounded driveway with a fountain gurgling in the center, the sunshine catching the water and reflecting rainbows. Stone steps led up to the front door, where Kerry and Warren waited for them, welcoming smiles on their faces. "Welcome to your new home for the next few weeks!" Warren smothered Nia in a hug she didn't ask for, and slapped Elijah on the back in greeting. "This is going to make you even more of a chick magnet than you already are." His voice lowered, though Nia could still catch every word Warren was saying. "I made sure we have lots of water activities." He winked at Elijah, who smiled tightly at him.

"I'm so excited." Nia heard the sarcasm in Elijah's voice, even if Warren didn't. Elijah walked around to grab his bags, stopping the production assistant from having to take it.

"Nia, I heard your bags were lost?" Kerry asked, some concern in her eyes.

"They were; the airline says it rarely happens anymore these days. So of course, it happens to me." She and Kerry shared a laugh. "They will reimburse anything I have to buy while they located it, though."

"Sounds like we should make a quick shopping excursion." Kerry smiled as Nia hefted her carry on over her shoulder. "Make sure you're really covered."

"I like the way you think." Nia smiled, and felt that maybe she'd have a friend on this thing, that wasn't Elijah. It was a good feeling.

Walking through the archway, they made their way over floating steps where colorful fish swam in the water between, and through the front door. Inside was a just as beautiful as the outside, the décor soft, romantic and tropical. Nia could imagine several intimate moments happening in any number of nooks and crannies. The living room was large and cozy, and the kitchen was something Nia wanted to get lost in. She was vaguely aware of Warren spouting off details as they looked around. "There's a pool out back, hot tub as well. And we've got a gym, so you can maintain your figures. We will be plying you with food and alcohol."

"Sounds like heaven." Nia smiled, shifting her bag to her other shoulder. Kerry noticed, and cut Warren off before he could go into any more details.

"How about we show you two your rooms? You can get settled in and explore a little before we have our team dinner after the production meeting later."

Warren jumped back in. "The production meeting! You aren't needed for it, but feel free to come and meet some new faces, hear some details-"

"I think Nia will need some time to find a few clothes, so the she might not have time for the production meeting." Kerry interjected.

Warren frowned. "Elijah though…"

"Has a busy schedule coming up, and should rest up before he has to charm thirteen women out their socks." Kerry steered them to the stairs. "We want to make sure the talent is well rested." Nia laughed as Kerry rolled her eyes and followed her up the stairs. Warren was about to respond when his phone rang, and he had to step away to take the call.

"How do you do that so effortlessly?" Elijah asked quietly, as they walked up the stairs. "Warren usually bulldozes over everyone and everything."

"Practice. You don't get to my position as a woman without learning a few tricks." Walking down the hall, Kerry went all the way to the end before stopping at two doors. "Anyway, since the two of you will be here the longest, you'll have the best rooms in the house. The girls are split between the rooms down the hall and on the first floor – they had a hell of a time setting up the beds in there. Crew is at a house a few doors down."

Nia opened the door on the left, and saw a beautiful suite that was basically the size of her apartment back in LA, probably bigger. It was decorated in teals and brown, with a few colorful accents here and there. There was a huge bed, desk, and cozy arm chair, and her own bathroom with a tub she wanted to crawl right into. Dropping her bag on the floor, she went and flopped on the bed, sighing at its softness. "I can get used to this."

"Right? I'm also so jealous of you." Kerry leaned on the doorway and smiled.

"Why is that?"

"Because you get to share the balcony with Elijah." Nia saw the doors to the side of the room and walked over, where she was greeted with sun, and a fantastic view of the water.

"Ok, I know this is going to make me sound like a bitch, but I'm really glad your other host broke both her legs so I can be here."

Kerry burst out laughing. "I'm glad you're here too. The other girl was such an Elijah James fan, I thought we'd have to keep reminding her she wasn't in the competition."

"You don't have to worry about me. He's attractive, but we'd never work."

Kerry quirked an eyebrow. "Why is that?"

"I don't like fighting over men. Especially when they've got a womanizer reputation." Those callous words felt wrong, especially since they'd just discussed being friends. Just as she opened her mouth to take it back, she heard *his* voice behind her that caused goosebumps to rise on her skin and her cheeks to fill with blood.

"Aw, that's too bad. I thought we had something special." Elijah stood in his own door, eyes shadowed by the cap he still wore.

Nia's heart jumped – she didn't think he would hear it, which made her feel even worse that she had before. Kerry leaned on the bannister, unaware of the tension that grew between Nia and Elijah. "Poor baby. Don't worry, we'll have lots of women here tomorrow that will stroke your ego."

"Looking forward to it." Elijah smiled, smaller and tighter than his usual one, before disappearing back into his room. Nia didn't want to feel bad – it was better to draw the lines now, right? But she still couldn't help wondering why he took that so seriously.

Kerry broke into Nia's thoughts. "I can set you up with a driver to take you to a few places to cover your wardrobe once you're settled in."

Nia pushed off the bannister, nodding. "I would love that." She couldn't worry about Elijah and his feelings. She wasn't here for him. Nia was here for herself, and to nail this job. And that's what her focus would stay on, even if that little voice in her head was telling her otherwise.

After going to a few different shops on the island and finding some temporary clothes, Nia made it back to the resort just as the production meeting was breaking up. She was slow to head back inside, absorbing the warm sun and fresh breeze that begged her to stay outside a little longer. The ocean was an impossible blue, the bluest of blues, and Nia could stare at it all day. Envious of the vacationing people stretched out on the sand, Nia decided she was going to be spending as much free of her free time on the beach as possible.

As she made her way to the house, one of the production assistants, Maddison, told her there was dinner set up in the crew house. Rerouting, Nia made her way down the gravel path to the crew house. The sun was just beginning to set, and a soft breeze carried the smell of barbecue to her nose, making Nia's mouth water. As she got closer, she could hear laughter coming from the house as a cacophony of voices spilled out of the open windows. The crew house wasn't as grand as the main house for filming, but it had a welcoming air that Nia immediately liked. It was light tan in color, with a slanted green roof and surrounded by tall palm trees and lush greenery. Light spilled out of the windows, which were opened to let in the fresh air. And the views it had of the water and mountains were stunning, of course.

For a moment, Nia hesitated before entering the house. It would have been easier to walk in with someone, and she knew that she was likely to find someone to talk to…eventually. She'd always hated the meeting part of meeting people. Even though she was a grown woman, Nia still got nervous when meeting new people. She didn't want to eat alone on this first day, but she'd screwed up already with Elijah, and Kerry was off somewhere with Warren and Isaac. Which meant Nia had to face a new group of people on her own. *You got this,* Nia told herself. She'd always been annoyed by the random pangs of anxiety, and had to remember to stay calm.

Taking a breath, Nia went inside and joined the line for the buffet style meal. The food looked absolutely delicious, barbecue, seafood and veggies, and a dessert bar that Nia couldn't wait to get to. As she was deciding between the barbecue pork and some sort of friend shrimp, a voice next to her sighed. "I swear, those grips are always first in line and take all the best options."

A small, purple haired woman stood beside her, frowning over the options. "I just wanted the chicken, and it's completely picked over."

"You snooze you lose Cynthia." A tall, brawny man was on the opposite side, looking over the table.

"What do you think you're doing Timmy? Everyone's got to eat first before you go back for seconds."

"More like thirds." Timmy, an incongruous name for such a large and built individual, snagged a roll. "I'm just waiting for you to come sit with me one of these days."

"I'm going to sit with my new friend here. You wouldn't want me to be mean to the new girl, would you?"

Timmy grabbed another scoop of vegetables for his plate. "That hurts me though."

Cynthia rolled her eyes, though she was clearly enjoying their interaction. "I have a feeling you'll live."

Timmy winked at Nia, before grabbing another roll and disappearing. Cynthia scooped a few bits of chicken onto her plate. "Want to come sit with us?" Her blue eyes focused on Nia, who smiled.

"I didn't realize I had a choice." That got a smile out of Cynthia.

"Oh, I like you. We're going to be friends, I know it."

Nia followed her to a couch, where a few other people sat. Cynthia introduced her to Pom, Ezra and Amy, the hair and makeup team, which Cynthia was the head of. They all made room for Nia, and she was folded into their conversation, a heated debate over which Chris was the best Chris in Hollywood. Nia cast her vote for Chris Evans, because duh. Relieved, Nia let the conversation wash over her, relived that she'd found a group of people who'd welcomed her so easily.

After dinner, Nia made her way back to the house, waving goodbye to her new friends. The sun was setting in a gorgeous burst of color, reds, pinks and purples streaking the sky. She couldn't help but realize her luck, to have been blessed with a job that took her to such an amazing location. Nia swore to herself to make the most out of this trip.

When the sun made its final dip below the horizon, Nia reluctantly wandered back into the quiet, big house, relishing the calm before the madness of women's arrival tomorrow. Nia had some prep work to go over, questions to look at, and she wanted to get a good night's rest. Bags under her eyes were not a good look on camera. Noticing the kitchen light was on, Nia walked in to see Elijah by the stove, uncorking a bottle of wine. He looked freshly showered, his hair still wet and curling against his head. Nia leaned on a counter and offered a hesitant smile. "Mind if I get in on that?"

"Are you sure I won't jump you and try to seduce you?" He grabbed another glass and poured.

"Eli, you can't really be mad about what I said to Kerry." Nia rolled her eyes. "You always did have the womanizer reputation."

Elijah carefully set the glass of wine in front of her. "If I could have expected anyone to understand me, it would have been you."

Nia chewed on her lip, watching the emotions play on his face. He looked as if he was…disappointed in her. She didn't like the way that made her feel. "Honestly, I wish I did understand you. But it's been years since I could actually say that I ever did, however partially. It's not like you ever really let me in back then. So what else am I supposed to go off of?"

"How about me, right now?" His eyes connected with hers, and a shiver of electricity ran down her, from her toes to the tips of her hair. In another lifetime, Nia might have linked hands with him, prolonging that intensity…but instead, she broke their gaze.

"You're right. And I am sorry for coming at you like that."

"It's fine." But there was still tension around his mouth, and Nia knew that it wasn't really fine.

"Are you sure?"

"Don't worry about it." Taking his glass, he waved briefly before heading towards the stairs. As Nia watched his retreating figure, she felt like there was a rock in her stomach. She did not like whatever this feeling was. For a moment, she thought about chasing Elijah down and talking more, but decided to let it go. She wasn't here for him. And maybe, the sooner they both realized it, the sooner they could act something like friends.

Nia left, determined to focus on her work, before doubling back for her forgotten glass of wine. She'd need it tonight.

The First Day

NIA

"Welcome to With This Ring, where thirteen lucky ladies will be competing in a series of wild and intense events for the love of celebrity bachelor Elijah James--"

"CUT!"

Warren cut Nia off, shaking his head. "This is great, it really is – but I need sexy. And give me a little attitude!"

"Attitude?" Nia knew exactly what he was asking but hoped that maybe, just maybe, Warren would surprise her. And maybe she'd be invited to the Academy Awards and actually win one. Both very unlikely things to happen at this point in her life.

"You know." Warren snapped his fingers. "Sassy. Bring the energy. Don't be scared to do your thing."

A place in Nia's stomach soured. They wanted 'sassy.' She was black, and Hollywood just loved to embrace the sassy black woman.

"Let's do it again. Roll it!" Cameras were trained back on her, and her cue was given. Nia froze for a moment before giving the lines again.

"Welcome to With This Ring, your favorite sexy show of the summer. Thirteen lucky ladies will compete in a series of wild tests for the heart of drop dead gorgeous Elijah James, but only one will win. Stick around and see who goes home, and who comes out with a ring."

"Cut. That was good!"

Nia barely managed to stop her eye roll. She hadn't changed anything about her inflection, refused to give it the stereotypical spin he wanted. It was a silent form of protest, but better than shrieking and whacking Warren over the head with a boom pole.

"Let's do it again, with even more sass this time."

Nia eyed the distance between her and the boom operator. If she was quick enough, she could grab the pole and shove it up Warren's ass before he knew what hit him. But her savior came in another form. Kerry's voice rang out from the monitors she was huddled around with a few others. "Warren, you can't keep telling our black hostess to be sassy."

He huffed. "There's nothing wrong with a little sass-"

"There is, and it's a PR problem waiting to happen. We got this shot over ten takes ago, let her have a break, alright? The ladies are going to be arriving soon and we need to keep the day moving."

Warren grumbled, but dismissed Nia, who shot a grateful look to Kerry. She shot off the set before Warren could figure out a way to make her say it again.

Making her way to the kitchen where craft services had set up a station of various snacks, Pom and Ezra smiled as Nia joined them. She found a bottle of water and took a massive swig, which was somehow the best water she'd drank. Looking at the activity around them, crew members were constantly in motion, setting up lights and microphones and adjusting decor in preparation for the arrival of the women. The first load was due to arrive around midday and it was just past eleven in the morning. Nia turned her attention back to the breakfast options, deciding on a bottle of orange juice and a muffin.

"A woman who's not afraid of carbs, I knew we'd be friends." Pom was grabbing a hot bagel that'd just popped up, hot potato-ing it from hand to hand.

"Whoever said carbs were the devil never experienced joy as a child." Nia smiled, popping open her juice.

"Exactly! Can you tell that to Ezra? He's terrified of them. Hasn't had a piece of bread since high school."

Ezra, who was sipping on a cup of tea, rolled his eyes. "Not terrified. I allow myself a bit of carbs every now and then. It's all about moderation."

As Ezra and Pom argued over what moderation looked like, Nia spotted Elijah out the corner of her eye (she definitely wasn't looking for him) talking with someone she hadn't yet met. He looked…good, damnit, and she hated that she was noticing it. Navy shorts that showed muscular calves, with a white collared shirt unbuttoned just enough to show a hint of his strong chest, and just the right amount of hair, that glistened like it belonged in a freaking blockbuster movie. It was unfair, how the simplest things looked like runway material on him. His eyes met hers across the room, and again Nia felt a warm sensation flood her body. Jumping, she tried to cover being caught looking him over by sweeping her eyes over the other people beside him and then turned her attention back to Pom and Ezra, faking interest in their conversation. "*Real* clever," she muttered to herself.

They hadn't spoken since last night, which Nia thought was for the better. It's not like she'd spent a good chunk of the night worried over how Elijah's face had looked when he'd overheard their conversation. She wasn't. Nia just couldn't afford let herself get distracted by him, not when her focus should be on nailing this job. So this distance was a good thing and would help her focus.

Nia successfully managed to avoid Elijah until the women started arriving at the island. She'd been in the green room, doing a last minute touchup on her makeup with Cynthia, before heading out into the hallway. Elijah was coming up the opposite direction towards her, and they ended up doing that awkward dance thing, trying to avoid being in the other person's path and moving side to side with each other. He finally stepped off to the side, letting her have the bulk of the hallway to pass through. "Hey. Good luck out there." A whisper of his hand landed on her arm before he pulled back.

Pausing she looked at him briefly. "You too." She ducked her head, heading for the door and feeling green heat from his eyes follow her. Looking back, she saw he was still watching her. Feeling off balance, Nia gave him a little wave before turning the corner.

Nia made her way out back to her mark by the gorgeous infinity pool, feeling better and off balance all at the same time. Taking a deep breath of the salt tinged air Nia counted to ten, forcing any and all idle thoughts from her mind. In the distance, Nia could hear as waves crashed against each other, creating a white noise for the thoughts beginning to settle down in her mind. Finally, finally it was quiet up there in her mind, and Nia let out a soft breath.

"Alright Nia, the first girl…sorry, *woman*, will be headed your way in less than five!" She hadn't even noticed Isaac speaking to her as she looked over the water. The two operators had their cameras trained on Nia, getting their focus perfected. Isaac stopped, listening for someone in his earpiece. He nodded and winked at Nia. "She's here now. Ready for the madness?"

Nia took a breath and turned on her smile. "Ready for whatever."

"Thirteen lucky ladies have just arrived on the island, ready to fight for love. Only one will succeed. Let's get ready to meet them - the first one is heading out now." Nia sparkled into the camera, feeling the warmth of the sun settling into her skin. The glass doors slid open and out came a pretty brunette, dressed in a red bikini and sarong. She slowly strutted her way over as if she were on a catwalk, soaking up every second the cameras followed her. Eventually, she stopped next to Nia, who got an eyeful of professionally whitened teeth that could pass for bike reflectors as the woman smiled into the cameras.

"Care to tell us your name?" Nia felt her eyebrows lifting and consciously brought them back down.

"Nicole Summers from Long Beach, California." Nicole finally made eye contact with Nia, giving her the once over before going back to her carefully posed expression for the cameras.

"Tell us, Nicole from Long Beach - why'd you audition for this show? "

"Because Elijah James is looking for love, so he had to meet me of course."

Ugh, Nia thought, though she nodded and asked her next question. "Why will Elijah fall for you over everyone else?"

Nicole gestured to her body, removing the sarong and fully flaunting her figure. "Just look at me."

Oh great, it was one of those thong bikinis. Nia made eye contact with the camera, a small smile on her face. "Yes, bold move coming out in a bikini for the first meeting."

Nicole's face was smug. "I know my assets."

"And now, so do we. Head on over to the cabana while we bring out the next competitor." Behind, she could see Isaac and John the boom operator smother a few smiles.

Nicole threw a look at Nia. "As far as I'm concerned, there is no competition." She slowly made her way over to the cabana.

"And just like that, Nicole has strong words to start the show. Let's get the next contestant out here."

A preppy red head bounced out, wearing a more reasonable sun dress, cowboy hat and boots. Though hyper, she was radiating good energy. "Hi! I'm so excited to be here y'all!" The red head barely restrained herself from jumping up and down before throwing her arms around Nia in a huge hug. "My name is April Montgomery, it's my first time in Hawaii, and I'm here to win me a man, woo!" The woo was punctuated with a little air pump.

Nia felt her personal bubble pop, and smiled ruefully as she broke away from April. "Aw, a hugger. What makes you think you have what it takes to land Elijah James?"

"I'm full of fun, know my way around a man, and there's never a dull moment when April comes to play."

"April, you are referring to yourself in third person?" Nia couldn't resist asking.

"Yep! Just one of April's quirks."

Just like that, April went from quirky cute to potential knife wielding psycho. As she wondered about Aprils other 'quirks', Nia took an imperceptible step away from her. "Alright April, Nia is telling you to go hang out at the cabana with our other contestant for now."

"You're getting the hang of it!" April waved before bounding away to the cabana.

"I'd give anything to be a fly on the wall when those two meet." Nia let a megawatt smile beam and Isaac let out a bark of laughter.

The next women out were actually twins, Samantha and Camille, and almost identical except for their hairstyles. Both dirty blondes, Samantha's hair was in a short, chic cut while Camille's hair cascaded down her back in waves. Their smiles were identical, however, and they moved in sync with each other. It was weirdly fascinating to watch.

"I want to say double trouble, but that wouldn't give either of you credit for making it this far. Who's the big sis?"

Samantha smiled. "I am, by three minutes."

"She never lets me forget it either." Camille rolled her eyes, but it was clear she was fond of her sister.

"Is there going to be any sibling rivalry in play here? Have you two ever fought over a man before?"

Samantha and Camille shared a look, before Camille spoke. "We're used to competing for everything, but it's anybody's game."

"We may be twins, but our personalities are opposite. I feel bad for Elijah, he's got to pick between us." Samantha linked her arm with her sister's.

"Ugh. Two cute. Two because, there's two of you? Bad joke, I know. Anyway, head on over to the cabana with the other ladies."

They took a quick break after the next two women, Olivia, a Korean American who was stunning but nervous, and Cristal, the first black contestant Nia had seen yet. Pom and Maddison made their way over to Nia, with Maddison popping an umbrella over her head to give some relief from the sun. Pom used a few blotting wipes, and gave her a little touch up. "These women are something else, let me tell you." She whispered, aware of the boom close by.

Nia could definitely agree with that. "They found some characters for sure."

Maddison rolled her eyes, and lowered her voice. "One of them is a real bitch."

Nia leaned in closer. "Did you get her name?"

But they were interrupted, Isaac coming back over to get back to filming. Pom and Maddison disappeared, and Nia got busy with the next cluster of introductions.

There was Charli, who seemed to be more interested in learning more about Nia than Elijah; Ava, who couldn't be as dumb as she acted, leading Nia to wonder if that was part of her 'thing'; and Tiffany, a conservative single mother from Texas who was looking for a father for her child.

Then came Lily Martin, a pretty caramel headed woman who was Nia's favorite contestant so far. At first glance, Lily looked like she was spoiled, but when she spoke Nia got the sense that she was level headed and had a good heart. Lily approached Nia with a warm smile. "I love your hair! Your curls are absolutely gorgeous."

"Thank you! Can you tell us why you think you're a good fit for Elijah James?"

Lily paused, thinking for a beat. "I don't know that I will be, honestly. I still need to meet the guy." She laughed self-consciously. "Maybe it'll be me, maybe it's someone else, but I'm just glad for the chance to find out."

Nia respected the fact that Lily was the only one who didn't assume she would automatically win Elijah's affection. A little wave of jealousy made itself known – she could definitely see Lily being someone Elijah liked – but she tamped that down. What did it matter to her anyway? *You're not here for him, and he's not for you.* Nia reminded herself. *If he finds real love, all the better.*

Danielle was up next, a bi-racial woman with pretty curls and golden-brown skin. Nia smiled, glad to see another woman of color. "Can you tell us why you think you'll be the one to win Elijah James' heart?"

Her answer was surprisingly…direct. "I'm a winner. I don't lose, I don't take prisoners, and I don't give up."

Nia's eyebrows rose. "You know this is a reality show, not a war, right? Some of these women could become friends of yours."

Danielle rolled her eyes. "Who was it that said love is a battlefield? She had it right."

Nia gave her a little credit for knowing Pat Benatar, at least until Danielle kept talking.

"And why would I take advice from you, someone who probably wasn't hot enough to be a contestant?"

"I'm sorry, what?" Nia barely stopped her jaw from dropping. The venom came out of left field, surprising her.

"It's fine, not everyone is meant to end up with a celebrity." Danielle said it with a smile, as if that would soften her words any. Nia could feel her face flushing, and said the first thing that popped in her head as she turned back to the camera.

"Spicy words from Danielle, who had to turn to a reality TV show to find love."

She got a sick moment of enjoyment as Danielle's face soured. "Excuse me--"

"You're definitely excused. Why don't you go sit with the rest of the contestants? Try not to bite any heads off." Nia turned away from Danielle, effectively dismissing her.

"Whatever, help." Danielle flicked her hair over her shoulder before sauntering over to the cabana.

The cameras cut, and Nia took in the shocked faces of the operators and Isaac. "I guess that's the bitch they were talking about."

Warren came out, clapping his hands. "I LOVED that Nia! Way to go, keep that same energy up. That shit is excellent for ratings."

Nia tried to smile, and managed some version of it for Warren who was muttering how glad he was that they'd authentically found their villain. She didn't like being bitchy back, but something in her had taken over the wheel. Nia wanted to feel proud for standing up for herself, but it didn't sit right with her to be a complete bitch, even if it was deserved. When they go low, you were supposed to go high, and Nia had met her right at her level.

Thankfully, she managed to finish up introductions with the last of the contestants (two women, Roxy and Molly, who was into the dark arts) unscathed before they broke for lunch. The women were left to eat outside and get to know each other, where they had stationary cameras and microphones positioned all around to catch anything that went on.

Now that she had a break, Nia managed to slip away upstairs to her bedroom under the guise of using the bathroom, hoping for a bit of quiet as she stepped onto the balcony. What she found was Elijah up there already. Before Nia could figure if she could sneak away or not, his deep voice froze her.

"Still avoiding me?"

The Same Page

ELIJAH

He'd heard, rather than saw Nia step onto the balcony. Turning, he caught her frozen in the doorframe and smiled at the caught look in her eyes. Elijah couldn't help noticing again how pretty she looked, especially in the sunlight. The pink of her dress warmed the brown of her skin, and he shouldn't be noticing how smooth it looked. He met her eyes as she started backing away.

Crossing his leg, he leaned back in his seat. "You can't keep avoiding me, you know. The island isn't that big." Nia frowned at that.

"I'm not avoiding you, I'm just making it easier to stay out of each other's way."

"That's avoidance, Nia."

She rolled her eyes. "Whatever. Besides, I thought you were mad at me."

Elijah could see she hadn't meant to admit that. "Why would you care if I was mad at you?"

Her eyes shifted to the water in the distance. "I wouldn't care – "

"I was mad at you." He got a perverse sense of enjoyment as she threw up her hands in exasperation, eyes darting back to him.

"So, I was right. Why give me a hard time?"

"Because you don't know why I was mad." Elijah shifted towards her, and her arms crossed over herself protectively. A small pang struck him, as he wished for the days when Nia had been open to him and not shut off and distant.

"Are you going to enlighten me?"

"Are you going to stop judging me?" He leaned forward, elbows on his thighs.

"I don't judge you- "

"You do." He stopped, trying to find a way to say what he needed to say without sounds like a complete tool. "Look, I know I was a dick to you in college and I in no way deserve your trust…but that was a while ago. I've changed since then. Sure I had my fun, who didn't? But that stopped when I met you, and I like to think that I don't treat women like real life single use sex dolls."

"I don't think that…" Nia chewed on her lip.

"It sure seems like it. And I can tell you that anything you've seen that looks like I'm a man whore is something that is creatively cultivated by my publicist."

It was a sore spot for him but he wanted to be completely honest with Nia. His publicist was always encouraging him to be seen with someone new, as it upped his desirability factor or whatever, and for a while, he'd gone along with it. He didn't sleep with all those women, despite what the tabloids reported. They were seen and photographed together and then parted ways, but Elijah had always felt weird about the interactions. He just wanted to settle down with the right woman eventually. Now, that's not to say he was a saint, (he was a man, after all) but he didn't want to be tainted forever by his past sins or fake news.

"Honestly, I don't think that." She shifted her weight to her other foot. "But can you blame me for being cautious? The man I knew last hurt me. Badly." She bit her lip, looking down at her hands before back at him. Seeing the raw honesty on her face made Elijah realize just how much he'd impacted her. He'd been reckless with her heart and she was the one dealing with the consequences.

"I know I did, but I can't keep apologizing for something I can't change now." He stood, and leaned opposite her on the doorframe and met those big soft brown eyes of hers. "What I can change is how I am now and going forward. But we won't make any progress if we're stuck in the past."

Nia's lips twisted as he watched her think about that. "I really want to ask if that's a line, because if it is, bravo."

"It's not." Elijah wanted to make that clear for her.

"I'll work on not putting you in a box, but don't you think it'd be easier if we kept some distance between ourselves?"

"No." The words were rushed out of him before she'd even finished the sentence. He couldn't, didn't want Nia to avoid him. "No. That would just make people wonder why we don't get on."

There was more than a little doubt was on Nia's face as he pressed on. "Think about it. People love drama. If they sensed there was something off between us, don't you think there'd be more speculation than if we were friendly?"

Nia slumped on the doorframe. "I hate to say you're right, but that makes a twisted sort of sense."

"All I'm asking is that you give me a chance to prove that I changed. You did. I think we owe it to ourselves to have an actual fresh start." Elijah could see it when she finally came to her decision.

"Fine. We'll be friends, be cordial and not cause any drama."

He smiled, relief flooding through his frame. "See how easy it is if you just agree with me?"

Nia rolled her eyes. "Don't make me regret this."

"I won't." Standing, he stuck out his hand. Nia hesitated, but slowly slipped her hand into his. "We're going to have fun these next few weeks." He turned her palm to his and dropped a spontaneous kiss there before dropping her hand and backing toward his door. "I'll see you down there."

Before Nia could change her mind and he could question why he'd kissed her hand, Elijah slipped out the door and back downstairs where crew milled about, getting ready to get started again from lunch. He was glad Nia had given him a chance, knew it shouldn't matter what she thought of him, but it did. And if Elijah was being completely honest with himself, he'd acknowledge that he wanted more than just friendship with her. Nia stood out to him in a sea of unimpressive women, and he was constantly drawn to her. So even if he couldn't act on it, Elijah wanted her around. It was a little selfish, a little self torture. He sighed. This would be a long few months of filming, but he had to get through it.

NIA

Nia made her way back just as crew were coming back in from lunch. The women were already rounded up by the pool, cameras in position capturing everything. As Nia was touched up by Cynthia and Ezra, Kerry gave her a few last-minute notes. "Nia you're going to go out first, welcome the ladies again, and then introduce Elijah, who's going to do his charming thing, and then get the game started. It's already two o'clock, so we want to get as much filming done before the sun sets."

It was hard to focus on Kerry as Cynthia prodded her face with various brushes. "You got it."

Warren poked his head inside, gaze landing on Nia. "Let's get started people!

Nia, we need you out here."

"She's coming now." Cynthia added a dab of color to Nia's lips before sending her outside. She stood just beyond camera as she waited for Warren to give her to go ahead. The women were discussing Elijah, of course, and what they thought he'd be like. Warren gave Nia her cue, and she walked into the area, a smile on her face.

"Did I hear someone mention Elijah James?" A few of the women clapped for her, which was weird, but nice. And then she realized the applause was for Elijah and laughed at herself. "Ladies, I know you're not here to hear me talk, so I'll get right to it. You've gotten to know each other, now it's time to meet the man of the hour. Let's bring out Elijah James!"

That got a huge scream from all of the women, and Nia was halfway afraid they would stampede her to get to Elijah, who made his way down the path and over to her. Elijah wore charm and sex appeal like nobody's business, and Nia could even feel herself start to get a little warm looking at him. But then Danielle actually powered through the crowd of women and was the first one in front of Elijah, sticking her hand out for him to take. Elijah spared her a smile, before taking a few steps back to address all the women.

"Hi ladies, I'm so glad to finally meet you all." Elijah's voice was smooth like a masseuse's hands gliding over your skin. There were various forms of hellos as the women soaked him up. Nia fell a little to the side as Elijah went around and met each woman individually, with what seemed like a bit of excessive touching coming from some of the women. April, of course, launched herself at Elijah in a hug while Nicole, Nia noted, made sure to press her entire chest along Elijah's.

Once he'd introduced himself to everyone, Nia stepped back in to the fold. "Now, I know you all want nothing more than to take Elijah and start figuring out the key to his heart, but we have a little game first: Never Have I Ever." Nia led them down the patio where a little game area had been set up. Benches were situated around a table, where each girl had a name card and ten hearts.

Samantha and Camille looked at each other and giggled while Ava looked a little worried. "What's the point of this?" Cristal wondered aloud.

"All relationships start with a getting to know you phase, the time where you're figuring out your potential partner and their secrets. The game is simple: You all have ten hearts, as does Elijah. The last five women standing win the game, and will have a beachside, candle lit dinner with Elijah tonight, while the others stay back home."

There were a few murmurs as the women talked this over. Danielle snorted, and looked over at Nicole. "Basically, the more boring women are the winners?"

Nia shook her head, a small smile on her face. "You are allowed to try and get other contestants 'out' of the game quicker." Some of the women definitely perked up at that.

"Remember to be honest - that's half the fun!" Nia turned to head off camera before throwing one last thing back. "I would say go easy on him ladies, but where would be the fun in that?"

The women drew random numbers to see who'd start first, and Samantha kicked off the game. "Never have I ever had an open relationship." Nia saw a number of hearts get tossed to the middle, surprisingly from quiet Olivia and the conservative Tiffany while Elijah kept all his hearts to himself.

"You never wanted to have some freedom in a relationship?" Camille asked Elijah, leaning toward him on the table.

"I'm not against open relationships, they're just not personally for me. I don't like to share." He winked at her.

Next up was April, who clapped her hands excitedly. "Yay, April's turn! Never has April ever stolen a man or date from someone else."

Danielle, Nicole and Tiffany dropped hearts, along with a sheepish Samantha. Elijah's eyebrows lifted. "Samantha? Who'd you steal a man from?"

Camille pointed a finger at herself, and there was a burst of laughter around the table. Samantha shook her head ruefully "It wasn't intentional, I swear!"

"My ass it wasn't!" Camille rolled her eyes. "She took Cameron Porter from me, who was supposed to be my date to senior homecoming."

"He'd thought he was asking me in the first place." Samantha threw back. Nia smothered a smile, enjoying the friendly bickering between the siblings. It reminded her of her and Yaya, who argued over everything but loved each other fiercely.

After that, the rounds flew by, with the women getting more and more targeted with each other. Elijah tossed in a heart when Ava mentioned stalking an ex on social media which Nia very much wanted to question him about badly about it. Thankfully, Roxy asked a few questions, though he didn't actually give any information that was useful. Molly said she'd never cursed anyone, which got a moment of silence from the group. Thankfully, no one dropped a heart for that.

Danielle cleared her throat, a soft *freak* falling in the silence. Molly's eyebrow raised at Danielle. "I could always start now."

Nia smothered a laughed at that as Cristal took her turn.

"Remind me never to mess with you, girl. Never have I ever gotten a tattoo."

A few more hearts were dropped at that, Elijah included, which surprised Nia. He'd been deathly afraid of needles in college. "What'd you get a tattoo of?" Danielle asked. Nicole and Tiffany giggled, as if Danielle had actually said something funny.

"And where did you get a tattoo?" Samantha added, wagging her eyebrows.

"It's small, but I got a tattoo on my bicep." Elijah rolled up his sleeve, revealing small block letters. "It says 'Never regret the things that made you smile.'"

A wave of delighted sighs went around the table and Nia couldn't help the simultaneous rush of warmth and goosebumps that ran across her skin, especially when his smile lit up his face.

The sun was finally starting to set in a fiery blaze of color when it finally came to Elijah's last heart and Lily took her time thinking of her question. She looked around the table with a small smile on her face. "Never have I ever been in love."

A couple hearts were dropped around the table, but Nia watched as Elijah thought about his answer, before tossing his last heart in the middle as the ladies whooped and cheered. April leaned forward, eyes more than a little glossy from the amounts of wine they'd been drinking. "Who was she? Was she your first love?"

Nia held her breath waiting for the answer. It mattered to her. A lot.

Elijah nodded with an enigmatic smile. "She was."

April heaved a huge sigh, followed by a delicate burp. "I hope I have love someday. Real love."

This did interesting things to Nia's stomach. Nia had known that Elijah had cared for her, but he'd never said those three words to her. And though she'd never said anything, it had mattered a lot, considering the length of time they were together. But if he'd said it, he would have had to define the relationship, which he wasn't big on doing at the time. But now Nia couldn't help wondering if it was her he was referring to, or if he'd found someone else after her that had won those words from him. It was eating her up, and she fought to keep her focus on the present. They weren't here to date each other, but they could be friends. And friends didn't worry if one of them had feelings for the other, past or present because romantic feelings had no place in a platonic relationship. Any and all thoughts that had no business taking up residence in her mind were banished to the back of her mind.

Nia almost jumped out of her skin when Kerry tapped on her shoulder. "That's your cue," pointing toward the table.

Putting on a smile, Nia approached the group and took note of who still had the most hearts in front of them. "Looks like we have our winners: Lily, Sam, Nicole and Olivia! Congratulations ladies! You four, plus Elijah, will be treated to an oceanside dinner that's being set up on the beach right now. The rest of you can go back to the resort and start enjoying your first night on the island. I know our four lucky ladies will." She managed to not make direct eye contact with Elijah, knowing that would break the focus she had on work.

The winning ladies cheered while the rest of the women wore various degrees of displeased expressions on their faces. Nia watched as the groups started to disperse, with Nicole practically shoving one of the other girls out the way so she could walk next to Elijah down to the beach. Nia noted the cameras getting that, along with her hand 'accidentally' brushing Elijah's ass before continuing up to his back. He jumped, before schooling his look of surprise. The other women trailed along, talking excitedly as they fought for Elijah's attention.

It was a perfectly romantic setting, with the sun almost fully set and a decadent table set up along the beach with torches and candlelight setting the mood but instead of watching, Nia turned and made her way back inside. She needed a glass of wine, and time to plan.

The Olive Branch

NIA

Nia woke up the next day refreshed and determined to keep things light between her and Elijah. It had to be normal to have old feelings resurface when you meet an old flame, but that didn't mean she could or had to act on them. Exes managed to be friendly all the time, so why shouldn't she and Elijah manage it? They were both mostly mature humans, so it shouldn't be hard to do. She made it through a quick self-led yoga session before showering and heading downstairs, where some of the women were already eating breakfast. It was a weird feeling only because she didn't want to get in the way of cameras picking up whatever was going on between the women, but it was where she was supposed to live so she'd find a way to deal with it.

After fixing herself a plate of scrambled eggs and turkey bacon with some fresh berries on the side, Nia made her way out to a sun room off the side of the house that was luckily unoccupied, and managed to enjoy her breakfast in some peace. It really was a beautiful house, with gorgeous tropical décor that worked so well with the views of the beach. She snapped a photo and sent it to the group chat with her friends along with a yawning emoji. That got a few laughs and jealous texts.

A little while later, a production assistant found Nia and brought her to the pool area so they could get the next game started. Walking out onto the terrace, Nia laughed when she saw what the women had to play. Outside, there was possibly the largest game of Twister set up that she had ever seen, with one side place precariously close to the pool. Nia silently bet that someone would fall in before the day was over. Kerry saw her and waved Nia over to the table she was at. "Good morning! Looks like a twister is in the forecast!"

Nia winced, and Kerry laughed at her expression. "Be warned, Warren is going to want you to use something like that for today's game."

"I'll make it work," Nia smiled, already planning for it. "I take it this game was his idea too? Someone is definitely going to fall in that pool."

"Actually, it was Isaac's idea." Kerry rolled her eyes but looked at him fondly across the patio, where he spoke with one of the set dressers. "Warren's idea was to oil them all up while they play." She gestured to the table filled with bottle of baby oil.

"Oh, someone's definitely going in the water then." Nia laughed, shaking her head. "I'm just glad I'm not playing that game."

"Same, girl. But you will be spinning the pointer and calling out the colors… with a front seat view of all the action."

Nia smiled, thinking about Danielle or Nicole falling ass first into the water before wondering if that was too mean of her. *Nah. Probably not.* "Is it wrong if that makes me a little excited?"

Kerry shook her head. "Nope, I know I am. Some of the women definitely started off on the wrong foot for me, so I'm hoping a few of them fall in myself."

"Points coming through!" A voice called behind them, and Kerry and Nia ducked out the way, letting a couple of camera guys pass by carrying equipment. The younger (and surprisingly attractive, Nia noted) of the two, threw a smile back at them, lingering a bit on Nia. He was tall, with dark wavy hair and a scruffy hotness that Nia liked. Kerry tried and failed to smother a huge grin.

"Looks like someone has an admirer already." She nudged Nia's arm, who watched the guy as they did some technical stuff with the camera lens.

"He was probably being polite," Nia started, before seeing the man look up at her, a slow smile spreading across his face.

"That is not a polite smile on Alex's face." Kerry fanned herself, causing a laugh out of Nia.

"Alex huh? He's cute." Maybe what she needed was a fling with a hot, available camera operator with the really strong looking arms.

"He's more than cute. If I weren't already taken we'd be having some non-polite fun." Kerry threw a pointed look at Nia. "And what happens on the island, stays on the island."

"Point received. Who's your boo?" Nia wondered if her hunch was correct. She'd noticed Kerry and Isaac were a little cozy with each other at times.

Kerry rolled her eyes but had a fond smile on her face. "Isaac, of course."

"I knew it! You two are adorable."

"He's alright." But Nia could see that Kerry meant more than that. She listened as Kerry recounted how they'd met as interns, and then met again by chance as adults, at a paintball course of all places. A small pang of not quite jealousy went through her as she wondered when she'd find someone to live out life with. It wasn't that she needed a man in her life, but she was at the point where she was ready to have someone to build with. Nia also knew she couldn't force things, and knew… hoped, that her time would come. Sooner, rather than later ideally.

A little later, the women and Elijah filed, out to the Twister board, all in swimwear. Nia noted the dark green shorts and open shirt he wore, figuring that she could still appreciate the man's looks, which were more sun kissed than they'd been a few days ago. Nia waited in a lounge chair with a sun hat and a beverage, courtesy of Kerry, who'd said Nia should be comfortable in the sun while the singles played games.

"Hello single people! The sun may be out but there's been a Twister sighting in the area." Warren did actually make sure she included that bit. "There can be some twists and turns that you have to adjust to in every relationship, so today we're going to have a little fun with that concept. You all are going to play a game of Twister. With Elijah."

The ladies giggled and eyed Elijah, who gave a charming smile and eager, "Alright!"

"The last woman standing gets to go on the first solo date with Elijah, so do your best to stay upright and on your feet." Nia grabbed the bottle of oil next to her and tossed it to the women. Cristal managed to catch it and looked at Nia curiously. "Make sure someone gets Elijah's back."

Smiling, Cristal took Elijah by the hand and started oiling his arms up. Tiffany grabbed another and started on his shoulders. Nia barely managed to resist rolling her eyes and the smile on Elijah's face, but knew if she were in his spot and the women were replaced with beautiful men…she wouldn't be complaining too much either. The rest of the women grabbed a few extra bottles and oiled themselves up. Nia's jaw dropped as Nicole bent down to crotch level and started rubbing Elijah's legs. "Like the view?" She pressed her cleavage shamelessly into his leg.

Elijah had a look of shock on his face, clearly at a loss for words. Nicole grinned, continuing to rub.

Samantha and Camille shared a look with each other while Roxy tossed a bottle of oil at Nicole's feet while beaming at her. "You forgot the oil, Hun. It might make it easier."

"I don't hear any complaints here." Nicole sniffed.

Lily came to the rescue, moving Elijah away from Nicole with a bottle of oil in her hand. "That's because he's in shock."

Once everyone was oiled up and shiny, everyone circled around the mat. Nia flicked the spinner and called out the first combination. "Molly: Right foot, yellow."

Molly went to her spot as Nia continued to call out combinations. "Don't be afraid, really get in there!" She cheered them on. Thanks to the oil, there was plenty of slipping as they tried to keep their hands and feet steady on the mat.

Elijah's turn came, and Nia spun the arrow. "Alright Elijah: Left hand, green." He slid in between the bodies, a few giggles as he bent into position, finding the green circle between a pair of legs. So far, none of the ladies had fallen yet and Nia was more than a little impressed. She knew she'd have been flat on her ass by now.

"We're getting real close here ladies." Elijah chuckled as he held steady. Nia flicked the arrow again.

"Danielle, Right Hand green."

Danielle, with a little smile on her face, moved her hand smack onto Elijah's ass.

Samantha rolled her eyes. "Wrong placement."

"I don't know, felt right to me." Smirking, she moved her hand to the ground and promptly slipped, causing Molly and Cristal to go down with her.

"First ladies are down! Sad to see you go, but the game goes on."

The three of them moved to the side while the game continued.

Isaac slipped up behind Nia and whispered into her ear a quick addition. "Warren wants you to go over there and add some more oil on them."

"More oil?" Nia thought they were oiled more than enough.

"Yeah, he wants more slippage to start happening."

"Whatever he wants." Standing, Nia grabbed a bottle of oil and made her way over to the board. "Seemed like a few of you were drying out, so let's add a little more oil here." She made sure to hit everyone a few times, despite hearing a few groans.

After that, the bodies started sliding like crazy. Camille went down next, followed by Lily, Tiffany and Ava.

Nia called out another combination. "Olivia, left foot, red!" Olivia tried and became the first one to fall into the pool. She came up sputtering, but good natured about it. Elijah even fell into the pool, sliding across the mat in what would be forever a memorable moment to Nia. She and a few of the girls got a solid laugh out of that imagery, at least until he dragged his soaking body out of the pool. That was enough to catch their attention as he toweled off. Nia dragged her eyes away from his impeccably muscled chest and back to her spinner, fanning herself discreetly. Looking at the camera next to her, she winked. "It just got a little hotter out here."

Eventually, it was down to April versus Nicole, and the girls were cheering them on. "April needs to hear y'all make some noise!" April yelled as she strained to keep her legs and arms in place.

"Down to the final two: who wants the first date bad enough? April, it's going to be left foot, blue."

April attempted to slide her foot to the spot but couldn't find any traction. In the most dramatic fall Nia had seen yet, April slipped and fell, somehow managing to slide backwards into the pool.

"We have a winner: congratulations Nicole!" Nicole threw herself at Elijah, trying to wrap her legs around him but only managing to slide down his body in what felt was a purposeful move. Nia aimed a smile at Elijah and Nicole. "Nicole, you've won a couple's massage with Elijah, followed by a romantic dinner…but first, a shower might be in order." She watched as the two of them were led away by one of the PAs, and shook her head. Elijah would have his hands full tonight with that one.

ELIJAH

Elijah didn't want to admit it, but he was already hiding out from the women. Out of sight in his greenroom, he tugged at the neckline of his tux while trying not to think about how much time they had left doing this. It wasn't that the dates were completely awful, (they weren't) but he was already tired of the subtle manipulations he could already see going on behind the cameras. Warren would come up and nudge him to go talk to one girl or the other, and he'd had to turn in a list of women he didn't want to be eliminated - only to be told that they weren't guaranteed to stay. He hated being manipulated, and could see that he'd be fighting against that for the rest of the show.

The date earlier that week with Nicole had been both predictable and surprising. She'd been shameless about parading her body around, which made him more uncomfortable than anything, but she'd surprised him with hidden depths that he hadn't honestly been expecting. It turned out she was a realtor with a penchant for making sure single parents found good, affordable homes for them and their children. That touched him, especially as he'd been raised by a single parent for the majority of his childhood. According to Nicole, drama had already started forming in the house. Each of the women were supposedly determined to one up the one before them, and there was already beef between some of the women.

An image drifted to him from earlier that week, back at the pool. It had been of Nia, relaxing by the side and calling out the colors for the game of twister, and he'd been taken with the urge to drag her into the game and have her body sliding against his. It was pure fantasy of course. She wasn't here for him and he had thirteen women eager to show how well suited they could be with him. But Elijah couldn't help the image from popping up at the least opportune moments, particularly on group dates when he should be learning more about the women.

As if he'd conjured her up, Nia stepped into the room wearing a stunning green dress that he committed to memory on the spot. It clung to her curves in a way that made him want to trace every part of her body and see where it led. It was more than her beauty that struck him though: there was something about *her* that called to something inside of him. And that affected him most of all. After a moment, he noticed she was beaming, almost bursting with happiness, and wondered what caused it.

"What's the grin for?"

Nia slipped onto the couch next to him, clearly eager to share whatever it was. He noticed the subtle, lovely scent of Shea butter and sweet almond oil that came with her, and something that was all Nia. "I just got off the phone with Lexie, my agent. I got an audition. A good one!"

"That's amazing! I want to ask what it's for, but I know you probably can't say." He leaned over and wrapped her in a hug, surprising her, and himself. He could feel his own smile matching hers, and was genuinely glad for her. It was always a great feeling getting an audition for a show that he'd really wanted to be part of, and knew those emotions all too well.

"I shouldn't, but I will say it's a drama pilot that has a great chance of making it to series."

"I'm really happy for you, Nia." An idea popped in his head and he said it before he'd fully thought it through. "I can help you with your part if you want. Be your reader."

At her surprised look, he explained. "Not that you'll need help, but I can read with you, give feedback. But only if you want." He tried to pass the help off as casual, but inside he really wanted her to say yes to this small thing. Elijah wanted, needed to spend some time more with her.

"The great Elijah James is offering to help a nobody prepare for a role? I'm honored." It was the sarcasm he was used to, but there was a smile behind it. He could see her thinking about it and prayed that she would say yes.

"I promise I won't overstep myself. I just wanted to be of some use."

Just as Nia opened her mouth to respond, Maddison poked her head in the room. "Ready for you two on set for the ring ceremony."

They both nodded, and Elijah stood, before helping Nia to her feet. She turned just before walking out the door. "You can help me. But no funny business."

A wave of relief passed through him. He didn't know why it'd meant so much for her to accept his offer, and later, he'd think about it in detail. Elijah grinned, before crossing his heart. "A little funny business, got it."

That little thing, knowing he'd be spending some time with Nia later made his mood brighter. It made it easier to get through the first ring ceremony, which dragged well into the night. Warren was constantly pausing and readjusting one thing or another, trying to make sure everything was perfect. He could tell Kerry and Isaac were beat, trying to keep up with him. By three in the morning, Elijah had managed to give rings to everyone, except for Olivia and Molly. They stood in front of him, as he held the last ring in his hands. Nia stood off to the side, a camera positioned in front of her. "One ring left, but two ladies stand before us. Whoever isn't offered a ring, will say her goodbyes and leave the island."

She paused dramatically, giving Elijah his cue to make his choice. "This is one of the hardest decisions I have had to make, and I hate to send anyone home right now, especially since I'm still getting to know everyone. But out of all the women here, I feel like I know you two the least. One of you, I feel stands out a little more than the other."

Elijah stepped forward and offered the ring to Molly, which he could see was a shock to her. "Molly, will you accept this ring, and another week on the island?"

Nodding, Molly let him slide the ring on her finger before wrapping him in a hug. She whispered in his ear, "I wasn't expecting that."

"I know." Elijah smiled at her, before letting her take her place beside the other women. On the outskirts of the filming area, he could see Warren a little shocked at his choice, which was what he'd wanted.

Behind him, he could hear Nia tell Olivia to say her good byes. He'd liked her, but she hadn't really shown much personality. Molly, who may or may not have been a witch, at least had one.

Warren came up, and slapped him on his back. "Good call not sending the flower child home right away. Don't want her putting any hexes on you. Or the show."

Elijah rolled his eyes. "Maybe I just thought she was nice." And maybe a little scared of being hexed.

"Whatever you say man."

Finally, Warren called for a wrap for the day. The women and crew dispersed, and Elijah was glad none of them tried to stop him for a conversation. He was beat. Heading upstairs, he made his way to his room, where he was surprised to see someone in his bed. Thinking one of the girls had decided to pull a stunt, he flicked on the lights prepared to kick them out when he stopped. It was Nia curled up in his bed, still fully dressed and completely knocked out. He figured she went into the wrong room and promptly passed out. She looked so tired, and Elijah didn't want to wake her. Tired as he was, Elijah was tempted to just crawl in the bed next to her. But he knew it would look bad if anyone were to see her in his room, and he didn't want to break her trust when she was cautiously giving it back to him.

Gently, he picked her up trying to disturb her rest as little as possible and walked her across the hall to her room. Nia barely moved in his arms. Laying her on her own bed, Elijah slipped off her shoes and unzipped the back of her dress a little so she could breathe easier. Placing a soft blanket over her, he couldn't help dropping a kiss on her forehead.

Nia sighed in her sleep, and wrapped her arms around Elijah's neck, pulling him down beside her. He didn't fight it, and let himself crouch next to her. Her lips met his, sleepy and full, and it sent a sound wave through him, an alert, a direct message: There was still *something* there. And he wanted to explore it. Badly.

Elijah let her lips brush over his again briefly, before pulling away. Much as he wanted to linger, he didn't, couldn't take advantage of her while she was basically asleep. He didn't want her this way, tired and unaware. He wanted her warm, and willing, knowing it was him giving her pleasure. Gently, he pulled away from her, and tucked the blanket higher around her before heading back to his room and to his bed. As he undressed, Elijah knew one thing: something had to give between them on the island, for better or worse. The last thought Elijah registered before he fell asleep was how nice Nia's scent was on his pillow, a small smile on his face. That night, he dreamed of Nia.

The Pool Game

NIA

Nia woke earlier than she'd wanted to the next morning with a fading memory of Elijah taking her to her room and tucking her into bed. The morning sun, still pale and dim, started to peek through her window as she remembered pressing a kiss to Elijah's lips. Her fingers came and touched them, as if she could still feel him on her. And then she buried her head in her pillow, embarrassment running through her mind. Did she actually kiss Elijah last night? Nia groaned aloud. But when she saw him later at the ATV excursion, Elijah acted as if nothing had happened, and maybe for him, nothing had.

The second week of filming quickly flew by, with Molly being eliminated the following ceremony. Nia found herself getting into a groove in the third week, and to her surprise, she was actually enjoying herself. She'd expected to be more bored than anything, but with her position on set, it was a fascinating juxtaposition of being both in front of and behind the camera and Nia had a great view. Watching the producers 'encourage' the women to have conversations that led to fights (the word manipulation was too 'negative') and see what the women did to get more time with Elijah was almost better than the NBA playoffs. One on occasion, Nia watched (with more than a little enjoyment) as Isaac whispered something to Danielle, who then went and picked a fight with Cristal, which led to throwing champagne in faces and security coming in to break up the ensuing fight. She might have to re-evaluate her stance on reality television - Nia could see why people got so addicted to show.

And some of the women, particularly Lily and April, had started growing on Nia. They'd sought her out, and despite the oddity of April's habit to speak in the third person, she actually really like her. The three of them would work out in the mornings sometimes, meeting up for beach runs and morning yoga sessions before filming started.

Elijah, true to his word, had coached Nia through her self tape, and he'd been very helpful. On one occasion, they'd met in Elijah's room the night after a particularly rough game of paintball, where Lily and the twins had been surprisingly agile and easily took out the other women. Nia had safely enjoyed the game from a distance, though it was interesting to see all the bruising that had already started on Elijah's arms. "If I didn't know any better, I'd say you were a delicate little flower with all these bruises." Nia teased as she examined his sculpted bicep for injury. For medical purposes, she reasoned. If she didn't know any better, she'd think Elijah was flexing for her.

"You wound me." Elijah shook his head but smiled down at her.

"And you've just proven my point." Nia smirked at him, and laughed at the face he pulled.

"Let's take it from the top smart ass."

Laughing, Nia pulled away and looked over the script she'd printed for her self tape audition. Taking a breath, she launched into the dialogue, putting as much emotion into it as she could.

"Why are you making that face?" Elijah asked, after she ended her dialogue.

Nia frowned, confused. "What face?"

He showed her the video he'd taken, to help point out things he noticed. "You have a tendency to do a little too much when you're gearing up for some emotional part. It's already there, I can tell, but you don't have to try so hard for it. I bet if you breathe a little and pull back some, it'll be much more powerful."

"So, you're saying I'm doing the most, basically?" Nia asked, flopping into a chair.

Elijah shifted an ice pack that was on his knee. "It would work for theater, but film is a different medium. Smaller movements work better."

Nia sighed, and wondered if maybe she should just back to her dad's business.

"And none of that negative thought process, it'll only trip you up more." Tossing the ice pack aside, Elijah walked over to Nia and pulled her up from the chair and shook her arms out. "Look at this like a love scene. I know your character is telling their boss why they deserve this job, and right now, it's looks exactly like you'd expect it to. Which would be fine for some people. But try it again, and let go of what it should look like, and think of it more as a last resort declaration of love. For this job."

An image of Elijah lingering over her popped into her brain, distracting her. Nia couldn't help but to glance at his lips, remembering how they'd felt.

Nia sighed, but nodded. "I'll try it your way." She took a deep breath a released it, ready to try again.   His hands gently squeezed hers before letting go, and Elijah held his phone up, trained on her face. This time, when she gave the words, she felt the difference – she'd let go. Instead of trying to put feelings in the words, she felt the words, let them feel real to her. And when she watched herself back, she'd even gotten goosebumps.

"That's it. That's the one. Very believable." Elijah's warm voice was right beside her, and she looked up into those emerald eyes that were warmed today with flecks of warm brown and gold.

"I hope they like it." He'd helped her unlock something, and to be honest, this was the best she'd felt about a self-tape in a long time.

Elijah's shoulder gently bumped hers. "You're really good, Nia. You've got something special."

"You think so?" Nia hated the note of uncertainty in her voice, and tried again.

"I mean, for this submission."

"In every aspect, but yes this submission as well." Nia tried, and failed to hide the smile that was breaking out on her face.

"Are you hiding a smile from me?" That slow, sexy grin started to slide across his face.

"Nope. No smile here." But Nia's own lips were betraying her, curving on their own accord.

He started to stalk her, and she tried to move to the other side of the bed and get out of reach. "Let me see the smile Nima."

The use of her family nickname for her is what got her. Nia couldn't help grinning at him for that. "I can't believe you remember my nickname." Nia didn't want to be touched, but dammit she was. She wanted to keep her walls up around him, but he'd been nothing but a good friend to her these last two weeks. It was like he was attacking every defense she had set up, and systematically working his way back into her life. Nia didn't like it…but also, she really did.

"I remember a lot of things about you." He leapt across the bed and grabbed Nia, tumbling them down and finding her ticklish spot underneath her arms. Nia broke into laughter, trying to avoid him but he was giving her no space. He surrounded her, his scent in her nose and strong body around hers. Elijah had used to tickle Nia when he'd been in a particularly playful mood, and it brought back a rush of memories to her. Managing to twist her body and get from under him, Nia pinned him under her hips and grabbed his hands. She was in no way a small woman, but knew that Elijah let her take control.

Their bodies heaved as they fought to catch breaths coming quick, and Nia became aware of just how closely they were pressed together. Some small part of her brain told her to lean forward, just a bit, and see if what she'd felt with the kiss was really or the product of a half lucid dream. Their eyes met, his eyes drop g to her lips and she felt something click insider her. This was a bad idea. She rolled off him and backed towards the door. Nia decided now was the perfect time to go get ready for today's filming. "Anyway. Thank you again for this. Hopefully something good will come out of it."

Her foot caught on something and Nia almost took a spill on the floor but caught herself at the last minute. "I should probably go get ready for bed. We've got that water volleyball thing in the morning."

Nia made it to the door and was just about to walk out when she heard a creak right outside. A light knock came, and she turned to Elijah with wide eyes. Danielle's muffled voice came through the door. "Elijah? Are you up?"

"Yeah, one second!" Elijah's whole body slumped at her voice, and if she hadn't been worried about being caught in Elijah's room, Nia would have laughed at his expression. As it was, she needed to get out of there, stat.

Quietly, she moved to the balcony, and out that door, leaving Elijah to deal with Danielle. She heard it open, and Danielle's voice float to the open air. Nia's heart was pounding as if she'd been caught doing something illicit, which was crazy. And almost being caught in his room? That was too close for her liking.

She managed to slip back into her room without issue and slumped into a chair. *Get it together,* Nia ran a hand through her hair. And she would, just as soon as she got over the warm, tingly feeling that had been lingering longer and longer the more time she spent with Elijah. She had to fight it to keep from growing, but the problem was, she didn't want to. Confused, Nia stared up at her ceiling. She wasn't supposed to be having feelings again for Elijah. That was not part of the plan. Damn him for being so cute and funny and sexy and caring…

She flopped over, pressing her face into the pillow. She had it bad.

ELIJAH

Elijah, after dealing with Danielle (which was more effective than a cold shower), managed to sleep without any other interruptions. The next morning, he knew he would be nothing but distracted today. His mind was constantly on Nia, as he dressed, made his way made his way downstairs, ate his breakfast. Something was shifting between them, and he was realizing that he wanted *more*. Elijah didn't want to classify them as old feelings – they were two different people back in college with different priorities – but he was more and more fascinated by the woman she had become, was becoming. He'd started to notice that he was more eager to see Nia on days of filming rather than the other women, despite all the time he was spending with them with the group and individual dates.

In staying with their 'friends' routine, (despite the kiss, which he still thought of) he'd managed to sneak in time with Nia here and there, and it was like a breath of fresh air to him. They'd been careful not to spend too much time together, but if he was being completely honest, him helping her with herself tape was just another way to spend some more time with her. Their conversations usually lasted well into the night, both of them usually to engaged to want to leave the other. He'd learned that she was as talented as he had suspected, if not more. And she fascinated him.

When Maddison invited him to set, Elijah made his way to the great room, stopping the admire the view of the ocean through the glass wall, the water such a pure blue that it made him want to grab a surfboard and catch a wave. Elijah moved out to the pool where he spied Kerry and Isaac by the monitors, watching the women as they discussed something about him. They smiled as he took a seat next to them, though Kerry went back to typing something out on her phone.

"How you are hanging in there?" Isaac asked. "The women running you ragged yet?"

Elijah laughed, and shook his head. "I'm just here for the ride."

"That's one way to look at it. Do you have your top picks for the one on one date this week?" Kerry asked, looking up from her phone.

"Does it matter? Warren's just going to pick whoever he thinks will work the best."

Kerry winced, unable to completely deny it. "He takes your picks into consideration."

"Glad to be even considered on a dating show." Elijah knew he was being dry, and also that it wasn't their fault. Easing up, he threw them a couple names. "Sorry, I know it's not you two. You can tell him Samantha or Lily."

"Thanks." Kerry gave him a grateful smile before diving back to her emails. "Oh, and hi Nia."

Elijah turned, hearing Nia's voice and got his first look at Nia as she met them by the pool, and any other thought he'd been thinking evaporated. Long, brown legs emerged from a light pink wrap thing, leading up to toned abs and glowing skin under an orange bikini top. He barely managed to move his eyes up to her face before someone noticed his brain short circuiting.

"Hey Kerry. Isaac, Elijah." Nia waved to them, but stayed standing. "Ready to get this pool day out the way?"

Isaac stood as well, stretching. "I know I am. Someone always gets hurt I feel like."

Elijah was still trying to get his brain to function enough to catch up with the conversation. Just as he was about to manage something, a commotion by the patio doors caught their attention. A couple of the camera operators were circling the group, and Isaac took a look at what was happening. Nia and Kerry left to get closer to the action. On the monitors, Elijah could see Samantha on the ground holding her ankle. A medic was beside her taking a look.

"Dammit Nicole! What was that for?" Camille stood, invading Nicole's space.

Nicole just fluffed her hair, clearly unbothered. "I can't help it if your sister is a klutz."

"You tripped her on purpose." Camille retorted, and Elijah had no doubt that Nicole probably did trip Samantha. "You were scared of our chances if both of us played volleyball today."

"Why would I care whether Thing One or Thing Two plays?" Nicole rolled her eyes to Danielle and Ava.

"Maybe it's because they were both volleyball champs in college and you were scared of a little competition?" Lily interjected, the cameras swinging over to her.

Isaac was glued to the monitors. "Warren is going to eat this shit up. He'll probably be pissed he missed it when he gets off that call." He let out a short laugh as the women continued to argue.

Samantha's voice broke in, as she was helped to her feet. "It's not that bad, just a sprain, but I definitely can't play.

Cristal turned to Kerry, who'd been on the sidelines watching the drama unfold. "Well, what happens now? We have odd numbers for our team."

April tapped her chin, thinking. "April has an idea! What if Nia played?"

All eyes landed on Nia, who was quietly taking it all in. "Excuse me?"

Lily nodded, warming up to the idea. "That could work! Would you be willing to play?"

"Um," Elijah watched as Nia threw a look to Kerry, who was thinking it over. He was literally on the edge of his seat to hear what she decided.

"That would work. It would be very interesting actually." Kerry nodded, giving the approval, and Elijah's heart gave an extra thump or two. He knew that it might be a bad idea to have Nia playing in the water directly across from him, but he also really, *really*, wanted her in the water from him. *Hopefully it's cold water.*

Tiffany looked at Nia, doubt on her face. "While that's great and all, can Nia even play volleyball?"

A small smile crossed Nia's face. "I may know a thing or two."

A couple of women clapped their hands, and Isaac slapped Elijah on his shoulder. "That's your cue man. Have fun out there."

Elijah didn't know how much he'd enjoy it. It seemed more like torture was in his future than fun. What happened next was the most erotically teasing, and fun game of water volleyball he'd ever played. He would normally call himself an athletic individual, but the sight of Nia in a bikini stalled his reflexes. Nia offered to serve, and drove a spike directly to Danielle who went under the water trying to avoid it. A few of the women snickered as she came up spitting out water.

"Hell yeah!" Lily high-fived Nia. "That was awesome!"

Silently, Elijah had to agree. Nia was great at volleyball, and he'd wondered how he didn't know that before. It was amazing to watch. He couldn't tell anyone anything he'd said to the women today, Elijah knew he was on autopilot at this point. His senses were filled with Nia, and he couldn't ignore it anymore. None of the other women attracted, or excited him the way she did and he was torn between doing the job he'd signed up for and taking a chance with Nia.

Nia's team won the match easily, despite a solid effort by the other one. Samantha and Camille both wrapped her in a huge hug, thanking her for the assist. "Where did you learn to play volleyball like that?" Lily asked, as they toweled off.

"I played in high school. We were regional champs three years in a row."

"That was something to watch. I had no idea." Elijah smiled at Nia.

"I'm just glad we, and by we, I mean Nia and Camille, kicked Nicole's butt." Lily gave a friendly nudge to Nia.

Kerry interrupted, "We need you all to get ready! Horseback riding on the beach in thirty minutes people!"

Nia waved bye to the women and disappeared towards craft services. Torn, Elijah knew he should go change…but he wanted to talk with Nia again. He knew he was a goner as he followed behind her.

NIA

At the crafty table, Nia held a small bag of trail mix and a bag of chips in each hand, debating. A charming voice spoke beside her. "Go for the chips, they'll be more fun."

She looked up to see Alex grabbing his own bag of chips. "Definitely, but which is better in the long run?"

He grinned, and shamelessly popped open his own bag. "Depends on what your priorities are. The trail mix might be healthier in the long run, but chips will leave you satisfied and happy with good memories."

"I do love a good memory," Nia smiled at him. He really was cute, with a dimple that appeared every so often in his left cheek.

"I have an idea, if you're game." A brief look of shyness passed over Alex's face before he schooled his expression. "Would you want to spend the dark day with me?"

Nia was surprised. She had noticed him looking at her every so often, but was in no way expecting to be asked out. She could hear Goldie's words echoing in her mind. *Find you an island man and have some island fun.* Maybe this would be a good way to start. "You know what, that sounds like fun."

"Perfect. Can I get your number?" He winked at her, and as Nia gave him her info, she waited to see if she felt anything…but nothing. He was hot, yes, but there wasn't anything really there. She sighed. Goldie would tell her to give it a shot, so she would. One of the crew members called Alex away, and he left with a smile on his face. "Hey Elijah, good game out there today."

Surprised, Nia turned to see Elijah behind her, and felt the zing course through her when their eyes connected. Of course, she felt something when she looked at him. There was an unreadable expression on his face as she looked him over. "Eli, I didn't hear you back there."

He shrugged, and grabbed a bag of trail mix. "Sounded like you were busy."

"Just talking. Did you need something?" She searched his face, an unreadable expression on it. Elijah shook his head before grabbing a bottle of water.

"No. Have fun on your date." He disappeared out the door, leaving Nia confused.

She didn't know why, but a small pang of guilt struck Nia even though it made no sense. They couldn't be together, so why did it matter if he'd overheard her being asked on a date? He was literally dating eleven other women right in front of her. *Was he jealous?* Nia tried to dismiss that thought, but it kept floating back to her. They'd agreed on friendship status, and she felt she was understanding him better than before. Which was why it felt as if he were jealous, even if he had no reason to be. They weren't there for each other.

Still, when Nia tried to talk to him later that night, he wasn't on their shared balcony like she hoped. The lights were dark in his room, and even though she sat out longer than she wanted to, he never came out to talk. Reluctantly, she went bak to her room, with the sinking feeling that Elijah might actually be avoiding her.

The New Resolution

NIA

After another round of eliminations (this time saying goodbye to Molly) Nia found herself on the deck of a yacht, a refreshing breeze blowing across her face as she soaked up the sun during the fourth week of filming. All she needed was an icy mai tai and the day would be utterly perfect. Below her, the women were in the middle of a cannon ball contest - this week had them doing water sports since Elijah loved the ocean. Nia smiled as she remembered the time when Elijah had dragged her to Rockaway Beach one summer in the city, and they'd had an impromptu beach day.

"We're going to the beach?" Nia questioned Elijah as they hopped off the subway car and began their trek to the coast.

"Hell yeah we are!" Elijah was grinning like a little kid, and his smile so radiant it made Nia catch her breath. "It's nothing like California beaches, but it'll work for today."

His hand had laced with her fingers, and they rambled down the boardwalk and into the warm, gritty sand. It was a perfect day for the beach, the sun hot and the sky so *blue, and Elijah was in a playful mood. They planted their blankets down and lay together, hot and smelling of sunscreen while looking at the few clouds in the sky.*

"That one looks like a pumpkin." Elijah pointed, drawing Nia's eyes toward a rotund cloud drifting by.

"Hmm, I get more of a formless blob, but we'll accept that answer."

Nia's sarcasm was rewarded with a quick tickle, making her laugh as Elijah moved to hover over her. Looking down at her, he dropped a slow, sweet kiss on her lips. "Last one to the water buys Mister Softee."

Laughing, they scrambled to the water, Elijah beating her with his head start.

"No fair, you cheated!" Nia pouted, splashing him a bit.

"I like mine with chocolate sprinkles."

Nia smiled as she thought about how they'd played in the cold water, and how they'd huddled together for warmth on the subway ride home. A huge splash followed by cheers sounded, breaking her reverie. She looked over the edge of the boat to see April coming up sputtering from the water, a grin on her face as Elijah gave her a score of an eight point five. As if he felt her looking at him, Elijah turned and found her easily. Even from this distance, she could feel the heat coming from his gaze, felt her heart speed up a bit.

Things had been a little awkward between them this week, and Nia couldn't help wondering why he was so put out. It wasn't that Elijah was mean to her, but he'd not been…as open as he once was. And she missed him. Nia had noticed that whenever she was with Alex, Elijah made a point to not be around them. Alex had been particularly attentive, well, as attentive as a person could be on a film set where he operated the camera. But he'd been making more and more of a point to show his interest to Nia, bringing her snacks and sending her messages throughout the day. While flattered, she wasn't feeling that spark or anticipation to be spending more time with Alex. He was sexy, in a scruffy sort of way, and made her laugh, but there wasn't anything else there. Goldie had advised her to have a few rounds of meaningless sex to get over her dry spell, but annoyingly, whenever she thought about sex with Alex, sex with Elijah popped up and took over more of her headspace and caused feelings she didn't want to acknowledge. So, Nia figured she would just never think about sex and be fine. Right.

Another splash, and an even bigger cheer this time. That one was from Samantha, with Camille cheering widely for her. Nia got a sudden pang of homesickness, missing her own sister. They'd talked as much as they could, but it wasn't the same as being able to spend time with her. Hearing footsteps, Nia looked up to see Kerry coming up the stairs. She flopped into the seat next to Nia, tossing her phone down, where it vibrated almost immediately.

"I'd hate to have a phone as active as yours." Nia commented as Kerry stared daggers at it while it buzzed on the chair.

"Tell me about it." Sighing, she grabbed it and tapped in her password. "I've got a new announcement for you to make today."

"What's that?" Nia sat up, curious.

"Warren is adding in another element for 'drama'. So today, Elijah is going to pick the first woman to have in the Dream Suite tonight." Kerry rolled her eyes, unaware of the sinking pit forming in Nia's stomach. "He thinks it's going to make the women even more jealous."

"Beyond jealous. They'll be even more obnoxious now." Dream Suite? That sounded like one thing to Nia: sex. And lots of it. Sex with Elijah popped up again, making Nia huff in frustration. *Settle down, girl.* "How is Elijah feeling about it?" She tried to sound more casual than she felt about it. Inside, it was like that unsure feeling when the barista is calling everyone else's name but yours, and she wondered if she'd been skipped over somehow.

"I don't know, but Isaac is telling him the news. But come on, I bet he's excited. One night, no cameras, and he's all alone with the woman he get to pick? Any guy would want that."

"For sure." Nia schooled her expression as best as she could, even though she couldn't deny it any more. She was jealous. And knowing that Elijah was probably going to sleep with one of the women tonight only put her in even more of a sour mood.

"We'll need you to make the announcement in about twenty minutes, so you've got a little time to think about how you want to present it." Kerry pushed off the railing, getting ready to head back in. "If I'm being honest with myself, I can't wait to see their faces." Kerry left, unaware of the storm brewing under Nia's exterior. She tried to push it off, but it wasn't budging. There was no way getting around it.

Twenty minutes passed, and Nia found herself in front of the women, looking at her with expectant faces. Her own features were schooled, and she was lucky enough to be wearing a pair of sunglasses that covered her eyes. Of course, she'd been positioned with Elijah right next to her to give the announcement, and could practically feel the heat coming off of his body. "Ladies, Elijah. We're spicing things up. Tonight, we've added another component to this challenge: The Dream Suite."

There were some eager looks on the women as they broke out into chatter among them. A look at Elijah showed a smile that she couldn't tell was real or for show. He looked at her briefly, some question in his eyes that Nia didn't want to answer. Instead, Nia passed a chain with a key on the end of it to Elijah, their fingers brushing slightly. Electricity ran through her at the touch, and Nia had to fight not to jerk her hand back at the contact. "Elijah will be giving this key to the woman he'd like to form a deeper connection with tonight. No cameras, no secret recordings, just pure private time. What happens after that is up to the two of you. Good luck ladies."

With a wink, Nia backed off and let them get back to their mingling. Danielle and Nicole approached Elijah right off the bat, slipping their arms in his and pulling him to the deck. And Nia did what she could do: watch, from the sidelines. She watched as he picked Danielle to stay the night with him in the suite. She watched as they linked hands, as Danielle stood on tip toe to press a soft kiss on his lips. The cameras captured it all, as the boat sped back to shore with the sun setting softly in the background. Nia watched as they got back, and the two of the disappeared into the guest house. She wanted to look away, needed to, but couldn't help herself. And when the lights turned off for the night, and Nia sat on her shared balcony alone with Elijah, Nia let herself think the words she'd been avoiding for far longer than she'd admitted: *I still have feelings for Elijah.*

Quietly, she made her way back into her room, and ignored the texts and calls from her friends. She'd deal with them in the morning. But right now, Nia felt that she was allowed to wallow, just a little bit.

NIA

The next day dawned with more clarity for Nia. She had feelings for Elijah, and after this week, there were only four weeks left on the island. That was four weeks that she had to keep it together until she got back to Los Angeles, where she'd hopefully be in and out of filming with him. And then after that, she wouldn't see Elijah anymore, and be able to get over him…again. Nia resolved to keep any emotion she had for him buried, and to be professional at all times. Her focus was this show, and furthering her career. Anything else was unnecessary.

With this resolve in mind, Nia met the day's work with more dedication. She managed to be civil to Elijah as they rode their van into Honolulu together, and didn't ask about how his night went in the Dream Suite. To be fair, Nia hadn't needed to ask because some of the crew asked him during the ride over. Pom had pounced as soon as the doors shut. "So…how was last night? Were sweet, sultry dreams made in the suite?"

Elijah had smiled a little and settled into his seat. "You'll have to wait and find out." They'd grumbled and tried to pry information out of him, but Elijah was surprisingly tight lipped.

Once they'd arrived in Honolulu, Nia and Elijah stood before the ladies where they were assembled in front of the Hawaii Theater and divided into groups of three. Nia smiled, and tried not to look too long at Danielle who wore a vaguely smug look on her face. *Did she look well rested from a night of wild sex or just sound sleep?* Nia tried to shake off those thoughts and focus on her words. "Ladies! I hope you've brought your detective skills with you. It's time for a Scavenger Hunt! You've been paired into teams – working with your partners, your goal is to complete the hunt and be the first to the end with all the items on the list."

Elijah chimed in. "For those who didn't know, I spent some time in Hawaii filming my first movie, so there's a lot of good memories here for me. The winners of this contest will have one on one time with me this week, as well as complimentary pedicures and manicures as part of my treat. Good luck ladies!"

Stepping back, he smiled at them. "Well, what are you waiting for? The game has started!" The women took off, scrambling in separate directions that as they went to find their first items. Elijah and Nia loaded back in the van with Kerry and Isaac, and were dropped off a few minutes away at a quaint little coffee shop.

As they got out the van, Nia turned to Kerry as a thought occurred to her. "Is it just me, or is this a convenient way to get them out of your hair for a bit?"

"Oh, it's definitely a way to get them away from us for a while." Kerry smirked as she looked up from her phone. "We need a break too."

"I love how your brain works." Nia let out a laugh.

Elijah tried to hold back a yawn, unsuccessfully. "So, what's next? We just hang out in the coffee shop until they figure this out?"

Kerry nodded. "Basically; the women stop here for a midpoint, and you'll be here to encourage them on before meeting them at the final spot at the marina. Some of us are going to go back to the house for a bit and get an hour or so of work done."

"I can handle that." Elijah smiled, before throwing a look at Nia. "Sounds like a nice break."

"Also, we'll have a dark day on Friday in addition to this weekend, so everyone can have a chance to mellow out a bit."

"Three-day weekend? Yes, please." Nia could definitely use a bit of rest.

"Some of the crew is going out Saturday night, you two should come with." Kerry's phone rang, and she excused herself back to the van, leaving Nia alone with Elijah. The hair and makeup team had disappeared into the shops, leaving Nia and Elijah alone for the first time on the island. She didn't want to be alone with him, and wondered how far ahead were Cynthia and the team.

Nia was just about to slide away when Elijah stopped her. "So, are you done being weird with me yet?"

Her head whipped over to him. "I'm being weird? You were the one who's been awkward all week." The audacity of the man.

His eyes crinkled as he acknowledged that. "It has been a little off between us. Can we make it right again?"

What was there to make right? A friendship that was only being maintained for appearances sake? Nia didn't know how to answer that.

"Here, let's go get a coffee and we'll talk." He pulled her into the shop, a little bell twinkling overhead and she had no choice but to follow.

ELIJAH

The shop was a cozy mix of island décor and items you'd find in your grandparent's house. Taking a deep breath, Elijah let the scent of fresh coffee wash over him. It was empty; Elijah knew that it'd been booked out for filming so he didn't have to worry about random people coming into the shop.

Nia dug her heels in as he tried to steer her to the counter. "I don't know what there is to talk about. You're hot and cold on me, Eli. That's hard to keep up with. And another apology doesn't make it better." He frowned at that, but had to wait to answer when he saw a familiar person coming from the back.

"Hi Leah! It's been a while." Elijah gave a warm hello to the woman behind the counter. She was middle aged with warm brown eyes and dark hair that was just starting to grey at the roots.

"Elijah James! I'm so glad to see you again." Stepping from behind the counter, Leah wrapped him in a warm hug. "I told you were going to be big, didn't I? And look at you now!"

Elijah laughed, as they broke apart. I never doubted you." He turned, bring Nia forward. "This is Nia, she's a…co-worker of mine."

Warm eyes took Nia in, and a small smile of approval graced her face. "Lovely to meet you Nia. I hope you know what you're getting into hanging out with Elijah."

"I know a little bit." Nia's voice was wry as she looked him over, causing a chuckle from Leah.

"Can I get you two a drink?" Leah asked, kicking into hostess mode.

"That would be amazing." Elijah turned to Nia. "Is your drink still a caramel latte, extra whip?"

Elijah could see Nia's brain fritz for a moment. "You remembered my drink?"

"Yeah, I could never get you to drink coffee the way it was meant to be." Elijah rolled his eyes in commiseration at Leah. "I'll do an Americano for my drink."

"There wouldn't be other flavors for coffee if they weren't meant to be drank that way!" But Nia was laughing, which was better than the quiet Nia he'd had all week.

Leah laughed at the expression on Elijah's face. "I'd tell you not to be so dramatic, but that's what you've made a career off of."

"Whose side are you on?" Elijah took a step back, his hand to his chest.

"You two go sit down and I'll have your drinks out in a moment." Leah patted Elijah's shoulder before disappearing behind the counter. Elijah led Nia over to a pair of cozy seats in the back and flopped down, enjoying the comfort of the chair.

Nia settled into the chair next to him, a smile on her face. "I like her. Is that why you picked this spot?"

"The official answer is this is where I found out that I got the leading role in *Never Die Again* and it changed my life forever."

"And the unofficial answer?"

"This is where I learned I'd be able to finally pay my mom back for everything she'd sacrificed to get me where I am today. She's been my biggest supporter, and I'm going to take care of her for the rest of her life."

Nia smiled, a sign of approval at that. "That's actually adorable."

"I have my moments." He let a small smile on his face though Nia didn't quiet meet it. He sighed, knowing he'd have to explain himself.

"What do we need to talk about Elijah?"

"I know you don't want another apology. And I know I was hot and cold with you."

"You were the one who wanted to be friends, Eli." Nia stopped as Leah came over with their coffees, smiling a bit of thanks to her. "That's what you said you wanted."

"What I wanted has changed." Elijah looked down into his cup. He could feel Nia staring at him.

"What do you mean it's changed? What could you possibly want now?" Nia's voice floated over to him, soft and tinged with curiosity.

"You." He looked up at her, locking eyes. "I want you, and I can't have you, and the thought of you going on a date with someone else is driving me up a wall." Elijah hadn't meant to say all of that, but it'd just came out. He wanted her, and he was damn sick of hiding it.

He could see he'd shocked her. Nia didn't say anything, and Elijah didn't want to push her anymore than he'd already done, so he waited, the sounds of the coffee machines whirring in the background.

"You can't want me." Nia whispered, anger creeping into her voice. "You are literally on a *dating* show, Elijah, where I watch you date women around the clock. And you don't want me going on a date with one man who is actually interested in me?"

"I know, I know. It's terrible, *I'm* terrible for even suggesting it." Elijah knew he was wrong, but couldn't help it. Hearing Alex ask Nia out had made him realize that *he* wanted to be the one asking Nia out, but couldn't. It' had sent him into a funk, and he hadn't handled it the best way he should have.

"Eli, this is insane." Nia's head fell forward into her hands, hiding her face from him.

"I know Nia. It makes no sense. But it's all I could come up with." Elijah wished she wouldn't hide from him.

"And what do you plan on doing about it? Oh right, nothing, because you have an obligation to this show." Her words were muffled behind her hands.

"Look at me Nia."

Her hands dropped from her face. "I'm not going to be used again, Elijah. You have eleven women at your disposal, one of which I'm sure you had plenty of fun with last night."

"Last night? Nia, I didn't do anything with Danielle. I told her I didn't like to sleep with people casually and slept on the couch. All we did was talk, I swear."

Confusion was on her face. "She made it seem like you did." Nia remembered hearing Danielle brag about Elijah keeping her up all night, and frowned.

"Whatever she told you and the other women was a lie. I did nothing with her." Her big brown eyes met his, and he willed her to believe him. "I couldn't do anything with anyone, because what I feel for you makes anything else pale in comparison. And I know you feel it to."

Nia rolled her eyes. "Don't be ridiculous."

"We're not going to talk about the kiss?" Elijah finally brought it up, having sat on it for a while. "You kissed me, not the other way around."

Her eyes dropped, and she bit her lip. "I was more than half asleep."

"I know that. But it makes me wonder what's going on in that pretty head of yours."

Behind them, the shop bell twinkled, and they turned to see Kerry strolling towards them.

"The first group, Samantha, Danielle and Tiffany is close to being here, way ahead of schedule." She shook her head. "I don't know if they're smart or managed to cheat somehow."

"That was fast." Nia stood, cutting off the connection between her and Elijah.

"They'll be here in about ten, so we'll get ready to meet them."

"I'm going to run to the bathroom really quick." With a tight smile, Nia disappeared before they could finish the conversation. Elijah watched her go, and wished he'd known more about what she was thinking, wishing that he hadn't agreed to this show so he could really see what was between the two of them. But he also knew he was being extremely selfish. He was dating other women, she was dating other men, and that was all there was. A little voice in his mind kept telling him *more* was the answer.

The Crazy Woman

NIA

When Nia made it back to her room after the Scavenger Hunt and Elijah and the winning team (Lily, Camille, and April) went off on their date, Nia had time to think about what Elijah had admitted to her. More like obsess, really. She tried doing a session of yoga, deep breathing, a glass of wine, but nothing dulled the fact of the matter: Elijah had feelings for her. So, she did the only other thing there was, which she had been avoiding, which was a call to Goldie.

She picked up on the first ring, and a high pitched, "NIA!" came through the line. Nia smiled, and sat on her bed, the glass of wine close by.

"Hey Golds. You got a minute to talk? I know it's getting late over there." A quick mental calculation told her it was ten thirty at night in California.

"Hell yeah I do, especially since you've been avoiding us!" A healthy amount of guilting was in Goldie's voice.

"Not avoiding, just thinking." Nia smiled, hedging a bit.

Goldie laughed, and Nia could hear her settling into her bed for the night.

"Trouble in paradise? Tell me everything."

"Yeah, well did your horoscopes predict Elijah James telling me that he still has feelings for me?" Nia took a sip of wine, still reeling. To her surprise, Goldie wasn't surprised.

"Of course he did. That makes total sense; your horoscope said that you were going to experience some bumpy paths on the road of love this month."

"I don't really know what to do with that information."

"Backup and tell me what happened."

Nia gave her the rundown of everything, from the sleepy kiss, to the low current of jealousy issues, to Elijah's admission of feelings. By the time she was done getting everything off her chest, Nia felt like she could at least breathe easier. And with it, came a little bit of clarity. She knew she was jealous, that she wanted Elijah. And she knew that by going after it, it would be risking this job that she'd fought so hard to get, and possibly burning a bridge. What Nia didn't know was if would be worth it all in the end.

Goldie soft snort snapped Nia out of her thoughts. "Didn't I tell you to guard your heart out there? Of course you go out and fall in love with him, typical Libra behavior."

"I never said I was in love with him." Nia drained the contents of her glass. "But there is definitely some strong like happening."

"Well, what are you going to do?" Goldie asked the question that had been floating around in Nia's head.

"I can't do anything about it. I mean, I can, but it has the potential to massively derail a ton of things I really want. But I could also be mad at myself for not taking the opportunity when I had it."

"You have to decide which opportunity is worth more to you. Do you want to do well at this job, or chase a road you've been down before?"

Nia sighed. "When you put it like that Golds, the answer seems obvious."

"It's up to you. I just don't want you to give up on something that you've been waiting for. What's happening with island boy? Are you still going on the date with him?"

"I guess so, but we haven't really had time to talk about it."

"Try it out with him. You won't know if what you have with Elijah is actually something unless you compare it with someone else. For all you know, you could be just feeling old feelings again, and not something new."

Nia had to agree, although it felt kind of close to using Alex to figure out her own emotions. To that, Goldie said, "Men use women all the time, and you can bet they're playing the field before things get serious. So before you get serious about Elijah, make sure he's what you really want."

A soft knock sounded at her door. Nia stood, wondering who it could be.

"Golds, hang on, someone's at the door."

Opening it, she was surprised to see Alex on the other side, a pink rose in his hand and a small smile on his face. "Alex? What are you doing up here?"

Goldie's voice came through the line. "Alex as in camera guy? Just say yes, girl. And make sure to tell me what happens." She hung up and Nia dropped her phone into her pocket.

"Sorry for interrupting, but I wanted to give you this," he passed the flower to her, "And say that I'm excited for our date this weekend and to spend some time with you." He really was cute, as he leaned in her doorway.

"Of course, I can't wait." She could do this. Maybe some space away from Elijah would help her be open to what Alex had to offer.

Alex smiled. "Ok great, this will be awesome, I swear." He started backing away. "I'm going to leave before you change your mind."

Nia tried to stop him before he got too far away. "Wait, what should I wear?"

"Wear something you can get sweaty in." With a smile, Alex disappeared down the hallway and Nia wondered what she'd gotten herself into. But this would be fine. It had to be.

ELIJAH

Just get through the day and you'll have a three-day weekend, Elijah thought as he jogged up the beach the next morning. He'd taken to earlier morning runs, due to some of the more persistent women tracking him down for extra one on one time, but he liked the early solitude. Elijah had enough to think about when it came to Nia and convincing her that they deserved another shot. It had been unfair of him to spring that on her, but he hadn't been able to resist himself. He was a big believer in signs, and the fact that the universe had seen fit to drop Nia back into meant a lot to him.

A low chirp sounded and he stopped, seeing it was Carter calling. "Bro." Elijah kept his greeting short as he caught his breath.

"How's it going on babe island man? Has Nia asked about me yet?"

Elijah rolled his eyes even though Carter couldn't see it. "What do…want?"

"You prepping for a caveman role now? Me, Carter. You, in running for Commander Hex."

"Wait a minute, what?" Elijah finally caught his breath. "Are you serious?"

"Hell yeah man! I'm not supposed to be telling you this, but the big guys are talking casting, and you're on the short list. All you got to do is not screw things up. No surprises, ok? You're looking good, and they just want to make sure you stay that way."

"Yeah, man. No surprises." But the news felt bittersweet: it was what he'd been working towards for so long, and the person he wanted to share it most with was Nia.

But she posed a problem. If he continued to pursue things with her, he'd mess up this job and be back at square one with the womanizer reputation he was trying to get rid of. Elijah could only imagine what the headlines would say about him doing a dating show and dabbling with the hostess still. It would not be a good look.

He made it through the day's date with Lily, which was the most fun he'd actually had on these dates so far. But Lily also wasn't over the top, like some of the women, and he actually liked her as a person. They'd went to the Wakiki Aquarium and looked at fish and sharks and whales, and talked about a little bit of everything. She'd stopped by the jellyfish, a slight squirm on her face. "I take it you don't like jellyfish?" Elijah asked, as the light from the tank glowed around them.

"Not a fan, not since one of my exes decided it would be fun to pick up a dying one off the beach and toss it at my head."

Elijah let out a disbelieving laugh. "I hope this was a middle school aged ex and not an adult one."

"He was of the adult variety." Lily had a small smile on her face as she shook her head. "He definitely left an impression though."

Elijah nodded, thinking of Nia. "I bet. It's funny what some exes leave us with."

He felt Lily looking at him as they continued on in the aquarium, the cameras not too far behind. "Do you have any crazy ex stories?" She asked, as they made their way to over to the next exhibit.

"No stand out crazy ones, although my college relationship might say I was the crazy one."

"Ah. Wild youth?"

"Maybe a little." Elijah did go wild after leaving college, a bender of sorts. He hadn't handled his mom's pain easily, and had turned to outside sources to deal with it.

"Well, you are looking to settle down, right?" Lily looked up at him, a tentative smile on her face. "I hope you are."

"Just looking for the right woman." He saw the kiss coming from a mile away, and knew it was coming. Warren had asked him why he hadn't been kissing the women, and Elijah hadn't had a good answer for him. Aware of the cameras on them, he allowed Lily to reach up and press a soft kiss on his mouth. It wasn't bad, but it just felt…wrong. Pulling away, he led her by the hand and they continued on the rest of their date.

NIA

"Two rings are left, but four women remain. Which ladies still have a chance to win over Elijah's heart, and which two must say aloha and head back home in a surprise double elimination? We'll find out more, after the break." Nia spoke directly into a camera, with Elijah behind her, about to decide between Camille, Charli, Tiffany and Roxy. It was well past two in the morning, and Warren hadn't been satisfied with any of the coverage the cameras were getting, so they'd been relentlessly adjusting position and reshooting. The crew was starting to get cranky at this point. It had also cooled off considerably, making the night even more miserable.

"Cut! We got that, let's move on to the final eliminations." Warren finally called, and Nia heaved a sigh of relief. All she wanted to do was crawl in her bed and sleep for the next several hours. Instead, she found a chair and kicked off her heels to give her feet a quick rest. They'd felt like they'd become a permanent, unwelcome addition to her body, and the thought of putting them back on made her want to cry. *Suck it up,* Nia told herself. *This is part of the process.*

All too soon, they were called back to their places, and Nia stood to take her position near the podium with the rings. She wobbled a bit, trying to slide her feet back into her heels and almost tilted over, but a strong hand was at her back to hold her steady. Through bleary eyes she saw Elijah, holding her steady until she regained her balance.

"Can't have you falling over." He said, though his own eyes were tired. For a moment, all Nia wanted to do was lean into his strength and rest against him for a moment. The thought was so tempting, she started to draw closer to him, at least until Maddie came over for her.

Breaking away from his touch, she mumbled a 'thank you' before making her way to her mark, the cameras in position. Alex had his trained on her, and he poked his head out, giving her a little smile before ducking back behind it. She was starting to forget there were cameras everywhere.

Warren called out action, and Elijah stepped before the women, still looking flawless in his suit. "Ladies. I have had a wonderful time getting to know all of you, which is why it hurts to have to send two of you home tonight."

The first woman he saved was Roxy, who almost crumpled to the ground in relief. She accepted the ring and threw her arms around, practically sobbing on him. Nia had to step in and pry Roxy away from Elijah, and helped her over to the row of women where she was given a few tissues to fix her face.

Charli was the first woman eliminated, though she didn't seem too surprised. Stepping forward, she gave Elijah a gentle hug. "While it was nice getting to know you Elijah, there is one other person I'll be sad to see go." Releasing him, Charli went over to Ava and pulled her into a tight embrace. Off camera, Nia could see Warren throwing fist pumps into the air, clearly thinking about ratings and the audience. Letting go, Charli added, "If you ever want to call me, you have my number."

Ava didn't answer either way, but Nia caught their fingers lingering together a little longer than strictly necessary. She thought it was sweet - someone should find love on this island if it wasn't going to be her.

Elijah smiled before facing Camille and Tiffany. Taking a deep breath, he began. "I feel like I haven't really gotten to know either of you that well. Camille, I know it can be difficult to open up and be vulnerable, but that makes it harder for me to find a reason to keep you around because I still don't know you very well. And Tiffany...I'm not sure you have what I need for life in the public eye. There seems to be so much drama that follows you around, and I don't know that I need that in my personal life."

Camille spoke up, a little wobble in her voice from tears she was holding back. "I want you to know that there is so much more to me than what you've seen, Elijah. Sometimes I need a little more time to open up to people, and I promise that if you give me another chance, I'll work on sharing more with you."

Tiffany stepped forward, elbowing past Camille. "Elijah, baby. You've got to give me another chance. You call it drama, I call it a little extra spice. If you're with me, I can promise you things will never be boring or predictable."

Nia could barely maintain her eye roll, and caught Kerry holding back a smirk off camera.

"The woman staying on the island is...Camille. I'm sorry Tiffany, but-" Elijah's speech was interrupted by Tiffany charging Elijah. He tried to dodge her, but the woman was relentless.

"How DARE you? Don't you know how precious I am?" Tiffany charged Elijah again, who was trying to take cover behind various set pieces.

"Tiffany, this is what I'm talking about- " He ducked as a glass was thrown at his head, and it shattered somewhere behind him. Nia was wide awake now, watching the madness unfold.

"You've got some nerve, your whole life is already full of drama, you, you…man whore!" Tiffany chucked another glass at him.

The cameras caught all of the melodramatic meltdown from Tiffany, who bitched, screamed, and toppled over several decorations in her anger. She had to be escorted off by security after throwing herself at Elijah, trying unsuccessfully to both hit and kiss him at the same time. Elijah managed to disentangle himself from her, but Tiffany was off balance and somehow fell into the pool, taking a security guard with her. Behind them, the other women were shocked; some, like Nicole and her gang, were amused, trying to hold back laughter.

"An evening to remember," Nia sparkled into Alex's camera. "Elijah said aloha to Tiffany, who said…several other things to him. Make sure you come back next week to see what more we have for you on *With this Ring*. Have a good night."

Warren, excessively pleased with how the night's events turned out, called it for the evening, finished for the night. After showering, and changing into shorts and a tank, Nia looked at her phone, which had a missed message on it from Lexie. The casting director loved her self tape, and wanted her to come in for an audition when she was back in Los Angeles. Nia stifled a happy shout, knowing how late it was. Seeing movement on the balcony, she saw Elijah standing outside looking at the ocean. Slipping her door open, she grinned at him. "Hey you." He was freshly showered, in grey sweat pants and a t-shirt, feet bare as he leaned on the railing.

Elijah turned, his eyes lighting up as she came to him. "Hey, sorry if I woke you up."

"You didn't. I wanted to say thanks for your help with my self tape, they want me to come in for another round when I'm back!"

"Of course they do, they'd have to be idiots otherwise." He wrapped her in a warm hug, his scent of clean soap and citrus wrapping around her as they rocked gently together. "I'm proud of you."

There was a warm feeling in her chest that kept spreading through out her body. This was happiness. This was exactly where she wanted to be at this moment in time. Nia felt her mouth pull into a smile. "Thanks. I couldn't have done it without you."

"You would have. You're amazing."

She looked up at him, his eyes hooded in the light, could feel him searching her face. Nia's gaze was drawn to his lips, and she wasn't sure who moved first, but they met, drawn together like magnets. The spark that had been between them ignited into full on flames as they kissed. Elijah's lips were familiar and new, all at the same time and Nia's brain was working furiously to commit this moment to memory. It was a slow, passionate exploration of the other person, and she could feel his arms tightening around her, his hands sliding down her back and cupping her behind, pressing her closer to him. Reaching up, Nia relished the silky feel of his hair, sliding her fingers through the dark mass. There were fireworks in her belly, a viral shut down her of brain that was focused only on Elijah.

This was everything.

This was what she was missing.

This was dangerous…

The kiss intensified, became nothing like the last one they'd shared. It was a conversation, of longing, of questions, of remembrance. His hands came up, cupping her cheeks as he tasted her, ruthlessly taking what he wanted and what she gave in return. Nia gave as good as she got, sliding her hands underneath his t-shirt and feeling the strength in his muscles, feeling how he tensed underneath her touch. It was too much, and yet, she couldn't get enough. This was what she was missing when Alex looked at her…

Nia pulled away, breaking their connection, breath heavy. That brief thought of Alex was enough to break her Elijah haze, bringing her back to earth and the cold reality - he wasn't available to her. And she didn't want to get caught up again. Beginning to pull away, she could feel Elijah's hands tightening on her hips.

"Stay." His velvet voice whispered, lips caressing her ear teasing a shiver out of her.

"I can't." She pulled away, breaking their connection and backing away.

"Tell me you don't feel this." Elijah gestured between them, eyes locked on hers.

Nia looked away, feeling every place he had touched her. "I can't." Feeling like a coward, she turned and went to her room, shutting the door on him and the look of pained desire on his face. Tired as she was, Nia barely slept that night, wondering why she had let it get this far. She knew there was nothing but pain on the other side of this thing between them, and yet…knew that she'd do it all over again.

The Zipline

NIA

Last night's kiss was still at the forefront of Nia's mind as she got ready for her date that day with Alex. When she'd finally fallen asleep, Elijah was even in her dreams, whispering sweet things and holding her close. Nia hoped that some distance today would help her calm down and look at things from a more rational manner. Grabbing her bag, she went downstairs determined to not think about Elijah James any more than strictly necessary. Spying Alex by the door, she put on a bright smile for him.

"Ready for some fun?" Alex wrapped Nia in a hug as she stopped next to him. *This is fine*, Nia thought to herself. *A perfectly decent hug.* Looking her up and down, Alex had a smug grin on his face. "I think you're going be pretty impressed with this date."

"If I say I'm ready, will you tell me what we're doing?" Nia asked, heading over to the production car they were going to take to this mysterious place.

Alex beat her to opening the door, and let her slide in. "That would ruin the surprise."

When he got in on the passenger side, Nia tapped her chin. "I could make an educated guess, based off our outfits, but I'll be surprised to go…on a hike."

"I'm not saying anything until we get there." Starting the car, Alex whisked her away, and Nia managed to keep her attention on him and not the other *him* for the most part. But much as she was hyper focused on conversation with Alex, she also realized that they didn't talk about anything that was really…interesting. Still, Nia was going to give it a chance, and time to warm up to each other. A slow burn was better than a roaring hot blaze anyway….

They drove along the coast, before turning into an entrance called Kean'e Farm. Curious, Nia took in the trees and mountain, wondering why this looked so familiar. "Is that where they shot those dinosaur movies?"

Alex grinned as he pulled into a parking space. "Jurassic Park? Sure is."

"What are we doing here?" Nia asked when the engine was cut.

"We're going to hike a bit, maybe ride an ATV." It definitely seemed like he was leaving something out, but she followed him to the registration counter anyway. "There is one thing I should mention."

April looked up at him, even more curious now. "What's that?"

"I know this is a date for us, but we won't be completely alone."

Nia was confused, at least until she heard her name being called from a distance. "Good morning, Nia!" Approaching them were Lily, Danielle, and none other than Elijah, who wore a ball cap and sunglasses as part of his 'disguise'. He had on a sleeveless tank and shorts, which showed off his muscles and made him look unfairly god like.

April was bounding to her, waving excitedly. "You guys, April can't wait, she's never zip lined before!"

Zip lining? Nia's breath caught, and she cut a look at Alex, realizing with trepidation what he had in mind. He obviously had no idea about her fear of heights, and had planned this whole thing for her.

"We're…zip lining?" Nia asked, trying to wet her suddenly dry throat and calm the drum that had taken residence in her chest. She wasn't going to die. Or maybe she would walk too close to the edge, the rope would snap or she'd trip and plunge to her sudden, steep death. Any of these were options, and they were fighting for the top spot in her brain.

"Yeah! I had planned a hike initially, but then I heard about this and how popular it was, and figured if we got a group together, we'd be able to get a nice package deal. That's why we have a few tag alongs - I hope that's alright?"

Nia's brain was flying even though she was frozen. More people meant more witnesses to a probable breakdown if she went through with it. "Totally fine." Her voice sounded high pitched, even to her own ears.

Lily added, "I hope it's ok that we're barging in on your date, we just heard the guys talking about it and wanted to get in on the fun."

Nia shook her head, brushing that off. "That's fine."

Frowning, Lily scanned Nia's face. "Is something the matter?" Nia could feel everyone's eyes on her, and she did her best to school her expression.

"What, are you scared of heights or something?" Danielle asked, a snarky look on her face.

Aiming for nonchalance, Nia shrugged, "Maybe a little, if I'm honest." She could feel Elijah's eyes on her, even behind his sunglasses, and wondered just how he'd found out about this date idea. "I guess now is as good a time as any to conquer a little fear."

April clapped her hands. "April believes in you, girl!"

Alex wasn't so sure. "I had no idea you had a fear of heights, is this going to be a good idea for you?"

Nia sighed mentally, but nodded. She didn't know how this was going to work out, but she was here, and not going to look like a little bitch in front of Danielle, or Elijah or anyone else. "I'll manage it. I'm sure it'll make a great story someday. If I survive."

Alex smiled and wrapped her in another hug before heading back to finish checking in. Nia focused on breathing and not on estimating how high the mountains were and what it'd be like if she fell from one of them in a freak accident. Those weren't helpful thoughts at all. She wandered a little away from the action to get some breathing room. She could hear Danielle mutter a 'wuss' to April, who jumped to Nia's defense.

Nia felt, rather than saw Elijah make his way next to her as she leaned on the fence and looked down at the solid ground beneath her feet. "You ok?" He asked, eyes trained on her face. Nia could feel the heat rushing to her cheeks, remembering their searing kiss from last night. It felt even sharper in the day light, and she just knew that there was no 'quick' way to get over this.

"Depends on how you define ok." Taking a deep breath, Nia asked, "How'd you find out about this excursion anyway?"

"I heard him talking about ideas with some of the camera operators, and tried to add my two cents."

"It would've been nice if you'd steered him away from this." Nia joked, looking up at the mountain they'd soon be climbing.

"Actually I did try, but remember we agreed to not give anything away about us? It'd be weird if I knew that about you."

Nia couldn't argue that logic. She was prevented from responding by Alex's approach, a shy smile on his face. "We can always back out if you want?"

Sighing, Nia saw the excitement that hovered behind the concern, and the smirk that Danielle aimed her way. That was just enough to make her swallow her trepidation and decide she would do the zip line. It seemed as if today, a fear would be conquered…or conquer her. "No, let's do this."

Following their guide, they rode ATV's through the trails and up the mountain, which perked Nia up a little bit. She'd always been a bit of a speed demon, and enjoyed the wind blowing around her as they steadily increase their ascent. The green of the trees and lush mountains were literally breathtaking, and it was amazing to see so much blue around them. Alex was attentive as well, enjoying the outing and constantly checking over his shoulder to make sure Nia was having a good time.

Once they reached the spot where the ATVs couldn't go past, they hiked up through a few trails, stopping briefly for a water break. Nia's anxiety only grew the higher up they went, and she was holding on by a thread trying not to panic. Their guide pointed out a few places where famous movies had been filmed, but Nia couldn't focus on what he was saying.

And then, they were at the top of the zip line. Johnny, their tour guide, moved them toward the overlook, pointing at the far end of the line. "We like to start off with the big one first, and then after that every other one gets a little easier."

"How tall is it?" Danielle asked, already suiting up to go down along with April.

"Five hundred feet off the ground."

Nia almost passed out. "Five hundred?" She edged away from the railing, determined not to look down, around or anywhere really.

April and Danielle moved to the launch point, where they were buckled in tight. Johnny and his coworker adjusted the straps, giving a final pull. "Are you two ready?" Johnny asked Danielle and April.

"April is ready for takeoff!"

Danielle nodded. "I'm ready!"

The two of them were pushed off, and Nia got a brief glimpse of them flying away before she sat down heavily on the ground. Alex and Elijah squatted next to her as Lily started to get hooked up into a harness.

"How you doing?" Alex asked, looking her over. "We can totally back out of this if you can't do it."

Nia looked at him, and saw the beginnings of disappointment in his eyes, and knew that he really wanted to do this. And she really didn't want to do this, but she was here now.

"Why don't you go ahead with Lily, and then you can cheer me on the way down, ok?" Nia stood on shaky legs and pushed him to the harness.

"Are you sure? You don't mind?" He hesitated, but not that long, she noticed.

A tight smile was all she could manage. "I'm sure. I'll either make it down or I won't."

"I'll buy you all the alcohol you need when this is over." Alex allowed himself to be buckled into the harness, clearly eager to experience this.

"Remind me to hold you to it." Nia watched as the final preparations were taken before Alex and Lily shoved off the platform, screaming with glee. She couldn't do this, what was she thinking? Right as she was about to tell Johnny to take her back down the hill, Nia felt Elijah's hands land on her shoulders, gently turning her to him.

"Hey. What's going on up there?" He tapped a finger to her forehead. His voice was low, soothing, and Nia leaned into him shamelessly.

"Just wondering how in the hell I ended up here." She exhaled shakily.

He tilted her chip up, meeting her eyes. "Focus up here and breathe. You can do this. You've done so much, this should be a piece of cake."

"I should've chickened out when I had the chance." Nia tried laughing at herself but it came out more wobbly than expected. Elijah's arms tightened, wrapping her in a hug that was sweaty and hot, but felt absolutely right where she wanted to be.

"You are the least chicken woman I know. And I know you can do this, you can do anything you want. But if you need to back this out, let me know and I'll ride down with you."

"You'd do that?" Nia mumbled against his chest. She felt him laugh as he rubbed her arms.

"I'd do anything for you." He whispered. And Nia knew that she was a goner, that she despite all her efforts, she as falling for him all over again. Despite everything she had did, against all her will, she found herself back in deep with him. "Let's fall together." His lips were warm against her cheek, and she shivered, the fear in her mind being replaced with the warmth in her soul.

She pulled back, taking a deep breath. Nodding at Johnny and the guide, Nia allowed herself to be buckled up into the harness, Elijah right beside her.

He held her hand until the moment they pushed off, his fingers slipping away as they were propelled down the line. She screamed, letting out all the fear and anticipation, flying through the air, feeling the exhilaration of it all, the freedom of doing something she'd been so scared to do. Elijah made it to the stopping point slightly ahead of her, and she flew to him, a huge smile on her face that his own matched. Nia was grabbed and released from the harness, feeling unsteady like she was relearning how to walk. And though it was Alex who swooped her up into a hug, it was Elijah's eyes that she met, and mouthed a *thank you* to.

The Club Outing

NIA

After making it back to the resort with minor issues, Nia managed to squeeze in a quick nap and recover a bit from her eventful morning. She'd sent a photo Alex had caught of her careening down the line to the group chat, and had woken up to a bevy of missed texts from her friends, ranging from enthusiastic to concerned.

GOLDIE: AHHHHHH, SO PROUD OF YOU!!!!!!

YAYA: Is that Elijah in the background? Did you really jump off a cliff for a man??

LEXIE: I'm both happy and slightly worried? What's going on out there? Update us!!

Nia smiled as she scrolled through messages, before typing out her reply.

NIA: It was a date with Alex, he didn't know.

LEXIE: But why was Elijah there?

NIA: Long story, but he invited himself along.

She deliberately didn't delve any further into why Elijah was there, since she was trying to make it make sense in her own mind. Checking the time, she saw that she needed to start getting ready for the night's outing. They were going to pregame downstairs before heading to a club in the city and she wanted to be ready for whatever the evening brought her. There was a tingle, an awareness of something changing in the air, but she wasn't sure what it was going to be. She dressed with more care than normal, applying flawless makeup and styling her hair to perfection, her curls actually cooperating for a chang. Slipping into her favorite dress, a backless forest green number that showed off her legs, especially when paired with the scrappy gold heels she'd borrowed from Goldie. Yaya had purchased the dress for her birthday last year, swearing it would make anyone stop and stare. And based off the looks she got as she went to the kitchen to join the pregame, it was a success.

Alex immediately found her, his eyes roaming up and down her figure. "If I had my camera, I'd be taking shots of you right now."

"Not necessary," Nia laughed, edging out of the way as his fingers brushed her back. She knew that despite overcoming her fear, that there was nothing between them and didn't want to lead him on any more.

"Uh, definitely necessary! Look at you!" Kerry's voice rang behind her and Nia turned, laughing as she fanned herself. "You are stepping on everyone's necks and I absolutely love it. Right Isaac?"

"Stunning." But his eyes were all for Kerry, who looked gorgeous in a little red jumpsuit that Nia immediately need to know where it came from.

Kerry leaned over and whispered in Nia's ear: "Elijah probably agrees, he hasn't stopped looking at you yet."

"Wait, what?" Her head turned, looking around until she spotted Elijah leaning against a counter, eyes hooded and smoky. She felt them travel her up and down, noting every single detail of her outfit, his eyes lingering on hers. Inside, she felt as if someone was tap dancing in her chest, a fire in her belly and heat in her veins.

Kerry nodded, fanning herself. "Ooh yes honey, you are going to break some hearts tonight. Wait, he's coming over here!"

They watched as Elijah crossed the room towards them, and Nia drank in the sight of him - and he was fine as hell tonight. They were matching in an unintentional way, his dark green jeans and black collared shirt left a little unbuttoned to show off his strong chest. But it was also just him – something about Elijah called to her, and she felt the answering call from inside, felt the connection between the two of them that wouldn't fade.

His smile felt like it was only for her though he addressed the entire group. "All of my favorite people in one spot. We'll definitely have the hottest party tonight."

Kerry tossed her hair over her shoulder. "You bet your ass we'll have the best-looking group on this island."

Nia could tell there were questions coming from Kerry's corner, and mentally prepared to face those. Once they were joined by the rest of the women who surrounded Elijah like a school of fish, they made their way outside to the vans that would take them into town.

Their stop was a club called *Waves*, which had an edgy beach vibe that Nia instantly liked. It was actually only a half hour walk from their resort, but considering the heels some of the women were wearing, a car made more sense. Inside the club it was dark and moody, with blue and teal lights lining the floors and booths. The dance floor was actually made of glass over a little body of water, and Nia could see colorful fish swimming underneath their feet.

A few booths had been reserved for their group and waitresses brought over a round of shots for everyone. Warren raised his glass and yelled over thumping music, "Let's party!"

After the third round of shots, Nia realized these film people could hold some serious alcohol. She could easily see them going all night if they wanted to, and they probably would. They started to make their way onto the dance floor, Kerry and Isaac dragging Nia with them. It was amazing to let loose, and was exactly what she needed as they moved to the heavy bass. But then she saw Danielle grab Elijah and started grinding on him in what could only be described as a fully clothed sexual act and her mood soured, just a bit.

Alex was constantly by her side, and for a while, Nia just let him be. She couldn't help noticing that April was also hanging close to him, and wondered if there was a little crush happening on her side. Deciding to let it play out, she yelled to Alex over the music. "I'm going to go sit!"

"What?" He leaned in closer to her.

"Me, sit!" She pointed to the booth.

Alex started to move with her. "I'll come with you!" But Nia shook her head.

"Stay! I'll be back!" She waved a little and dodged moving bodies until she made it to the booth and collapsed in a grateful heap. What she really wanted was a cup of water, but there weren't any waitresses around and she didn't feel like braving the masses at the bar either. *In three minutes I'll get up*, she decided, wanting to give her feet a little bit of a break. Much as she loved these heels, they were murder on her toes.

Not two minutes later, a glass of water was set on the table in front of her, and Elijah slid into the booth next to her. "I thought you might need some water, from all the heat you've been making out there."

"That is literally the worst pickup line I have ever heard, Eli," Nia laughed as she gulped the icy water. "I'll let it slide since you brought me water."

He slid a little closer, and she felt his leg press against hers under the table. "You're torturing me, you know." Elijah was closer than strictly necessary, his arm resting along the top of the booth, right behind her. "That dress, and you…are just awe inspiring. I know it's a bad idea, but will you at least dance with me?"

Inside, a battle warred. She knew it was a bad idea, knew that she wouldn't be able to hide her feelings in public - but Nia really wanted to dance with him. "You've already have so many people to dance with." She whispered, not sure if she was agreeing or pushing him away.

"I haven't danced with the one person I wanted to yet." He held his hand out to her, waiting for her to close the gap. "Dance with me?"

Nia felt her hand sliding into his, and he pulled her onto the dance floor, away from their group and she followed, unable to help herself. The music had shifted into something sultrier, more seductive, and Nia felt the energy pulsing between them, growing stronger by the minute. He drew her into him, his arms sliding against her back as they ran briefly down the side of her thighs before up to her hands. Elijah twirled her, before bringing her back against him, her front pressed against his chest. Their eyes connected, locked only on each other. There were questions there that she didn't have answers to yet. Unable to answer them, Nia shifted in his arms, allowing his body to press along her back, creating a blanket of warmth from head to toe.

It felt as if it was just the two of them on the dance floor, their bodies moving in perfect sync as if they'd been apart only days instead of years. Nia didn't notice the looks they were getting from the people around them - all she was aware of was the music, Elijah and how they moved together. Some small part of her brain was telling her to ease off, but the louder voice told her to cling to him, at least for this moment in time.

Something had changed since this evening, or maybe even before that.

Or perhaps it was just the past, coming back full force. Maybe what Nia felt for Elijah had never actually left. What Nia did know was that she wanted to stay next to Elijah for as long as possible.

Someone cleared their throat right next to them. Danielle stood, a predatory look on her eyes as she assessed the competition. "Can I cut in?" She'd obviously deemed Nia a threat, making Nia aware of the looks some of the crew were giving them.

"Um, sure. Go for it." Elijah's grip on her tightened, before letting her go.

Danielle began a deliberate grind on Elijah, who reluctantly danced with her, which was Nia's cue to leave. She wandered off the dance floor trying to calm her beating heart. By the bar, Alex was deep in conversation with April, who looked very into each other, his hand resting on her thigh for a moment. When she had suitable brain power, she would process that. Later though.

"That was some dance," Kerry remarked, as Nia approached the booth.

"Tell me about it." Nia sank onto the cushions, her feet thankful for the brief reprieve though her mind was still racing. She couldn't remember their chemistry ever being that high off the charts, even back in college.

"If you two had been out there any longer, we would have had to call the fire department with all the heat you guys were producing. Must have been some dance."

It had been; Nia felt her cheeks get hot just thinking about it again. "I think I need another shot."

"I think I need a cigarette after watching you and Elijah dance." At Nia's look, Kerry backed down a little. "Drinks on me."

For the rest of the night, Nia tried her best to ignore Elijah, trying to have fun and forget about their moment on the dance floor. Their eyes kept colliding with each other despite their various dance partners, each very aware of where and who the other was with.

Giving up for the night, Nia waved off the offer of a ride back to the resort, figuring the walk back to the resort would be the best way to clear her head. The night was gorgeous, a slight chill in the air as the moonlight caught the waves and reflected back diamond tips. Watching the waves and standing upright was starting to become a little too much for Nia, who felt as if the world was swaying underneath her feet. Spying a gazebo, Nia carefully headed that way in search of a chair. Or something to lie down on.

Inside there were nice lounge chairs that called her name. Stretching out, she didn't notice the shadow in the corner of the gazebo until he cleared his throat. Nia screeched, falling off the chaise in an ungraceful thud. Looking past the hand that helped her up, she saw it was none other than Elijah. Steadying herself as much as she could despite her tipsiness, Nia focused on him in the dark. "What are you doing out here and not at the club?"

Elijah smiled down at her. *Damn him and that smile.* Nia broke out of his hold and tried to lean against a pillar, but it kept moving for some reason. "Why are you damning my smile?"

It took her a moment to realize that she'd said it out loud. "You didn't answer my first question."

He laughed at that. "Maybe I'm meeting someone out here and you just interrupted."

Asshole. "Well don't let me get in the way of a midnight hookup."

"I'm not an asshole. You just didn't ask who I wanted to see."

"I think I need some fresh air from all this B.S." More like she needed to figure out the mess that was her emotions. Nia tried to push away from him, but his arms tightened around her. "Let me go."

Elijah studied her, longer than she would have liked, before letting her go. He settled against a pillar of the gazebo, a small grin on his face. "You're drunk."

"Am not." Nia tried to cross her arms, but somehow failed at the simple task. "I've just been enjoying a few drinks with some of my fellow co-workers."

"They know how to drink, that group."

"I've noticed that." Nia slumped into her seat, head suddenly dizzy. Closing her eyes, she just prayed that things would stop spinning. He moved beside her, his body an anchor that she leaned against.

"Hey, are you good?" Why was he here to witness her drunken disgrace?

"I'm fine. Just leave me alone." Despite her words, his presence was comforting.

"You never could hold your liquor."

"Liquor is meant to be drank, not held."

"Funny. What kind of friend would I be if I left you like this?" She could hear the smirk in his voice.

I don't want to be just your friend.

The thought crossed Nia's mind before she could stop it.

That was the crux of it all, really. She'd never wanted to be just friends with Elijah, but here they were, acting like that's exactly what was going on between them.

They were both silent for a minute, listening to the waves crash onto the shore. "I don't want to be just friends either." Elijah whispered.

Nia struggled up, trying to make some space between them. She damned her drunken self for saying things she had no business saying aloud.

"Where are you going? "Elijah asked, watching her struggle against him

"Away." Damn her feet for not listening to her. She managed to stumble out the gazebo, the fresh air hitting her face and bringing with it a wave of alertness she desperately needed.

"Let me help." His voice was soft in her ear.

She needed to sleep. Or throw up. Maybe she'd know what she was doing if she just took quick nap. "Fine, you can help me."

A warm strong arm wrapped low around her back, as he started to steer her back into the gazebo but she resisted. "Fresh air."

"Got it." Elijah guided her to sit in front of the gazebo, where he let her sit in his lap, his arms going comfortably around her waist in a way that made her feel extremely secure. "Sleep. We'll head back inside a little bit later."

How was he so warm? She snuggled in deeper to his arms, and his head came to rest over hers. Nia managed a garbled thank you before nodding off, safe in his embrace and the sounds of the ocean lulling her to sleep.

The Cabana

NIA

Slowly, Nia pried her eyes open. It took a minute for her to place her surroundings – why did the ocean sound so much closer than usual? The last few memories of the night came rolling up to her feet like the incoming tide. The bar, the dance, and more recently, Elijah, who was still cradling her in his arms. They'd fallen asleep together on the beach, and Nia guessed it was a few hours later. Craning her neck, she snuck a glance at Elijah, trying not to disturb his sleep. The moonlight was exceptionally kind to Elijah, highlighting his lips, cheekbones, soft, smooth skin.

"Do you like what you see?" He spoke, his eyes still closed.

Nia froze, caught in the act. "Sorry. I didn't know you were up."

"I was just resting my eyes. I love the sound of the ocean." Those eyes of his opened, gazing at her with a gentleness that made her insides go mushy. "How are you feeling?"

Stupid. Nia thought to herself. "Better now; thank you for sitting with me."

"Anytime." As she looked at him, Nia knew one thing for sure: she wanted this man. This good, flawed man – she wanted him for herself. But she knew that he wasn't hers to have, that at the end of their time on the island, he would be packing up to start a new life with someone else. And Nia wanted *something*, anything, that she could hold onto for just a little while longer.

"Ready to go inside?" Elijah sat up, dusting the sand off his body as best as he could.

Do something, her brain scolded her. *Anything*! Her lady parts begged.

Mouth frozen, Nia looked into Elijah's eyes, and saw answers to questions she hadn't the courage to voice. He came a little closer, his arm going back around her as they sat, her legs draped over his. Nia leaned in, a hand pressing on his chest, not to push him away, but to feel the rapid heart beating inside.

"Nia..." He whispered, his breath brushing against her forehead.

"I just..." Her mouth closed the distance between them, and it was like lightning struck. Lips collided, molded together, a fusion of two people meant to be together. His big hand came up to cup her cheek, still protecting her, holding her gently despite the strength in his kiss. Nia moved to straddle his lap, connecting their bodies through the layers of clothes, that made her beg for more, more, more. He pressed his hips into hers, and a soft duet of moans escaped their mouths.

This was more.

This was everything.

This was too much, and not enough.

Later, Nia might say that she was making a mistake, taking what she could from a man who wasn't going to be hers, a man who'd hurt her in the past. But after everything they'd been through together, Nia had become more and more assured that he had changed, for the better. They were drawn together, despite distance and time. And tonight, she would allow what would happen to happen.

Nia's arms skimmed his back, feeling those strong, supple muscles as she slipped his shirt over his head, tossing it somewhere behind them. His neck was there, vulnerable, strong, and she couldn't help leaving a mark, feeling especially territorial. She bit it softly, leaving a trail of fire up his neck as he murmured sweet words to her. Right at the base of his neck she left her mark, a soft love bite that made her feel fiercely pleased to see on his skin. *Mine.*

ELIJAH

Elijah clamped his hands around her waist as she trailed kisses and love bites along his neck. That had always been his weakness, and Nia knew it. His abdomen was taut, his control razor thin as he tried not to completely ravish her on the beach, even though that was all he'd been thinking about as soon as he'd seen her this evening. She was stunning, in a way that the other women simply couldn't compare to. It had taken every ounce to still pretend like he found other women fascinating, when the only one he wanted was off limits to him.

Nia's hips grinding down onto his stuttered his thoughts. "Fuck, Nia." His hands grabbed her waist, letting her feel what she did to him. What they could do together.

"Babe…I want to see you." His hands hovered at her top, which she used to help drag it off and over her head. *Dear god, she wasn't wearing a bra*…and a little twinkle caught his eye. "Is that a nipple ring?"

Nia bit her lip, unsure of his reaction. He could feel her watching him, but all he could do was lean forward and suckle her breast into his mouth in response. It was so unexpected, the last thing he'd expected from Nia. Her hands came to cradle his head, as she set a slow, smooth grind on his lap.

"I want you inside of me." Her breathy voice filled his ear.

Inside he rejoiced, before a thought came to him. "I don't have protection."

He rolled them over, coming to a stop over Nia who was under him in the sand. His hips rolled, pressing against her hot core. "But I can do this."

Elijah lowered, trailing kisses down her body as he found his way to her sweet core, feeling her stomach tense until he finally tasted her. She groaned, and he stopped, a whisper away from her heat. "Quietly," he whispered, before pressing his mouth against her and doing his best to make her scream.

Elijah focused on her, every part of him invested in the lovemaking his mouth was doing with her body, and it was a powerful feeling, making this strong, beautiful woman feel something so primal and instinctive. He was playing with her and teasing out every possible bit of enjoyment he could. And when she crested, he kept going, building it higher and higher until she cried out, before letting her come back down to earth.

He brought his body back up her, a slow slide, as her legs opened to hold his body against hers, and pressed another tight, firm kiss to her lips. He felt her hands unbuckling his pants, her hands slipping him out. "Nia, you don't have to – "

She shushed him, laying his length against her stomach and grinding her hot core against him. They moved like that, a slow steady pulse, her heat close but not where Elijah wanted to be. He moved faster, thinking of when he'd eventually be able to slip inside her, feel her surrounding him completely, tight, warm, wet –

With a low grunt, he pumped a few more times before releasing himself on the sand, throbbing, but still wanting more. They lay together, spent, the moon their guardian and the waves their music. And when they'd caught their breath, they'd dressed, wiping off as much sand as possible before heading back into the house, creeping in silently so they didn't disturb anyone who might be sleeping.

He stopped Nia at her door, tilting her chin up to read her expression. Wide brown eyes met his, vulnerable and unreadable. "Knock knock, who's there?" Elijah dropped a soft kiss to her forehead.

"Aren't I supposed to say who's there?" Nia laughed softly.

"Making up our own rules here." The collective we fell easily from his lips. For him, that was what made sense, the two of them together.

But he could see she wasn't ready to talk just yet. Lowering gently, he waited to see if Nia would let him kiss her again. Her lips met his, and he put as much feeling as he could into it before breaking away. "Goodnight."

Reluctantly, he let her go, at least until Nia's fingers caught his, and backed him into his room. He barely remembered to lock his door behind them. Elijah drew her back to him, his lips meeting hers as they kissed furiously in the darkness. He lifted Nia to the dresser, setting her down there and she wrapped her legs around him, bringing him tightly to her. He could feel himself thickening again, pressing against his pants and begging for the pleasure only Nia could bring him. But a creak in the hallway broke through his lusty haze, and he froze, waiting to see what it was. Nia held still, having heard it too, the sound of footsteps approaching.

Faintly, he heard someone knocking at the door and he cursed whoever it was.

Helping Nia off the dresser, Nia pushed past him towards the balcony. "I've got to get out of here."

"Wait." Pulling her back, he risked one last kiss before letting her disappear onto the balcony and out of sight.

Straightening his clothes as best as he could, he opened the door where Danielle was unsurprisingly on the other side. "I thought you'd might like some company." She purred, trying to push her way inside his room.

"This isn't a Dream Suite night, Danielle." He kept the doorway blocked, not letting her inside.

"We could make our own dream suite." Her finger trailed down his chest, aiming for seductive but it did nothing for him.

"Not tonight." Elijah gently removed her hand from his pants, and she pouted, stumbling back. She'd definitely had more than enough liquid courage at the bar. Danielle stumbled a little catching herself on Nia's door.

"You should get some sleep." He added as Danielle stood on shaky legs.

"It's not sleep that I want." As she was advancing to him again, Nia's door opened, and she peeked out, a robe wrapped around her.

"I thought I heard voices out here." Nia's glanced between the two of them, eyebrows raised. Danielle straightened, clearly not expecting anyone else to be around. And, Elijah noticed, not as drunk as she had initially appeared to be.

Elijah barely resisted rolling his eyes. "I hope we didn't wake you. Danielle was just about to leave."

"Oh, Nia. I didn't know anyone was in there." A questioning look passed over her face. "I never realized how close you were to Elijah."

"Close enough." Nia smiled, tight, before waving. "I'll leave you two alone." Her door shut, leaving Elijah alone in the hallway with Danielle.

"Goodnight, Danielle." Elijah backed into his room, and shut the door. After a second thought, he locked it for good measure. When her last footsteps faded away, he released the breath he'd been holding before stripping off his clothes on the way to the shower. He thought about heading over to Nia's room, but reconsidered, considering how they'd almost been caught.

This is what he'd been missing.

It had always been Nia for him.

It would always be Nia for him.

And he had to figure out a way to make it real. He couldn't lose her again.

Mine. Elijah's brain was stuck on Nia. As he stood in the shower washing the sand off his body, he could still remember every part of their night with searing detail. He knew what he wanted – and had no shame in going after it – but now, things were different. Elijah had just wanted a taste, but didn't expect to feel…addicted to her. And they hadn't even fully slept together. That was the problem with telling himself he'd be happy with just a taste. Nia wasn't a one taste, then keep it moving type of woman. And now that Elijah knew what he was missing, his body craved more.

More Nia, more them.

More.

He didn't know what would happen these next four weeks. But he knew that he'd be an idiot to let Nia slide away from him again. Elijah just had to figure out how to keep her close.

The New Feelings

NIA

Stretching, Nia woke up to the bright sunlight coming through her open windows, realizing how late it was. Last night had been the fifth elimination ceremony (Roxy and Cristal both were sent home), and they'd gone late into the evening to say goodbye to Cristal and Roxy. And then, once filming was done, Elijah and Nia had stayed on their balcony, blankets wrapped around them as they watched the sun rise, fingers entangled gently. Elijah had finally peeled himself away once the sun tipped the horizon, dropping a sweet kiss on Nia's lips.

The two of them had really connected these last few weeks, sneaking whatever time they could together. It was strange to think how close they'd gotten, but it had just felt right, coming back to their Happy Place, as Nia had deemed the balcony. They talked, vented, learned more about the other. Cautiously, she'd started opening up to him. Nia knew that she was setting herself up for hurt, especially since they didn't have a shot in hell of being together, but she couldn't help herself. There was something hopelessly idyllic about being on an island with Elijah, with secret looks and shared jokes that were just for her that made the days go by faster, even though he was still 'dating' other women. And then they talked, sometimes all night, learning more about each other, only for the spell to be broken at dawn.

Deciding to go for a walk, Nia dressed in workout clothes and ran into Kerry on her way out, who asked if she could tag along. They set off along the beach, feeling the sun beginning to warm the air. *I'm so blessed to be here,* Nia thought. She couldn't help the grin on her face, which Kerry commented on. "What's with the dental ad smile? Did I miss something or are you just really happy to walk with me?"

Nia shrugged, but that didn't make the smile go away. "I'm just in a really good mood."

"Does that good mood have anything to do with Elijah?" Kerry asked, which made Nia's heart skip a beat. Was it that obvious that they were into each other?

"Why do you say that?" Nia hedged.

Kerry didn't say anything for a minute, the silence almost overwhelming as Nia's brain raced, thinking of all the scenarios where she and Elijah were caught and thrown off the island. "Whatever we talk about out here stays between us?"

At Nia's cautious nod, she continued. "I noticed that you and Elijah seem to be pretty close, which I love, by the way. And I also happened to notice that you two went to the same college, around the same time." Kerry stopped, picking up a sea shell off the sand.

"We did go to college together." Nia wanted to play her cards close to her chest. She wasn't sure where Kerry was going with this. The only positive was that it didn't seem like she as going to lose her job over this...

"But why act like you don't know each other? Do you have history or something?"

For a moment, Nia was silent, debating how to answer that. "Can I ask why you're so curious?"

"If I could find out as easily as I did, others might. And others might get curious as to your history, and assume some things."

Nia tried to sigh but it came out as a puff of breath as they paused, looking out over the glittering ocean. "We had history in college that...didn't end well. And both figured it would be easier if we didn't bring that baggage into this job."

Kerry nodded, "Understandable. I take it the baggage is not an issue?"

Nia let out a short laugh as she shook her head. "Not today, no."

"Also, can I say that I just totally ship you and Elijah together? I know I shouldn't be saying that as a producer on a dating show, but you two do look good together. Even if it didn't work out." There was no censure in Kerry's gaze as she met Nia's eyes.

"Thank you - you won't tell anyone about this, will you?" Nia barely glimpsed at the view, focusing on Kerry. "I don't want anyone to think less of us...or me."

"The women always get the blame when things go wrong. I won't say a word though, I swear. And I'll deflect if I hear anyone trying to bring it up."

Nia sighed, relieved. "Thank you."

"Of course." They fell silent as they took in the view. "And if there was anything budding between the two of you, presently, I would try my best to find a way to make it work."

"What -" Nia's eyes shot to Kerry, who wasn't looking at her.

"Only if. I could never forgive myself if I stood in the way of love. Actual love, not fabricated for television love."

Nia was silent for a beat as she processed this. Obviously, Kerry knew more than she was letting on…but was supportive of it for some reason. "Thank you."

"Of course." After a moment, they silently turned back to the house as the tide rolled in.

ELIJAH

In a word, Elijah was distracted. He was happier than he'd been in a while, and it was thanks to all the time he'd been spending with Nia. The dates he had been on with the other women this week hadn't even resonated in his mind, and Elijah found himself having to turn up his acting to make sure he was still convincing everyone else that he was falling for one of these women, but he hated having to do it.

Speaking of dates, Elijah tuned back in on what Samantha was saying. They were having dinner right on the shore of a private beach as the sun set in one of the most romantic settings yet, Elijah found himself constantly thinking of Nia, wondering what she was doing. He pushed the lobster around on his plate that they weren't allowed to eat for 'sound purposes' and laughed a little to himself, thinking how Nia would lament that perfectly good food going to waste all for the sake of television.

"…maybe two or three. Elijah? What do you think?" He started, remembering that he was not on a date with Nia, but with Samantha, who looked a little put off that he wasn't paying her enough attention.

"I'm so sorry, I was admiring the view." He'd been looking down at his plate and they both knew it. Luckily, he'd caught the tail end of her sentence, a question about if he wanted children.

"Cut!" Warren interjected. "Let's try that again, and Elijah, let's focus, yeah? Roll cameras!"

This time, Elijah managed to be more present in the conversation. "I wouldn't mind a few kids." He aimed a smile at Samantha, but thought about Nia. Wondered if she wanted children, before questioning what the hell was going on in his mind. He'd never actively thought about kids - he liked them, and his own had always been metaphorical things rarely thought of. But it wasn't as scary of a thought as it had been before, especially if the woman was Nia.

More and more, he wondered what would happen if he just called it quits, and chased after what growing between them. But then he thought about the jobs, the money that was on the line, and how so many people had invested in this project, and hated to put it all to waste. But he had no idea how to make it work without hurting someone in the process. Which made him refocus back on his date with Samantha. He still had a job to do.

Back at the house, he noticed Nia was more quiet than usual, letting out a sigh every so often. He wondered what was on her mind; she'd been happy enough telling him about the audition, but after that, she'd withdrawn a little. They sat in his room as clouds were starting to roll in, making outside a little too chilly to sit, the television playing softly in the background. After her third sigh, he pulled her into his lap and held her close. "Hey, what's going on up there?"

Though he couldn't see her face, he could feel her thinking. "Kerry knows."

Elijah frowned. "Knows what?"

Nia gestured between them. "About us."

"What makes you say that?" Elijah frowned, thinking they'd been pretty circumspect.

"She basically alluded to the fact that if there were ever something happening between the two of us, she'd find a way to make it work." Nia worried her lip as Elijah thought about Kerry's little hint. It made him smile, knowing that she was on their side, however subtle she was being.

"I knew I liked her." Elijah smiled, though it was short as he realized that Nia was still worrying about something. Tilting her chin up, he saw the worry lingering in her eyes. "What?"

"Are we making a mistake here? You've got projects attached to this and I'm just starting to get more auditions…what if we're starting something that could stop all of that?"

Elijah understood where her worry was coming from and that they should be careful, but he also wanted to test the waters a little. "What if all these projects didn't matter as much to me as seeing what we have together?"

Nia sat up and frowned, shaking her head. "Eli, I don't know what's going to happen with us, but you are not going to give up something you've been working towards forever just for a shot at us. If we work out, great, but we both deserve to have our dreams actually realized."

He sighed, knew that she was right. "I just hate that the moment you come back into my life is the one time I have to be super careful."

"Are you actually glad that we…reconnected?" Nia asked, a little unsure, a little hopeful.

"*Yes.* I'm so glad." There was no hesitation. Elijah knew that she was what he wanted, and somehow, they'd figure out a way to be together.

Nia's lips split into a smile, and with the soft moonlight glowing over her skin she was breathtaking to him. Elijah dropped a soft kiss on her lips, glad that he could do this much.

"I know I should be worried about all my obligations, but all I can think of is being with you right now. We can worry about the other stuff later."

Nia, still a little uncertain, nodded and curled back into his side. "Let's stay in the now." She whispered.

A small voice told him it might be all they had together.

The Thunderstorm

NIA

"Wait, you hired a psychic for tonight?" Nia and Kerry were watching the crew scramble to set up an indoor area for the night's filming. Overhead, thick clouds were brewing outside, promising a storm. Up until now they'd been pretty lucky in terms of good weather for filming, but tonight that had all changed. Some news outlets had been projecting a tropical storm, but it was still on the move and not entirely on course to hit the island. Production had decided to keep on schedule for filming unless the storm worsened, especially as this was the second to last week of filming with only five women left in the competition. Nia had no idea where time had gone, but she was sad to think that her time on the island was almost up. But it had been much better than she'd anticipated, and was ready to see her family again.

Kerry adjusted one of the wine glasses on the table. "Warren's idea. Honestly, I really like it." Kerry paused to give some additional feedback on the set up of the tables. "We're going to make it social media friendly by letting viewers vote on who they think they pick to be the winner."

"That'll be fun." Nia tried to make sure her face was neutral. It was getting harder and harder to not let her feelings for Elijah slip out. Increasingly so, she was beginning to think of him as hers, which was not productive. Nia had had to watch her jealousy, knowing he was just doing his job…but that didn't mean she had to like it.

Deliberately, Nia set aside those thoughts and turned back to the present, taking in the activity going on. The living room had been turned into a dusky, moody area, with colored scarves thrown over lamps, cozy pillows on the floor. And things with her and Elijah were…wonderful. She looked around the room, expecting to see him back from the walk he'd gone on earlier, but not finding him.

Just as she was about to mention it to Kerry, Isaac popped up and vocalized her very thought. "Have either of you seen Elijah?" He looked at his watching, gauging the time.

Kerry shook her head, while Nia replied. "Last I heard he was going down to the beach for a walk."

"In this weather? It'll rain any second." Isaac shook his head. "I'll go track him down." Before he could leave however, Cynthia stopped him.

"So, April has some sort of skin condition going on that you need to see. Probably just a rash, but it looks gnarly."

Isaac sighed. "Of course. This night is going perfectly."

"I can track him down, it's not like I have anything to do." Nia volunteered.

Kerry was pulled away by another crew member. "That's a great idea!"

Isaac hesitated, "Would you? If you don't mind, that would help so I can keep the PAs where they are."

"Of course, I'll go reel him in."

"Thank you." Isaac smiled gratefully before disappearing with Cynthia.

Heading out the back doors, Nia headed down towards the beach. Over the ocean, lightning struck, and the waves were getting choppier by the minute. *Where the hell is he?* Nia wondered. She checked the gazebo, but no one was there. The beach was completely empty at this point. On a whim, Nia decided to check the crew house, wondering if he'd made a pit stop in there.

As she headed up the steps, fat rain drops started falling down, drenching the porch and sand. She spotted a figure inside, and upon entering, saw that it was Elijah. He was in the living room, blinds partially drawn and seated on the couch. Actually, he was fast asleep on the couch, softly snoring. Quietly, Nia walked over and gently shook his arm. Sleepy green eyes opened, and a soft smile crossed his face as he realized who it was. "Did I fall asleep?"

Nia sat on the cushion next to him. "You did, and production couldn't find you so they had to send in the big guns." Her arm broke out in goosebumps as his fingers trailed along it.

"Your skin is so soft."

A flash of light in the dark room illuminated his face, focused on hers, before the crack of thunder followed.

Elijah looked over at the windows and the rain that was beginning to pour out of the skies. "I guess that also means you're stuck here with me." His eyes connected with hers, and Nia could feel something growing between them. Their fingers tangled together, making their own sparks that shot through Nia's body.

Dimly, she realized her phone was ringing. She managed to answer it before the last ring, seeing Kerry's name on the line. "I found him. But the rain is pouring."

"Thank god. Are you two safe?"

"We're holed up in the crew house for now." Elijah brought her fingers to his lips and pressed a kiss to each tip.

"Stay there. It sounds like this storm isn't going to stop any time soon, so we're having everyone hunker down until this blows over."

"We can do that." Nia managed to keep her voice composed. "We'll head back when it starts to ease up."

Hanging up, Nia felt Elijah sit up, his body coming to cage her in his warmth. His scent was all over, and she found herself leaning into him. Rain pounded on the windows, competing with the blood that was pulsing through her body. His lips brushed her ear, warm breath flowing over her as he whispered, "What do you think we should do with this free time?"

Nia balanced herself, pressing a hand into his muscled thigh. "Something very fun? Maybe even athletic."

Elijah let out a soft chuckle. "I can handle that." His big hand cupped her cheek, bringing her eyes to meet his. "Only if you're sure. We don't have to do anything you're not ready for."

Nia thought about everything they'd been through, all the time and things they'd learned about each other, and how it led them to this moment. A small, tiny part of her wanted to hesitate, to pump the brakes, and cool things down…but the larger, more vocal part was demanding she lay on the gas and rev up this fire that'd been simmering between them for the longest. Nia was tired of living with a bunch of what ifs, of maybes, of uncertainty. She knew she wanted this, wanted him. And that's how simple it should be.

Pulling away from him, she saw the disappointment in his eyes as she went to the door. The lock clicking into place had his eyes darting to hers, a question in his eyes. Nia slowly made her way back to stand in front of him. His head fell to her stomach, pressing a soft kiss there as she ran her fingers his hair. "I really want this."

Elijah pulled her down to him and they closed the distance, lips meeting and crashing together like the thunder that raged outside. Elijah's kisses weren't tentative or soft or exploratory. These were fiery, passionate, filled with the urgency of missed years and time and pent up fervor that had been building for what seemed like ever.

And if it was all they ever got together, she was determined to make it worth the effort. Elijah grabbed Nia by the hips, lifting her over him and she sunk her weight onto the hard erection that strained for release. He groaned into her mouth, and responded by grinding up into her, earning a mirrored gasp from her. Nia let her hips start a slow roll, intending to drive him wild. "Nia…" He warned. She laughed breathily, doing it again and loving the sounds he made. Suddenly she felt the world shift; Elijah was flipping her over and underneath him on the couch.

She couldn't press close enough to him, a wave of emotion rolling over her. It was warm, like sun heated breeze that made her feel safe, wanted. Elijah was grabbing her thigh, bringing her leg around his hips and allowing him to press his hard length more directly against her core. Her skirt was slowly running up, Elijah's hands gliding across her thighs revealing inch by inch as he moved to cup her behind. He slid a thick finger inside her, easily gliding in and spreading her wetness around. Her mouth dropped open as he slid another in, setting a slow pump along every nook and cranny. Nia's fingers shook as she tried to unbutton his shirt, desperate to feel his skin against hers. Finally, *finally*, she met the smooth strong skin of his back, and let her fingers trail there, marveling in him, in them together. Unbuckling his pants, she stroked him, taking her time, feeling him her hand, completely vulnerable to her.

Nia was falling for him, had fallen hard, completely letting him in again. In all the years since him, there had been no one else who had even come close to making her feel like he did. Some people found love, lost it, and found it in another person. Nia couldn't help but wonder if he was still her person. The thought, not as scary as it should have been, was drowned out as he sucked the tip of her breast into his mouth, edging a primal cry out of her. God, he knew how to make her feel good. Right now, she would do her best to enjoy it.

ELIJAH

Elijah was glad. So, so glad. And he was not going to mess this up. Not this time. Nia's legs tightened around his hips and he let out a soft curse. She was driving him crazy, in the best possible way. They moved with a harmony borne of two people whose bodies remembered each other, discovering new things. He pulled her dress over her head, and groaned when he saw her pink bra that held her breasts up to perfection. Leaning down, he tasted one brown nipple, rolling it around his mouth and relishing the moan it brought from her.

"...Just like that," her breathy moans filled his ear. His hand came up to play with her nipple ring, teasing her until her hips rolled uncontrollably against him. He kissed his way down her body, leaving little love bites along the way.

Mine, he thought. *She's mine.*

Reaching his target, he slowly slid her underwear down, laying a kiss on every part revealed. He could feel her fingers sliding into his hair, nails scratching his scalp and felt the fire in him ramp up. Elijah worshiped her, lifting her legs over his shoulders as he feasted on her core, dragging greedy moans from her. Soft pleas fell from her lips as he teased her higher and higher, before pulling away. That turned her pleas into curses, and he laughed as he continued to tease her, until she fell over the cliff in a climax that had her legs clamped around his head, trembling with spent passion. When she finally stilled, he rose back over her, pressing a soft kiss to her lips, his own still wet with the taste of her. Nia slid from underneath him, pushing him back to the couch and crouching over him. She was like his own goddess sent to show him a taste of heaven, and he wanted as much as he could stand. Nia's hands trailed down his chest, shaking a little. "Come here." Elijah pulled her closer, feeling the silky warmth of her body sliding against his. "Shit. Condom. Pants."

Between kisses, Nia mentioned, "I'm on birth control, by the way and clean." She dropped a kiss on his neck, delaying his response for one blissful moment.

"You are?" He gritted out. She bent over to grab his pants off the floor, but he grabbed her by the hips. "Wait." Their eyes met. "I haven't gone without a condom in a long time. I haven't trusted anyone that much."

"It's fine, I understand." Nia moved again, but he stopped her.

"I trust you. I always have." He knew it in his bones, knew it was true. Nia was always someone he had trusted, could trust with secrets, fears, intimacy. And he wanted to feel her, nothing between them. Her eyes locked onto his as she realized what he was saying.

"Thank you," came her whispered answer. And then she lowered herself onto him, sinking her warmth along him. Elijah's head fell back, eyes closing as he focused on the two of them joining together. They moved together, Nia riding him for everything he had. The only sounds in the room were their mingled breaths and the sound of thunder to shatter the silence around them. His hands gripped her waist as she came again, grinding on him as spasms racked her body.

Feeling his own orgasm rising, he was glad she was there with him. They came together, a shared cry of passion as he felt, their worlds colliding, and Elijah knew that he wouldn't be able to let her go. *Not again*. Spent, he collapsed onto the couch, tucking Nia into his side.

Everything had changed. Elijah couldn't imagine being with anyone else at this point. Nia had fallen back into his life at the most random, opportune time, and he didn't, couldn't see a life without her. Even if it meant he wouldn't get the job, he knew it was the right thing to do. Nia was worth more than that.

The Psychic

NIA

Nia woke slowly, with Elijah gently stroking her arm. She couldn't help the soft smile that ran over her face as their eyes connected in the dim light. He dropped a kiss to her lips, before whispering, "Sleepy eyes."

A laugh escaped her. "Someone wore me out."

"I had some making up to do." His smile was only a little cocky, but Nia loved it anyway.

"A few more tries and we'll be even." She noticed that the rain had slowed, and it was dark out.

"Tonight." His eyes were green fire. "But we should head back before anyone comes to find us."

Nia wanted to stay, but knew that he was right. They'd already been gone long enough and too much longer would make people suspicious. "Stop being so responsible."

Elijah laughed as they sat up. "Trust me, I would much rather stay here with you."

They found their clothes and managed to right themselves to a presentable form. Things had definitely changed between them, but she didn't know how it would affect their current lives, or even if it would. It was a major risk, letting him like this when she didn't know where it could go. But it was almost like she didn't have a choice; Elijah had a permanent spot on her heart and he'd taken it back. Nia just hoped she wouldn't get burned again.

They stood at the door, not ready to head back to the main house. Elijah took her hand, lacing his fingers with hers. "Are you ready?"

"I'm not sure." She bit her lip, looking down at their hands. "I'm not sure how this works. Or if it even should work."

His hand came under her chin, tilting her face until she met his eyes. "We're going to make it work."

Unsure, she let him kiss the doubts away. Nia thought she heard a creak somewhere in the house as they pulled away from each other, but the wind had started to pick up again outside. Taking each other's hands, they ran out into the rain and wind. For now, she'd take each day as it came, and worry about the future later. Hopefully, hopefully, things would work out for them.

Back at the resort, Nia and Elijah ran up to the glass patio doors. They were soaking wet, which Nia was thankful for. Maybe now no one would notice how Elijah had completely ruined her hair and makeup. She dropped his hand, breaking their connection. There was no need to advertise what they'd done back at the crew house or how their relationship had changed; it would only cause more questions when all Nia wanted to do was take a hot shower. Kerry was the first to see them by her post at the door, throwing it open and tossing warm towels at them while directing a few PA's run to grab them something warm to drink for them.

"Thank the sweet baby Jesus you two are safe!" She wrapped Nia up in a quick hug. "I swear Warren was going to kill me if anything happened to Elijah, and I don't know what we'd do without you Nia."

Nia managed to keep her smile relaxed. "You're definitely right about that."

"Is there any update on the storm, or are we calling it for the day?" Elijah asked while toweling off his hair, unreasonably sexy despite being soaking wet.

Kerry rolled her eyes. "We're still going to go for it. The rough patch is past us for the most part, so unless there's a lightning strike too close, we'll shoot tonight. The psychic predicted it actually."

"Or maybe she checked the weather." Nia rolled her eyes while Elijah and Kerry laughed.

There was a commotion in the doorway as the remaining contestants started to realize that Elijah and Nia had made it back. A few of the women ran up to Elijah, wrapping him in hugs and fighting to have their not so subtle whispers of concern be heard over the women next to them. April was definitely the loudest of the bunch, projecting her voice as if she were participating in a local community theater production. "April is so happy you two are back! We just couldn't believe y'all got stuck out there!"

Danielle squatted down, rubbing Elijah's legs dry. "We've got to make sure you don't catch a cold." She winked at him as her towel creeped higher up his thigh. Elijah jumped and shifted away from her.

"I uh, appreciate the concern Danielle. I can take it from here."

Nia held back a laugh and decided now was the perfect time to excuse herself without too much attention. "If we're still filming tonight, I'm going to take a shower and change into some dry clothes."

Kerry agreed. "Good idea - I'll try and help lover boy over here lose the crowd. We don't need him catching a cold."

"Pajamas!" Warren was darting by, clipboard in hand. "Everyone change into pajamas! We're making this a sleepover shoot!"

Escaping, Nia managed to get through a shower and into her favorite college sweater and black leggings before it was time to head downstairs. The lights had been dimmed and electric candles were strategically placed to give the living room a soft, mysterious glow. Cushions and blankets had been placed on the floor around a small table with candles and small plants, and a little stick of incense burning. The other ladies were already seated on the floor, talking and eating slices of pizza. Cameras were picking up their dialogue, and Nia silently found a spot off to the side to stand.

Alex caught her eye behind his camera and sent a wink her way before ducking back down. She knew she need to figure out a way to kindly let him down and resolved to do it before the weekend was over. Or maybe she'd ghost him. As Nia was debating her options, she heard a familiar voice speak softly into her ear. "I don't like the way he looks at you."

She felt a huge smile come over her face. "Is that a touch of jealousy I'm hearing?" Nia could hear the gentle laugh from Elijah that warmed her from the inside out.

"Maybe. Actually, it definitely is."

"This coming from the man that currently has five girlfriends?" Nia turned a caught a smolder from Elijah. His eyes were on her mouth, and she took a step back, not sure if he'd try to kiss her again at this point. "Pretty possessive."

"There's only one I want." His words were a low murmur, only for her ears. Before she could respond, one of the production assistants found them and brought Elijah over to sit with the other women, and Nia over to a side room where she would enter from. Inside was a woman of average height, with soft lavender curls that stopped at her chin. Hazel eyes met Nia's, who knew who this had to be. "You must be Seraphina, the psychic."

Seraphina nodded, a smile on her face. "I am, call me Sera. And you must be one of the people lost in the storm."

"Guilty," Nia smiled. *Word traveled fast*. "That storm hit much faster than I thought it would."

"It came when it was needed. Rain is cleansing; perhaps it was a sign of the start of something new." There was a mysterious smile on Sera's face that made Nia wonder if she might actually be legitimate.

Nia was a breath away from asking what she meant by that when they were invited out to set. Leading Sera, Nia made her way into the living room. "Ladies, Elijah, say hello to our special guest Seraphina. She's going to take a peek into your futures…and maybe she can see if one of you belong in Elijah's."

Sera smiled warmly at the group. "Thank for the introduction. I'm excited to see what we discover together, so let's get started."

Nia started to move back out of the shot, but Sera stopped her with a hand on her arm. "Nia, I'd like you to sit in on this as well."

"Me? Are you sure?" Nia felt her eyebrows raising. Sera nodded, linking her arm in Nia's. She threw a look at Warren and Kerry in the back who shrugged, giving her a thumbs up. "Sure, why not."

Another cushion was brought out for Nia and the group made room on the floor for Nia. She couldn't help noticing some of the looks thrown between Danielle and Nicole and was glad she wasn't seated next to either of them. She had no idea why Sera wanted her to be part of this, but she was going with the flow.

To the left of Nia, April was slightly more skeptical as she took in the relative normalcy of Sera. "I thought you were going to be in a bunch of robes or something like that. With a like little crystal ball or some tarot cards."

"A crystal ball would hardly be useful. I read energies, auras. It's much more accurate." Sera's eyes crinkled as she smiled. "How about we get started? Everyone, please join hands together."

Lily grabbed Danielle and Elijah's hands on the other side of the circle. "You don't need to touch us all individually?" Nia felt Sera's warm hand surround hers, and April's hand beside hers.

"No, not for this. All you need to do is close your eyes and relax. Focus only on the sound of my voice." Nia closed her eyes and let the tension out of her shoulders. Slowly, silence fell around the small group, and Nia could almost forget that they were in the middle of filming. There was only the soft patter of rain outside, so soothing that Nia almost dozed off.

Softly, Sera began to speak. "Someone here is not here for the right reasons. You seek fame and fortune over true love."

Nia couldn't help but think she knew which woman she was referring to.

"Elijah, your mind is not yet made up. You know who you want, and yet, you hesitate. The woman for you is here right now, but only if you make the move."

Nia could hear Danielle snort softly beside her. "Duh."

"This goes beyond a dating show – the woman you pick has the power to change your life. Pick wisely, for you may not get a second chance."

Nia risked opening her eyes and got a peek at the frown that marred Elijah's face. His eyes were still closed, but he looked surprisingly unsure.

Sera continued to speak, bring up some things about auras and love before falling silent. "You all can open your eyes now."

Nia blinked her eyes open, taking in the people around her doing the same. Lily was the first to speak. "Do you know who is going to win?"

Sera looked around the table, lingering on Nia for what felt like the briefest of moments. "I do." The group made a few noises, looking around each other. "It will be revealed when the time is right. I don't want to influence anything unnecessarily."

Danielle rolled her eyes at Nicole "How convenient."

Sera smiled at the two of them, before adding. "What I can do is write the name of the woman Elijah will choose at the end of the contest and seal it for you. You all are welcome to open it on the last day of filming to see if I am correct or not."

Nia nodded, liking the idea. "I love that."

Seraphina stood and took a small bag to a table a little way away from them. She pulled out a piece of paper, and scribbled something on it before pulling out an actual wax stamp kit and sealing the note. "I'll give this to Nia to hang onto, and she can do the honors on the big day."

Nia stood, taking the letter from her. Seraphina met her eyes, and was that a look of concern there? Nia wasn't sure.

"Thank you for all of you time." With that, she gathered her things up and left. Nia left the group to allow them to digest and speak about their time for the cameras. She found Kerry in the back, nursing a large glass of wine. "That was something. Should I give this to you to hang on to?" Nia passed the envelope to Kerry, who tucked it away in her clipboard.

"Yes, good idea. Warren practically wet himself he was so giddy about that envelope."

Nia stretched, feeling some lingering soreness from that afternoon's *activities*. "I wonder if she'll get it right?"

Kerry took a long drag from her glass. "I hope he does." She met Nia's eyes, a little note of concern on her face. "I really hope he does."

Patting Nia on the shoulder, Kerry left with Isaac as they talked about dailies and final edits of the first few episodes. Nia went out to the deck, watching the rain drop into the ocean, wondering if she was doing the right thing by taking up with

Elijah again. She liked him, a lot. And yet there was a little voice inside her head that told her the more involved she got with Elijah, the more it would hurt when this all eventually imploded in their faces. But Nia knew that if she didn't see where this could go between them she would regret it. Sighing, she disappeared back into the house, heading toward the stair.s Nia could figure it out. She always did.

ELIJAH

Elijah heard the door open, and saw Nia's silhouette enter the room, deep in thought. He shifted in his chair and watched her almost jump out of her skin. The light flipped on and he watched the tension leave her body when she saw that it was just him. Elijah stood, crossing the room to her and pulling her into his arms. "You scared the shit out of me Eli."

"That was not my goal." He rested his cheek on her head, loving the scent of mango and coconut in her hair. Nia smelled like summer and sunshine, a tantalizing combination.

"What was your goal, as you wait in my dark room for me?" Nia quirked an eyebrow at him.

"Is it wrong to admit I didn't get nearly enough of you this afternoon?" Elijah dropped a kiss to her lips and Nia backed to the bed. He pressed a soft kiss on her stomach.

She smiled down at him and ruffled her fingers through his dark hair. "A girl likes to hear things like that every now and again."

For a while, there wasn't anything said between the two of them, only breathless whispers and gasps as they tried to keep quiet. Once spent, Elijah drew Nia into his arms as they caught their breath. It was well into the night, and he knew they should get some sleep, but there was a lingering thought on his mind that he couldn't get rid of. *Nia was spectacular*. Elijah hadn't known that he could feel as much as he did with anyone, hadn't expected to come to this island and actually find someone he could potentially see himself with in the future. But now, he knew what he wanted, and couldn't wait to say it.

Elijah propped himself up on his elbow, looking at Nia's sleepy face in the moonlight. "You know how Seraphina said I was wrestling with what my decision would be?"

Nia cautiously nodded, more alert now. "Mmhmm. I remember."

"I'm not going to pick any of the contestants"

"What do you mean?" Nia sat up, looking at him.

"For the sake of completing the show, I'll finish and get to the final round of competitors. But at the final ring ceremony, I'm not picking anyone. That way I get to be with you."

"Are you serious?" A smile was beginning to form on Nia's face. "You'd do that? What about your reputation?"

"You can't blame me for not wanting to settle for mediocre love, and most dating show couples don't last that long anyway. But I know I want to give us a chance, and I can't do that if there's someone else in the way."

"So after the show, we'd just…be together?"

"If you'll have me." Hope bloomed in Elijah's chest as Nia nodded, and curled back against him.

"I'll have you." She whispered, and he met her lips with a kiss. This was what he wanted. A chance with Nia. And somehow, despite the odds, they would make it work.

The Hiccup

ELIJAH

CARTER: **Heads up, this was NOT my idea.**

Elijah frowned at his phone as he walked over to the crew house a few days later. He'd been called into a meeting with Warren, Kerry and Isaac who had some update to share with him.

ELIJAH: What are you talking about?

The ellipsis bubble popped up as Carter was typing, but then he got another text.

NIA: I can't believe we stayed up all night. I had fun ;)

Elijah smiled as he thought about the last few days. He and Nia had been on a reconnecting spree this last week in Oahu whenever possible. After filming ended each day, they spent a lot of time talking on their balcony, watching the moon sink into the water and the sun start to rise. They shared secret looks during filming, and spent their nights holed up in either of their rooms. For some reason, Elijah felt like they were on borrowed time, and he didn't want it to end. He was earning her trust again, and he had to make sure she knew she wasn't an idiot for doing so.

ELIJAH: Let's do it again ;)

"Elijah! We're meeting in here." Warren called, breaking Elijah's focus on his phone. Warren was in a loud floral print shirt as he waved to Elijah. Another text came in from Carter, and he took a quick look as he walked into the room.

CARTER: About Lily...

Frowning a little, Elijah put his phone away and sat down in one of the chairs around the table. He noticed Kerry's frown which was different from her normal face in phone habit. She looked at Elijah with a look he couldn't quite identify when Warren started speaking. "It's crazy that we're at the last week on the island, right? I know I'm going to miss this place."

"Me too, but I'm ready to get home. What's on the agenda for today?" Elijah looked around the table.

"I'm going to put it bluntly - you're going to pick Lily to win the competition."

A clock ticked somewhere. "I'm sorry, Warren, what was that?"

"Lily - she's going to win the competition."

Carter's text made more sense now. "Am I missing something here? I thought I got the final decision." Elijah caught Kerry's gaze, and she nodded.

"Technically yes, you do."

"So, what's the deal? Why do I have to pick Lily?"

Kerry sighed. "Lily is the niece of Chris Parker, the head of motion pictures for Annex Media Group. He thinks this will be good to 'launch' her career and wants to strike a deal."

Warren took a sip of his coffee. "Parker wants to strongly encourage you to make this decision. If you make him happy, he'll make you happy by casting you as the lead as Commander Hex. You'll be set."

So many thoughts were racing in Elijah's mind, but the one at the forefront was: Nia. He'd told her he wasn't going to pick anyone to win so they could be together. But this was the opportunity he'd been looking for, what he'd been hoping would happen since he first started his acting career.

He barely noticed when Warren kept talking. "You've got this in the bag man, just think about the big picture. Plus, Lily is a catch. The marriage won't be so bad."

"Marriage?" Alarms were blaring in his head.

"Yeah, but it doesn't have to last. Weddings are excellent for ratings. Give it six months, a year tops."

"I need to think about this." Elijah stood, shaking his head.

Warren opened his mouth to say something, but Kerry interjected. "Of course you do, it only makes sense. Let us know what you decide."

Elijah excused himself, heading outside and down to the beach. The last thing he wanted was to be ambushed by another one of the women looking for 'quality time' – except, now he knew that his choices were actually limited. He wasn't sure what to do, absolutely did not want to give Nia any reason to doubt him again. And looking at his phone, Elijah wanted answers. Elijah called Carter to try and find out more about this mess. He answered on the second ring. "I was wondering if you'd had the meeting yet."

"What the fuck, Carter? Whose idea was this?" He shifted his feet deeper into the warm sand.

"It was Chris Parker's idea. I overheard some of them talking in the kitchen and connected the dots."

"Fuck." Elijah picked up a shell next to him and threw it into the water. "Fuck."

He could hear Carter pause on the line. "What's the problem?"

"Why would there be a problem?" Elijah muttered.

"Eli, come on. You wouldn't be this bitchy about picking someone for a literal dating show unless there was a problem."

Sighing, Elijah gave in. "Do you remember Nia?"

"Which one was she? The hot waitress, right?"

"She's the host here."

"Don't tell me you've been fucking the host this whole time?" Carter groaned into the line. "Is that why you don't want to pick Lily?"

"Not the whole time." It didn't mean he hadn't wanted to.

"Dude, I thought you agreed to no drama, remember? That's the only way all of this works."

"It's not like I wanted this to happen." Elijah stood, and paced down the sand. "Trust me, we both avoided it as long as we could."

Giving Carter a shortened version, Elijah briefly detailed their relationship on the island and what the promised Nia, and how the deal with the producers would mess it all up. Once it was all off his chest, he let out a pent-up breath. Elijah hadn't realized just how much tension he'd been carrying around with this, and just wanted to let some of it go.

"Making promises that you can't keep?" He could practically see Carter shaking his head. "To your ex-girlfriend? That's dangerous, man."

"I know." Elijah sighed, looking out over the water.

"Look, I'm not one to get in the way of love, but there's an obvious solution."

"I'm listening."

"Ask her to wait."

Elijah frowned. "I don't think she'd go for that."

"Look, you're already waiting now, right? What's a few more months until it airs? That way you can still get the job, and the woman."

It was an option, but Elijah didn't know if it was the best one, and he voiced it to Carter.

"I know it's not as fast as you wanted, but you both signed up for certain obligations during this show. So if she's a professional, she should understand." There were a few voices in the background. "I have a meeting, but think about it."

The phone clicked, and Elijah was left alone with his thoughts again. He didn't know what he was going to do, but he knew he'd have to decided quick.

NIA

On her way out to the beach for a jog, Nia bumped into the women who were also dressed in workout gear. "Let me guess, group workout?"

Camille nodded, glum. "I swear I've gained five pounds since I've been here." Nia couldn't see any difference, but knew the feeling.

Danielle rolled her eyes. "I've kept my same routine up as much as possible. Just because we're on an island does't mean we're on vacation."

Nia was glad there was only a week left on the island with Danielle before she'd finally be home. Lily made a face at Danielle. "If only we were all as dedicated as you. Besides, I know Elijah thinks you look fantastic."

Nia nodded. "You look great to me. All of you do. I don't know how Elijah is going to choose." Ok, that may have been a little too much, but Nia was still in a good mood.

"Want to come workout with us Nia?" April asked.

"Sure, why not." Nia felt a little guilty at her thoughts and resolved to be as positive as possible.

They set off, heading to a hill towards the front of the resort. Danielle suggested they run up and down the hill ten times, with pushups in between. After the first few times, Nia and Camille were both out of breath. Annoyingly, Danielle was barely panting. She must really have been working out. Nia was surprised when Danielle waited for her at the bottom of the hill, and ran along with her up to the top. If Nia was being honest, she pushed herself a little faster, so she didn't look as bad next to her.

On the way down, Danielle started up a conversation. "So…have you liked getting to know everyone here?"

Nodding, Nia tried to catch her own breath. "Yeah…nice."

"I'm just a little jealous of you, actually."

"Why?" That was surprising; the last thing Nia expected Danielle to admit was jealousy. They made it to the bottom of the hill and dropped into a quick ten pushups before running back up the hill.

"Because you get…to watch us be crazy…and spend time with Elijah."

Nia wasn't sure if she was out of breath due to the exercise or Danielle's poking around.

"I don't spend…that much time with him."

"Really? I would. Especially if our rooms were right next to each other. I'd have some fun." At the bottom of the hill, Danielle took a sip of her water bottle. "We have limited access to him. You don't."

"Elijah is too busy to hang out with me." Nia was on high alert, wondering what Danielle was getting at.

"I'd find time to get to him." Danielle laughed, aiming for self-conscious but coming out more threatening. "Don't tell anyone, but that time you ran into me outside his room wasn't the last time. I went back again, but he wasn't in the room." They sprinted up the hill again, and the whole way up Nia wondered what exactly Danielle knew. On the way back down, she kept asking questions.

"You went in there?" Nia gasped, stopping for air.

"No, the door was locked. I'm surprised you didn't hear me."

"I must've been sleep." Nia murmured. Internally, her thoughts were racing – was she sleep or being slept with?

"But come on, what healthy male wouldn't want some female company after two months?"

"True." Nia flopped in the grass, stretching her legs out in front of her. Danielle folded herself next to Nia, taking a drink of water.

"The question is, who has he been spending time with? None of the other girls have fessed up to anything." Danielle shrugged, bending over her leg. "Whoever she is, she's lucky as hell."

"If there's even a she." Nia watched as Danielle smiled, as if she knew all her secrets.

"I'm sure there is."

The conversation ended as the rest of the women flopped on the grass beside them, breathing heavily and ready to head back to the resort. To top it off, they ran into Alex on the way back to the house. She hadn't really spoken to him since the night at the club, and knew it was time to say something. So when he suggested they talk for a moment, Nia agreed. They went out onto the patio, settling into on a couple chairs that faced the water.

"I feel like we haven't gotten any time together." He leaned forward, elbows on his knees. Alex really was attractive, and Nia was only a little sad she hadn't been able to muster up any feeling for him.

"I know, things got away from me." Nia sighed. "Look, Alex…I'm being honest, I think we're just better off friends."

Alex nodded, looking down at his hands. "It might be best. But if you ever decide you want to change things, you have my number."

Nia laughed at the shameless flirting despite the rejection. She was about to remark on it when she saw movement inside. It was Elijah, walking through the kitchen, grabbing a bottle of water. The look on his face was a little troubled, and Nia wondered what had happened to put it there.

Alex looked over his shoulder and saw where Nia's attention was diverted to. "Not you too? Seems like that man has all the women half in love with him."

Shaking her head, Nia tried to deflect. "I'm not half in love with him." She was afraid it was actually more than that.

"If you say so. But be careful. I don't want to see you getting hurt." Alex stood, patting her shoulder. "You deserve someone who's all in."

Nia couldn't argue with that. She just hoped that everything would be fine. It had to be.

The Desires

ELIJAH

After what should've been a nice group date turned into a heated argument between Danielle and Camille about who was spending too much time with him, Elijah wanted nothing more than to go back to his room, wash off the wine that had spilled onto him and curl up with Nia. Unfortunately, there was another Dream Suite tonight so he wouldn't be sleeping in the same bed as Nia today. Elijah was feeling the urgency to spend as much time with Nia as possible, especially after Chris Parker's offer.

The soft breeze blowing through the open window of the car was welcome from a hot day. Warren and Kerry were in the back seat, talking about ratings and other technical things he wasn't fully listening to. As they turned into the driveway, Elijah was ready to run to the shower when he heard his name called by Warren. Shifting in his seat, he looked up at them. "Elijah, we need you to pick Lily for tonight's Dream Suite."

Frowning, Elijah shifted in his seat to face them. "Why is that? I thought we'd agreed on April."

"It would be weird for you to pick Lily to win if you never even took her to the suite." Warren spoke as if the Lily decision had been made already.

"I didn't realize I'd chosen her yet." The car stopped, and Elijah made to open the door.

"Jim, can you give us a moment alone in the car?" Warren spoked to the driver, who left Elijah alone with Warren and Kerry. "What's the deal man? I don't get it, Lily is the obvious choice. Who are you holding out for?"

"I'm not holding out for anyone." Elijah huffed, but he knew it was a lie. He didn't want to hurt Nia, but it's not like he could come out and say that they'd been dating this whole time.

"Warren is right." Kerry spoke up, a sympathetic face on. "Even if you don't choose Lily, which is your choice, it would be strange not to have her go to the suite at all. Early polls are showing her as a crowd favorite."

Sighing, Elijah agreed. "Fine, I'll take her."

"Thank you." The words were only a little sarcastic as Warren slid out the car.

"One more week?" Elijah looked at Kerry, opening his door.

"On the island. We still have LA photography to do." Groaning, Elijah slid out the car and ran upstairs for a quick shower before heading back down. Unfortunately, there wasn't time to talk to Nia before filming started, and he sat with the women before taking Lily off to the Dream Suite. It was actually a little cabana off to the side, not too far from the crew house. Lily held his hand all the way to the door, where Tiffany, the sound utility waited to take their mic packs for the night. She smiled at the two of them before disappearing back up the beach to the main house.

Inside, there was a box of pizza and a few bottles of wine situated on a small table in the room, which was mostly a really large bed covered in white linens and a bathroom with a tub and robes. Lily perched on one of the stools and peeked inside the box. "At least there's food." She grinned at Elijah before taking a slice.

"True. I think some people had more wine than they should have." Elijah loosened his tie and snagged a slice as well. It was pepperoni, and he smiled; an image of Nia curling her nose at eating pork popped into his head. He'd always thought of it as more pepperoni for him.

"What are you smiling about?" Lily wondered, and Elijah shook his head.

"Nothing in particular." An awkward silence fell over the room as they ate. Elijah opened a bottle of wine, pouring them each a healthy glass. He was trying to figure out what to say to her. It would have been easier if it were April – she was her own source of entertainment, and could talk uninterrupted for hours. Lily, wasn't like that. And he knew she would start to ask questions if he didn't somewhat keep up the role. But Lily beat him to the punch.

"Why don't you do anything with the women in here?" She wondered as she chewed on the crust.

"Who says that?" Elijah wondered what exactly went around about him with the women.

"Everyone you've taken in here. They all say you don't do anything, barely even make out. It's fascinating."

"Fascinating? Most women would think I'm hiding something."

Lily curled her legs up under her in the chair. "Are you? I don't know, you could be. But I think it's kind of sweet. I always thought it was gross when you see bachelors screwing their way around the women before choosing someone to break up with less than a year later."

"Interesting." Elijah offered Lily a bit more wine before he poured himself a bit more.

"What's it going to be with us? A little light canoodling? Sleeping on separate sides of the bed? Or all out banging?"

Elijah laughed, despite himself. "You are something else." He did like Lily, but more in a sisterly affection than a romantic one. In a different world, they might even be friends.

"That's what my family tells me." Smiling, she went into the bathroom.

"What does your family think about you doing this show?" Elijah shook off his jacket and took a few pillows off of the couch.

"They're fine with it, I suppose." Lily came back out, wrapped in a big white robe. "I never told anyone, but I do have an uncle who's a pretty big producer connected to the show."

"Is that right?" Elijah watched as Lily flopped on the bed. "Is that why you're on?"

"God, I hope not. I told him absolutely no meddling." She yawned. "I like to get places on my own."

"But why a dating show?"

"I do want love. But, dating sucks these days, if you haven't noticed." She looked over at him. "You probably haven't, actually." That got a laugh from Elijah. "The cynic in me figured why not try another form of dating and get some exposure from it?"

"That's one way to do it." Elijah stood, stretching.

"But you're not going to sleep with me?" Lily yawned and slid under the covers.

"No, I'm not."

"Fair enough. I'm going to sleep now. I love April, but the talking extends to her sleep as well."

Elijah made his own way into the bathroom, shutting the door behind him. Lily didn't know anything about her uncle's string pulling. It made him feel a little bit easier, to know at least that she wasn't in on it. With a clear conscious, he would pick

Nia. It set him at ease finally, and he could breath. By the time he got back out to the room, Lily was asleep. He curled his big frame up onto the couch, and settled in for the night.

NIA

After Nia had gotten back from the group date, which Kerry had let her tag along with and snag a few bottles of local wine, she treated herself to a nice long bath before propping herself up on her side of the balcony to watch the sun set. On a whim, she called Goldie, who answered immediately. "Please tell me you're coming back soon? It's so boring here without my roomie."

Nia laughed as she put in her ear buds. "Goldie, I'm sure you've been glad for some space for your harem of men."

"While that might be true, no one's there to bother me about cleaning schedules and bedtimes and all of that."

"You might want to call your mother if that's the case." The two of them laughed together.

"Any new updates on the Elijah front? I expected way more from you two than just a kiss."

Nia smiled, "Hold on, let me go back inside before we talk about this."

A high-pitched squeal came over the line as Nia went back in, closing the door behind her and flipping on the television. After Danielle's little bit of snooping, she didn't want to make it any easier for anyone to find things out.

"Shut up, did you two…? I knew it! Wait, I'm switching to video call, tell me everything."

Nia flopped stomach first onto the bed as Goldie's face popped onto the screen. "Well, there's been more than kissing. We might be actively…" Nia wiggled her eyebrows in a way that made Goldie's jaw drop and do a little fist pump.

"Yes! How often?"

Nia thought back over the last couple of weeks and smiled. "…Often."

"I knew it!" Goldie grinned. "You always fall off the map a little when you're getting good dick."

"Crass, Golds." But Nia could help the smile on her face. "Can I tell you something else?"

"There's more?" Goldie clutched her heart. "I don't know whether to pass out or grab some popcorn."

Nia lowered her voice to a whisper for this next pick. "He says he's not going to pick anyone, so he can be with me."

Goldie paused, jaw dropping. "Wow…that's major."

"I know, I didn't believe it at first myself. But he says he wants us to have a chance, and doesn't want to miss this moment."

Goldie chewed her lip a little, thinking. "And do you really believe he's actually going to do it?"

Nia sighed, flipping over to her back. "Part of me says yes; it's been so much fun these last days, and we've talked and bonded so much better than we ever did in college. But another part of me thinks it's crazy to think he'd do something like that. His work means everything to him, and I just wonder if I'm enough for him."

"First off, you are brilliant and I don't want to hear you doubting yourself. You were enough back then, and you are enough right now, and anyone who's not an idiot can see it." Goldie pointed a finger at Nia to emphasize her point, making Nia smile.

"Thanks Golds."

"What I do want you to do is be careful. I know things are great right now, but our gut speaks to us for a reason, so if there's a little uncertainty there, don't ignore it. I'm happy for you, but I don't want to see you get hurt."

Nia sighed, knowing Goldie was right. "Ugh, this will all be easier when we're back home and there's real life to distract us."

Goldie laughed softly at that. "Life isn't meant to be a distraction, it's meant to be lived and experienced fully, the good with the bad with everything in between.

That's what makes it special."

The Wishing Stones

NIA

The end of the week came much faster than Nia expected, and with it, Nia's last night on the island. In the morning, she would be catching a flight back to Los Angeles in order to make it on time for her audition. She was sad to be leaving the island and her little bubble of happiness, but was also very ready to get home and see her family and friends.

At the last ring ceremony, it had come down to Danielle and Camille in the bottom two. Nia had her hopes dashed when Kerry muttered that Danielle had to stay on, because she brought the 'drama', so there was no surprise when Camille was sent home. "How much of this is staged again?"

"All of it." Kerry shook her head. "It's all for show really."

The two of them watched as Elijah took back the ring from Camille, who tearfully hugged April and Lily goodbye. Stepping out to her mark, Nia spoke into the cameras. "Another tearful goodbye, but we have our three finalists: Lily James, Danielle Winters, and April St. John, all vying for the heart of Elijah James."

After a quick retake, Nia moved on to the last bit of the evening. "Before we say goodbye to this beautiful island, there's one last thing we want to do. Let's head down to the beach."

This last bit was added on as a little impromptu session, so none of the contestants we expecting what was about to happen. The small group followed Nia down to the beach, cameras following close behind. One of the production assistants passed Nia a basket before darting off camera.

"Ladies, Elijah – what I have here is a basket of wishing stones." Reaching into the basket, Nia pulled out a small grey stone with a soft white line running through it. Beginning to pass out stones, Nia continued. "Wishing stones let you do the obvious – make a wish. It can be any wish, for love, success, your heart's desire. Probably for Elijah." There was a small laugh from April and Lily. As she passed Elijah to his stone, she tied not to react as Elijah's fingers grazed hers as he accepted his stone.

"Legend has it that in order for your wish to come true, you have to give it away. Make your wish, and toss it in the ocean, give it to a loved one, and we'll see if it comes true." She left them there, making her way behind the cameras to watch what would happen.

There was a solemn quiet, the sound of waves crashing against each other the only noise in the night.

April sighed. "Do we have to? They're really pretty."

"If you want it to work, yeah." Lily took a breath and marched closer to the shore, and tossed her rock into the waves. Slowly, April and Danielle followed, tossing their rocks into the ocean. Elijah was the last one, reaching his arm back and tossing it out to the water.

On the way back inside, Kerry caught up to Nia. "I know you're out of here in the morning, and there'll be a car waiting for you out front at nine to take you to the airport. How're you feeling? Nervous?"

Nodding, Nia took in a deep breath of the salty air. "I'm kind of nervous, but excited for this audition."

Pausing at the back door, Kerry leaned on the railing. "You're going to do well, I know it."

"At least one of us has faith in me." Nia rolled her eyes but smiled. "Thank you for that. And everything really."

"Of course. Actually, there was something I wanted to mention – "

"Kerry! Mind if I steal you away for a moment?" Warren interrupted Kerry's train of thought. "We need to talk parents."

"Of course. We'll see you back in LA, Nia." Though she looked like she had more to say, Kerry left with Warren while Nia went inside and up to her room.

Checking her phone once she got back to her room, there were messages from Lexie, Yaya, and her parents, all of them excited for her coming home. Smiling, she hopped in the shower, washing away the layer of salt water and sand that had accumulated from the beach. Stepping back out, she felt more than saw Elijah's presence in her room. "Sneaking in now?"

He lounged on a chair in her room, flipping through channels. "I couldn't wait to see you." He'd changed into a pair of sweats and a t-shirt and was barefoot.

She stepped over to him, and he pulled her down into his lap. "Did you forget the last eight hours we just spent filming this little thing called a TV show?" His arms went around her.

"No, but I couldn't do this down there." He sighed, holding her close. "I like doing this."

Nia laughed against his chest. "Careful, some people might call you a softy."

His lips pressed against hers before he responded. "Only for you." They kissed, longer, her arms going around his neck to bring him as close as possible. She felt her towel slipping but made no move to adjust it.

"What if someone comes to the door?" She traced a path along his neck, eliciting a soft curse from him.

"I locked the door. Mine too, so you're stuck with me."

"Oh, no." The gently sarcastic words were the last things said as he carried her to the bed.

Elijah lowered her down, and she watched as he took off his clothes, before covering her with his perfect body. They fit together, like lost puzzle pieces finding their place. His hands traced a path along her arms, lifting them above her head, fingers interlaced before taking her mouth. Her legs widened, letting him press closer to her. She was ready for him, but he still slid down her body, tasting her, dragging soft cries that she had to muffle with a pillow.

Once he felt her tremble and shake, she pressed a kiss on the inside of her thigh before rising a flipping her over to her stomach, trailing soft fingers down her spine as she caught her breath. A crinkle of foil sounded, the she felt him covering her, which should have made her overpowered, but instead made her feel safe. He sunk into her warmth with a soft groan, reveling in her heat, and she in his hardness, anchoring her to him in this moment. His legs came up behind hers, firm and sturdy, opening her wider to him as they moved together.

This was softer than the last few times they'd slept together had been. She felt like the walls she'd had up were crumbling, and he was making his way back in, nestling at the spot in her heart that still had his name marked. Whispered words of pleasure fell from his lips, as he tortured her with slow, hard strokes that urged the fire inside of her higher and higher.

"More…please…" She begged, but he took his time. He switched their position, turning her back to her back. She linked her legs around his waist, trying to draw him closer, tighter, harder, but he laughed gently, refusing to be rushed.

His big hands slid down her torso to her hips, where he held her still, using her, torturing her, watching her eyes as he slid in and out of her, setting a faster pace. She couldn't help but be entranced, their eyes locked together, breaths coming in time with each other. There was something there, something that was begging to break through, but it was too much, the emotions threatening to make her say something crazy. Breaking, Nia closed her eyes, tried to avoid it.

His hand came down between them, to the spot where she needed it most, bringing her over the edge. And with it, a thought floated to the front of her mind, overwhelming and reassuring at the same time. *I love you.*

The thought stayed with Nia, as their breaths slowed and a quiet lethargy settled over the both of them. It had snuck up on her, not the loud, face first falling that she expected like the first time they'd met, but a quieter, slower burn that had slowly taken over.

She'd thought Elijah had fallen asleep, his breathing was so steady, until she heard his deep voice in her ear. "I love you."

Surprised, Nia froze as thoughts raced around in her mind. *Did she hear that right?* Shifting so she could see his face, wondered if he'd say it again.

But he was asleep, snoring softly in the night. Nia doubted he would even remember what he'd said to her in the morning. She could feel a smile threatening at the corners of her mouth, as a flood of warmth rushed over her like waves rolling up the beach. Because she knew what he didn't - that she was there already too. Knowing that he wouldn't hear it, but feeling like she still had to say it, Nia dropped a kiss on his chest as she snuggled back in his arms.

"I love you, Elijah." It felt…right. Even though they couldn't be public with it just yet, even though he was sleep when he said it, Nia knew that she loved Elijah, and that when the show was over, they'd find some way to be together.

The Speed bump

NIA

"Hey Ma, can I get them digits?"

"Coming in at five feet nine inches and slim thick is Nia Austin, back and ready for action!"

"That's my bestie!" Nia heard the cacophony of noise as she made her way over to baggage claim, the smiling faces of Goldie, Lexie and Yaya all headed her way. Unsurprisingly, she felt the sting of tears at the corners of her eyes. Even though she'd been able to communicate and talk with her friends and family, it had nothing on actually being with them in person. Nia really missed that. Spreading her arms out, she was almost toppled over by the hugs that surrounded her. "Next time I got to Hawaii, all of you better be there with me."

"You bet your ass I'll be there!" Yaya squeezed Nia a little tighter. "Mom has done half the promotion for the show already, anyone who breathes within walking distance of the restaurant knows about it."

"We're so happy you're back." Lexie grinned as their hug broke apart. "LA is not the same without your special brand of sarcasm."

Nia laughed as bags started rolling down the belt. "You'll be seeing that special brand on screen soon enough."

Lexie cut right to the chase. "Girl, we need all the detail between you and Elijah, because you look well-tended to."

Nia's thoughts went to the long goodbye that had taken place between her and Elijah before dawn that morning, and couldn't help the little smirk that came over her face. Elijah's goal had been to tire her out so thoroughly that she would sleep the whole flight home…and he'd succeeded.

"Is that a hickey?" Yaya asked, as she grabbed one the of the bags from Nia.

"It is! What is this, high school?" Lexie shook her head though she was grinning. "We definitely need details."

"I just got my suitcases and you guys are already grilling me? Just for that, I'm keeping the gifts I brought back for myself." Nia gripped her carry-on bag tighter as Goldie fake lunged for it.

"As your sister, I'm legally entitled to anything that's yours." Yaya added as they made their way outside into the bright LA sun.

Lexie rolled her eyes. "I don't think that's how that works."

"I'll take Lexi's too."

"No, you won't." Nia laughed as they went out to the temporary parking area.

They loaded into the car, all talking over each other as they filled in Nia on the latest gossip and happenings since she'd left for Hawaii. Goldie had two boyfriends she was juggling, Lexie was in talks to sign another client, and Yaya had been trying to convince their dad that she could handle the business whenever he decided to retire.

"But when do we get to talk about Elijah?" Goldie salivated. She was a woman determined to pry every single detail out about Nia's sex life.

"When I'm back in my apartment with a glass of wine and some takeout."

"Done." She hit the gas, causing them to shout at her to slow down. Nia was glad to be home.

They made it back to Goldie and Nia's apartment in record time, ordering food on the way so that it would be delivered when they arrive. When Nia had a glass of chilled white wine and a plate of Chinese food in her lap, she felt ready to tackle the subject of Elijah.

"Your demands have been met. Now tell us everything." Lexi said, curled up with her own plate of food. They sat around the living room table, takeout boxes and bottle of wine liberally placed all over.

"Fine." Nia sipped her wine, wondering where to start. "Obviously, we've slept together."

"Details!" Goldie said around a bite of lo mein.

"I think what she meant to say was how did it start?" Yaya clarified.

Nia filled them in, on their ups and downs, on how he was always there for her, how he'd opened up to her on the island. It was really amazing, she reflected, to see how much he had changed from the person she'd known in college. Yaya practically swooned when Nia told them about the first time they actually slept together at the crew house. That night still made her flush to think about. Nia did skim over some of the more personal details he'd shared, wanting to keep some things just between the two of them. And Nia also didn't add in how she felt something shift between them the last night she was there.

When Nia was finally finished, her friends were silent, digesting the whole story. "Girl, live your best life," was all Lexie could manage.

Yaya poured herself another glass of wine. "What now? Have you two talked about how you're going to make this work now that you two are back in the real world?"

"He's said he's going to back out, and claim that he hasn't really found what he's looking for." Nia could hear the hope strung tight in between her words.

"And you know he's going to do that?" Lexi asked, pragmatically. "His track record isn't the best when it comes to saying, 'this is my woman' for longer than a few nights – not just to you, but in general."

Nia plucked at a loose thread on her sleeve. "I know that. But he's honestly changed so much, it's like he's not even the same person. And it's like, I love the man he's becoming."

She realized what she'd said as soon as she said it. Goldie cheered, almost spilling her wine. "You love him?"

"I didn't say that." Nia's thoughts were working overtime.

"But are you thinking it?" Lexi asked, studying her thoughtfully.

Nia knew what she and Elijah had told each other, and but it felt to new to share with anyone else right now. And it was scary to admit that.

"You don't have to answer us," Yaya gave her an out and Nia smiled at her sister gratefully.

"But we want answers," Goldie added. "Eventually." She amended when she saw Lexi's look.

"Thanks guys. I definitely did not expect to feel anything beyond hate when it came to Eli, but I don't know. It feels…different this time."

"Just be careful, yeah? He's hurt you once, and I'd hate to see you go through that again." Yaya said, adding wine to Nia's glass. She was only two years younger than Nia, but Yaya had been there to help pick up the pieces the last time he'd made a fool out of her.

Goldie speared a shrimp with her chopstick dramatically. "And if he does hurt you, we hurt him. No questions asked."

"And we'll hide the body. Now, let's finish eating - you've got an audition tomorrow to prepare for." Lexi said, effectively switching the conversation topic.

Nia smiled, grateful for friends that understood her. She snapped a quick selfie with of all of them, catching each one of them in their element – Goldie pouring another glass of wine, Yaya picking through the leftovers and Lexie flipping through the channels. This was her tribe, her people, and maybe Elijah would be joining that group with her. Smiling to herself, she sent the picture off to him, with simple message.

NIA: HOME...MISS YOU ALREADY.

ELIJAH

After a stunning morning goodbye, Elijah went for one last run on the beach, feeling filled with energy. Something was different between him and Nia now. She still seemed a little gun shy about being in a relationship with him, but he would wear her down with time and determination. It would help when they were back in Los Angeles, and he could spend some real time with her when they weren't obsessively filming. As much as he loved Oahu, the stunning beaches and crystal blue water, he couldn't wait to be back home where the smog thickness was only rivaled by the number of tourists on the street.

He slid into the house, intending to take a shower and finish packing a few things when he ran into Lily in the kitchen, who was heading out with her camera. A large smile lit her face when she saw him. "Back from a run?"

"Just a little jog before I head out. Staying loose." He grabbed a bottle of water from the refrigerator.

"This has been an amazing few weeks, right?" Lily leaned against the counter, and he became very aware of how she was watching his every move.

"Better than I expected." *All thanks to Nia.* Elijah couldn't help the small smile that came over his face when he thought of her. This morning, before he'd slipped off back to her room, he'd woken up feeling contentment for the first time in a long time. The faint light from the rising sun had cast her features in a glow, and he couldn't help kissing her awake for one last goodbye. Alright, it was more like two. He had to tune back in to what Lily was saying."

"-- I know we're not on camera or anything, but I wanted to say that you're an amazing guy. Even if it's not me, I just hope you pick the right partner for you to build a future with." Her smile was genuine, and Elijah felt a little twinge that he wasn't going to pick her. Lily was honestly a good person, and he didn't want to hurt her if he could avoid it.

"Thank you for that. Means a lot."

"Also, do you know if anyone has Nia's number? I didn't realize she was leaving so early, but I wanted to exchange information. She's such a great person, right?"

"She's amazing." Realizing the amount of emotion he'd put behind those words, he tried to cover. "I think I have her number, it should be in my phone."

"I don't have mine on me, but can you text it to me?" She called out her phone number, and the whoosh went through the air. "Thanks. I can't wait to be reconnect with my phone." Lily sighed wistfully. "Anyway, you have my number now too. Make sure you save it." With a smile and a wink, she went off the porch leaving Elijah in the kitchen.

He shook his head, heading upstairs to his room. That was probably the smoothest way anyone had gotten his number, even if he didn't intend on using it.

He took a quick shower, changed into some fresh clothes, and was just about done packing when he heard a knock at the door. Setting down his bag of toiletries, he opened it, and Isaac and Warren came bursting in. "Hey Isaac, Warren. What's up?" They both were obviously worked up about something, Warren setting up a computer. Elijah watched as Isaac paced the room, and waited for him to say something.

"We have a problem Elijah." Warren stopped and looked Elijah over.

"And what's that?"

Warren pulled up a video on the screen and hit play. It was a clip of him and Nia in the cabana the night they went out. It had caught *everything*, and Elijah slammed the screen down.

It felt like someone punched Elijah in the gut. "What the hell – "

Warren whirled toward him, stabbing a finger in his chest. "Remember how we went through orientation, and how there are going to be cameras everywhere? We literally meant everywhere. The hallways, the balconies, the beach cabana. *Everywhere.*"

The full meaning of Warren's words sunk in to Elijah's fog filled brain. He sat heavily on a chair, trying to figure out what to say.

"You couldn't keep it in your damn pants, James? You had to go and fuck the hostess too?"

Elijah saw red and stood, fingers curled into fists. "Look, I don't know what you saw between us – "

"Everything, obviously."

"But you should know that Nia and I have history." That made them both pause.

Isaac folded his arms across his chest. "Define history." There was a bit of curiosity in his voice. "You two…were together before the show started?"

"We went to college together. She was my girl for a few years."

Isaac let out a puff of air. "Why the hell didn't you say anything during the casting process?"

"Because I didn't want our past history to affect her getting the job." Nia deserved so much more than she'd gotten, especially after the way he had treated her. She was a brilliant actress, and Elijah knew with the right timing and momentum, she had the capacity to go far. His phone buzzed, but he was too shocked to look at it now.

"While that's very kind of you, you're now in hot water with the big dogs." Warren leaned on the counter, pulling a silver flask from his pocket. He toyed with the cap, not taking a drink immediately. "I could show this to Chris Parker up top. You'd lose that fancy high profile job of yours." He took a swig from the flask. "You were supposed to be wooing Lily and letting her win. That was the plan."

"I didn't say I agreed to it." Elijah hadn't actually said he would do it, they'd just assumed.

Warren shook his head. "You're not getting it. Apparently, Lily actually likes you, has been talking your name up to Parker from day one. And if you pick her, only to dump her later for Nia? People will be very upset, and feel used. I'd feel used, getting you this job only for you to screw my show over."

Oh. Now he understood.

"What are you saying?" Elijah perched on the arm of a chair, watching Warren and Isaac carefully.

"If you don't set this thing with Nia to the side and focus your attention only on only Lily, I don't know what I might do in retaliation. Whatever it is, it won't be good, for you…or Nia for that matter. My petty streak is the size of the pacific. That footage can end up in the wrong hands…maybe even on the show."

The unspoken words were clear – if Elijah screwed up Warren's show, Warren would screw up not only his career, but Nia's as well. He'd trash both of their reputations, and Elijah wouldn't ever let that happen to Nia. Her career was just getting started, and he'd crawl over hot coal before exposing her to something like this.

"You can't be serious." The idea seemed crazy to Elijah.

"Do you want to find out?" Warren stood, pocketing the flask again. "Look, all you have to do is pick Lily, woo her for a while, let's say a year. I won't have to use any unflattering footage, and maybe after that, you can separate later claiming differences or whatever. Her star will be fine, your role will be fine, and my show will be fine. Got it?"

Elijah could only nod as he watched Warren and Isaac head to the door. This is not what he had in mind – he'd figured it would all be so simple, but obviously that was not the case. He thought about Nia, how she would feel if he asked her again to be the backseat. *Not happy.*

He barely noticed as Isaac stopped at the door. "Look, I feel for you. But this is your career that we're talking about. You've worked hard for it – are you really going to throw it away for a woman?" Elijah didn't even respond to that. The door clicked behind him.

Elijah flopped on his bed, defeated. He'd thought they'd been so careful, so subtle...at least he'd thought they had. And the fact that the cameras had got some intimate moments between Nia and himself made him feel disgusting. Suddenly, he was ready to leave the island, now, before anything else could happen. Feeling his phone buzz, he picked it up and saw a text from Nia. It was a selfie of her with her friends back home. A wave of longing came over him as he looked at her smile. Elijah loved that smile, loved the way it lit up Nia's face. And he'd do anything to keep it there, even if it warred with his desire not to hurt her. Some protective instinct kicked in – Elijah would do whatever it took to make sure Nia came out of this unscathed.

The Dissapointment

NIA

Nia didn't think she could hold her breath any longer. She was at her audition waiting for her name to be called. Goldie had made her some super healthy breakfast that she could barely eat because of her nerves and she'd downed a cup of coffee on the way over. Her mom and sister had both sent their well wishes, and she was just trying to stay calm and not freak all the way out.

Her phone buzzed with a text. It was Elijah.

ELIJAH: GOOD LUCK TODAY.

Nia smiled, glad for his support. He'd been a little quieter since they'd made it back to Los Angeles, but she figured he was catching up with friends and family. She knew she had been doing the same thing. She started to type out a reply when the door opened and her name was called. It was like everything inside of her sunk to her gut and started tap dancing on her intestines. Taking a breath to balance herself, Nia walked into the room with a confidence she didn't completely feel, remembering Elijah's coaching of her from the island. The room was simple, still somehow bright despite the blinds being tightly shut. Off to the side was a table where four people sat, watching her come in. Nia was introduced to her reader, a small woman with glasses, and told she could start whenever she felt like it.

With a small breath, she poured her heart into the words, feeling like it was her best read yet. Nia's confidence grew, and she felt herself slipping deeper into the character. But then, she stumbled on a few words - and her groove was shaken a little. She kept going, but made it, finishing up her monologue with a whisper, waiting to hear what they said. The four people at the table were silent, looking over one another. Nia felt a little sinking feeling in her gut, but remembered to stay confident. Thanking them, she gathered her things up and was about to escape when a voice stopped her. "Ms. Austin?"

"Yes?" Nia turned to look back at him. He was seated in the middle, and had a small smile on his face.

"We'd like for you to come in for the next round of auditions, next week. Your performance was excellent."

Did he just say -

"Seriously? I mean, thank you." Inside Nia was cheering and doing mental backflips.

"We'll give more details to your agent, but let's chat soon."

Nia blessed them with a huge smile, before leaving the room. The tap dancing in her stomach had turned into cheerleaders doing cartwheels inside, but like, cartwheels of joy. Her fingers were itching to tell someone, anyone, about this huge thing. As soon as she left the building, she dialed the first person she thought of.

"Guess who was called back for a second audition next week?" The sunlight hit warmed her skin as she slipped her sunglasses on her face.

"What?! I'm so happy for you babe." Elijah's voice was full of excitement for her. "I knew you'd kill it."

Nia couldn't help the huge grin that spread across her face. "I mean, all of your island coaching definitely helped."

Elijah laughed, but Nia thought she sensed some tightness in his voice. "You would've done it without me."

"Maybe. Probably. But still, thank you." Nia slid into her car, starting the ignition. Elijah had gone quiet on his end, and Nia chewed her lip. "You ok?" She asked as she pulled into traffic.

"Yeah, I'm great. Perfect."

"Are you sure? You sound a little…off." Nia's blinker accented the brief silence. When Elijah did answer, it wasn't an answer to her observation.

"Do you feel like celebrating?" His voice came over, a little brighter.

"What'd you have in mind?"

"Come over to my place and I'll make you dinner. Eight o'clock?"

"Dinner sounds good, but I feel like there's something missing?" Nia let a little question trace her voice. She couldn't help wondering if something had changed between them, and wanted their little bubble of time on the island back. Already it seemed as if something had changed, but she wasn't sure what it was exactly.

"I'll have desert too." She could practically feel his wink through the phone.

"Perfect. I'll see you at eight."

Hanging up, Nia tried to shrug off the weirdness, figuring she was overanalyzing things. Of course, their relationship would look a little different, if you could even call it a relationship. They were back in the real world, with obligations and roadblocks and had to figure out how to move forward. Nia just hoped they could figure it out soon.

After called Lexi to let her know the good news, Nia made it to her parent's restaurant, to see them now that she was back in town, with the bonus of good news to share. Lexi was thrilled for her, and was already plotting and figuring her odds of actually landing the role. "Get your ass home so we can celebrate tonight!"

Nia laughed. "You'll have to get in line, Elijah already asked me to come over tonight."

"Are you really going to let some dick get in the way of your girls?"

"Well…"

"I don't blame you, I would too." Lexi laughed. "We'll celebrate tomorrow."

"Perfect. I've got to go, my family is expecting me for lunch."

Laughing, Nia parked at *Dinner at Nigel's* and went inside. Despite what her father thought, she did love the restaurant – it held tons of memories and it was always nice to work with her family. But it wasn't what fed her spirit, and she was determined to do what she loved.

The place was quiet during midday, her mother requiring that they close the restaurant between the hours of two and four so they could have a little rest and eat lunch like civilized people. It helped that those were slow hours anyway. Yolanda was seated in a booth near the front when Nia entered, looking over the nights specialty menu. "Nia! You can't ever leave me like that again!"

They met in the middle, Nia being pulled into a warm hug despite towering over Yolanda. Her mom had always smelled like cinnamon and spice. "Mom, I wasn't even gone for that long."

Nia laughed as her mother squeezed her tighter. "It was long enough! And you hardly called!"

"I called you at least twice a week, and we Face Timed too."

Her mom always gently nagged her, but Nia knew she didn't mean any harm. Yolanda had always be supportive of her daughter's dreams, and it was one of the things Nia loved most about her mother.

"Where's Yaya?"

"She's back in the kitchen with your father."

"She's actually walking out with our father," Yaya announced, referring to herself in third person. "And she put her foot in this macaroni and cheese."

"I thought we talked about this whole third person thing." Nigel said, rolling his eyes at his youngest daughter's antics.

"You talked, Yaya does her thing." Yaya set down the she carried and doubled back to the kitchen. "She is grabbing the rolls, and then we can eat."

Nia snickered. "You sound exactly like one of the contestants, who while sweet, sounds crazy when she uses third person."

Yaya paused. "How crazy are we talking?"

"Somewhere between sleeping with the doors locked and you might need professional help." Nia snagged one of the rolls as Yaya thought about that.

"I see your point. Won't happen again." They laughed together.

They sat down at their corner booth, which was the biggest, coziest one in the restaurant and managed to have a somewhat civilized conversation over baked chicken, macaroni and brussel sprouts. They caught up on everything about Hawaii, the contests, the people. Nia was so glad to be back with her family.

Yolanda brought up the Elijah thing midway through. "How was it, working with that boy?"

"Boy? You mean Elijah? Mom, he's older than me."

"And he's definitely not a *boy*." Yaya snickered into her asparagus.

Nia kicked Yaya under the table, a warning not to say anything extra. "It was fine, we managed to be civil, all things considering."

Yaya chocked on her glass of water, and managed to dodge Nia's incoming foot. She winced as it connected with the booth.

"I actually made a few friends there that I wouldn't mind actually seeing out here in the real world."

"This is that boy that dumped you as soon as he got a part?" Nigel cut in. "Now does all those action movies?"

"Dad, you know who he is. But it was nice working with him." Nia could feel herself getting a little defensive and settled back down. Her dad was just being protective – lord knows she was a mess after that breakup.

"At least he made something of himself." Nia paused, setting her fork down on her plate.

"What's that supposed to mean?"

"Nothing honey, I'm just glad to see someone found success from this whole acting thing."

"Nigel." Yolanda's voice cut though the tension, but Nia wasn't having it.

"No, dad, say what you want to say." Nia's arms crossed as she leaned back in her seat. "It's never stopped you before now."

Nigel set his fork down, looking directly at Nia. "He has a successful career; maybe you would too if you would just do what you're actually good at.

A direct hit. "I am good at this. If the show gets picked up, they'd want me to come back another season, so that's great – "

"You know how fickle this industry is, and it's not like you're getting any younger. You're almost thirty and still chasing pipe dreams."

Yaya tried to diffuse the situation. "Dad come on, that's not fair to Nia – "

Nigel kept on as if she hadn't even spoke. "I'm sick of watching you struggle when there's something perfectly good here with the restaurants that can support you as soon as you are ready to put in some real work."

She felt like she was seeing red. "What I do is real work. And it's not like I'm asking you for handouts."

"What you do is get paid to play make believe and temporary at best. When are you going to grow up and accept that the real world it out there? I just want to see you thriving, and I'm not convinced that acting is going to give you the life you deserve." Rationally, Nia knew her dad was just being protective and worrying about her future, she got that. But Nia wasn't thinking realistically right now, angry as she was. She was tired of defending her career path to people, tired of doing what was expected, tired of it all.

"Dad that's your plan for me, not mine. When are you going to let me live my life and stop trying to force me to live yours? Just because I haven't made it yet doesn't mean I have to give."

Nia knew it was below the belt, but she was furious. Her dad was constantly belittling her dreams and she'd had enough. She stood, grabbing her purse to leave. "If you would just stop harping on me for a minute, you would see that you have everything you need to run this business properly right here, starting with Yaya."

"Yaya has her place in the business – "

"Yeah, and you won't let her show you what all she can do." Nia looked over to her sister, who was watching the whole thing in silent shock. "You keep trying to drag me back here dad, when Yaya is right here, doing all the right things, and yet you won't give her the recognition she deserves."

"Yaya knows her place. You should learn yours."

Nia strode to the door, her head shaking. "I have. I just wish you'd support me for once in your life." She stopped, looking back at Nigel. "What happened to the man that told me I could have whatever I reached for? Because I don't know who this one is anymore."

She left, before she said anything else she regretted. She could really use a drink now.

ELIJAH

Everything was a mess. Elijah could smell smoke burning from the stove, and he dropped the cutting board when the fire alarm went off, spilling garlic and parsley all over the place. Swearing, he ran to the stove where he turned off the eye, where what was formerly an amazing tomato sauce was now burnt nothing, steaming in the pot. He sighed, opening a window to let out the smoke while he tried to get the beeping to stop.

His phone rang, in the middle of all of this, and he was glad to see his mother's name roll across the screen. "I messed everything up."

"I just left an hour ago, how bad could it be?" Rebecca, Elijah's mother, laughed over the

Elijah looked at the mess that was now strewn around his kitchen and sighed. "Very. The sauce is gone." It was more like a dark sludge that would never fully leave his pot, but she didn't need to know how badly he'd messed up. He pulled out his phone and started ordering delivery.

Rebecca laughed. "You never were any good in the kitchen, but bless your heart for trying." She had come over to help Elijah with a nice homemade dinner for Nia, helping him make her classic spaghetti and Bolognese sauce with her secret garlic bread recipe. But now he needed to go to Plan B. "I just wanted to check in and make sure you had it under control, but I guess not."

"I know, I know." Elijah began scraping everything into the garbage can. "Warren called and I got distracted." Warren was trying to make sure Elijah didn't screw things up for the both of them, asking if he'd spoken to Nia yet about how they had to stop dating.

"Are you sure that's what you want to do? I thought you liked this girl."

"I do mom." More than you know.

"What's the deal then? It should be simple."

"But it's not just me this thing affects. It affects Warren and his job security, Lily - it's not just me." Elijah could hear his mother sigh on the phone.

"Talk to her. Let her know where you're coming from. I know you'll say the right thing." He wished he had his mother's confidence.

"Thanks mom."

'But feed her first - your father would tell you to never argue with a woman who's on an empty stomach. He learned that from dealing with me"

"On it. Delivery should be here shortly."

"Good. Love you Eli."

Hanging up, Elijah set to work straightening up his demolished kitchen before Nia arrived. He was midway through when he heard the buzzer - someone was downstairs. Thinking it was too soon to be the food, he went to the intercom, where he could see who was down there on the screen. It was Nia – and she looked upset.

"Hey, you're early. Come on up." He buzzed her in, and tried to minimize the mess as best as he could, before grabbing a bottle of chilled wine and opening it, pouring her a glass just as he heard a knock at his door. He took a breath, and opened to let in Nia, who seemed on the verge of tears or rage, he couldn't tell. She slipped in, wrapping her arms around his waist, his automatically coming up to hold her. She sighed, and went still. He couldn't help his hand rubbing a gentle trail along her spine.

"What happened?" Elijah asked, when she finally looked up at him.

"My dad happened."

"Uh oh. Here, hang on a second." He let her go briefly to grab her glass of wine, and brought it to her on the couch.

"You're amazing." She took a sip, as he settled down next to her.

"Tell me about it. Your dad, not how amazing I am – unless you want to?" That earned him a small smile from her.

"You know you're great, stop fishing for compliments." He settled his arm around her, letting her lean in to him. Nia sighed and continued. "I just wish he would support me when it comes to the things I want to do. It was fine when I was all part of the family business, going according to his plan, but now that I'm trying to do my own thing, acting's not a real job."

"Why would he say it's not a real job?"

"Because it's not useful."

Elijah never understood when people dumped on the arts. Sure, they weren't saving the world like doctors or scientists, but they kept the joy and heart that people needed, and couldn't imagine a life where there were no arts to be enjoyed.

"My dad was perfectly happy when I was part of the business, hell, part of someone else's business, but this - he can't be happy for me. I don't think he thinks I can make it." Elijah could hear the hurt in her voice, and in that moment, wanted to do whatever he could to prevent hurting her like that.

"You are one of the most focused and dedicated people I've known, going back to when I first met you in college." The buzzer rang again, and Elijah paused to let up the delivery guy. He didn't see the look of happiness Nia gave him.

After grabbing the food and setting it on the table, Elijah was wondering how much he should share with her. "You know it was my idea to have you sub in for that one girl when she got sick for the short we did in college?"

"What do you mean?" He could feel Nia's eyes on him. "I'd seen you around campus several times, and I just always thought you were this driven, talented individual. I couldn't work up the courage to talk to you at first. The short film seemed like a good way to break the ice."

"Are you serious?" Nia pushed up off him so she could look him in the eyes.

"You wanted to work with me?"

Elijah nodded. "I knew if anyone would take it seriously, it'd be you, and you just had this quality that make people want to know what you're thinking."

"I never knew that." He could see the gear turning in her head.

"Well, now you do. Which is why I'm so sure you'll make it, with this audition, and others, because you have that quality that makes people want to support you, like you're going to succeed no matter what's in your way."

All of a sudden Nia wrapped her arms around him and he was suffocated in a hug by her. "You're too good to me, you know that?"

"You deserve the world." Her lips pressed against his softly.

"Thank you. Sorry for taking over tonight. You'd said there was something you wanted to tell me?"

Elijah paused, thinking about the contest, and how now was definitely not the time to tell her he couldn't see her. Not now, when all he wanted was to make her part of his forever. "Nothing important. I'm just glad you're here, and super thrilled that you were called back. Let's get on with the celebrating, yeah?"

He'd tell her about Warren knowing about them later. Right now, he just wanted to enjoy dinner with his lady.

The Family Dates

NIA

"It's pretty ironic that we're meeting Danielle's parents at a church of all places." Nia commented to Kerry as the stepped out the van into the parking lot of a medium size church. It was a nice building, with flowers and palm trees lining the front path which lead to a double door entrance with colorful stained glass. It was pretty early in the morning on a weekday, and the lot wasn't as full as it could be.

"Why, because she's such a bitch?" Kerry snorted, before adding, "Sorry, Jesus." She paused. "Actually, you know how you made her."

Nia laughed as they started toward the doors. "She is though. I would have never guessed her to be a pastor's kid."

"Fun facts they don't tell you. I'm pretty sure this was Warren's idea too."

"It definitely was." Warren had opened the doors just as they reached the top of the stairs. "Let's get this done, we still have two other segments to film today."

They were filming the meet the parents segments today, gearing up for the final ring ceremony that they would film that weekend. It was wild to know that they were almost done filming, and Nia could only hope that summer brought around more projects once pilot season was over. Nia was tagging along to briefly interview each couple, asking how they stood with each other and what their chances of being picked by Elijah were. She knew they didn't stand a chance, but work was work.

Warren turned down a corridor, leading them out to a back garden area where the cameras had been setting up the meet and greet area. It was a little garden party, with a quaint tea tray situated on a lace table cloth with tiny finger foods surrounding it. Nia quietly chuckled at the mental image of Elijah trying to be comfortable in such a…delicate…environment.

Nia listened as Warren pointed out where she would be hosting their interview, and her point questions to ask. She couldn't help but notice when Elijah and Danielle arrived, and gave a small smile in his direction. Warren gave her a look, but it was hard to interpret, and left her alone before she could ask. He'd been rather distant to her since they'd made it back to Los Angeles, and she hadn't quite figured out what the issue was. Nia watched as he went and spoke with Elijah, hushed but fervent, and couldn't help but notice the tension rolling between them. *Interesting*.

More interestingly, she saw a tall-ish woman arrive with them, who bore striking resemblance to Elijah, even from a distance. Pointing her out to Kerry, who confirmed who it was. "Rebecca, Elijah's mom, is coming along with us on these meet the parents, so she can also vet the ladies. Cool, right?"

"My mom would love to be on television, she'd soak it right up." Nia noticed the woman was looking her way curiously, and sent a smile her direction. They were introduced briefly, Rebecca giving Nia a friendly smile before being pulled away for filming to begin.

The cameras followed Nia, who walked with Elijah and Rebecca as they made their way into the church where Danielle and her family waited. "There's nothing like meeting the parents to get the nerves up, but it's a necessary part of the courtship process. Elijah, what does having your mother here with you today mean to you?"

Elijah shared a smile with his mom. "My mom means the world to me. She's given so much to make sure I got where I am today, and I can't imagine her not getting to know the woman I'm going to marry." His eyes lingered a little on Nia's, before continuing. "I'm so glad she's here today to meet all the women I've been spending so much time with."

"And I'm glad to meet all of them." Rebecca added, patting Elijah's shoulder. "It's about time my boy settles down. I need a few grandchildren soon!"

Nia laughed as Elijah groaned. "Let me get married first, ok mom?"

They paused as Danielle came out, a wide grin on her face as she threw herself into Elijah's arms, planting a huge kiss on him. "I missed you so much baby."

Smothering her own groan, Nia addressed Danielle,

"Danielle, you have come this far and now it's almost time for Elijah to meet your parents. What role do you expect your family play in your lives?"

Danielle paused, looking up at Elijah through her lashes and linking her arm with his. "My family means the world to me. I love my parents, who have taken care of me since day one, and I want a husband who can take care of me. And I'll take care of him."

After a few more questions, Nia left them to head to their table for tea, where Danielle's parents were situated, two very proper, but nice looking people. She distracted herself by looking through her email, hoping to see something from her audition, with no luck. On the monitors she heard a bit of commotion and saw that Danielle was snatching a napkin and dabbing at her skirt. "Daddy, you're such a klutz!"

"I'm so sorry sweetheart." Danielle's father was passing napkins to her.

"You better replace this daddy! It's Prada." Danielle sat, pouting as her father promised to buy her new clothes. Nia could feel her eyebrows raising as she shook her head.

Thankfully, the rest of the morning went fairly smoothly, their tea ending with Elijah and Danielle going off to talk by themselves for a moment.

"That's an interesting girl right there," a warm voice mused next to Nia. She turned to see Rebecca beside her, watching Elijah deftly handle Danielle and her parents.

"I had a teacher who always said 'interesting' is a placeholder word for something you don't want to say." Nia smiled, looking at her fully. Rebecca laughed, a lovely sound that reminded Nia of Elijah's laugh.

"Your teacher sounds very wise."

Nia found it easy to talk with Rebecca, who was more than willing to entertain her with stories of Elijah's wild youth that Nia tucked away in her memory. In return, Nia shared a few moments of her more dynamic auditions, as well as a few stories from hers and Elijah's college days. They were still gabbing when he came over, catching the tail end of a story Rebecca was sharing about Elijah's senior prom date.

"…and then, poor Eli finally realized that the girl had actually expected him to love her duct tape dress! The girl gave him a boutonniere made out of paper and duct table!"

Nia was practically in tears when she realized they had company. Elijah stood next to his mother, wondering what had them both in stitches. "Please tell me you're not sharing embarrassing stories again Mom." Nia looked up and realized filming had finished for Elijah and Danielle. The crew was wrapping things up and Danielle was heading away with her parents in tow.

"It's my privilege as a mother to share embarrassing stories." Rebecca's eyes twinkled at Nia.

"You could've explained your aversion to duct tape a little bit sooner you know." Nia grinned. "I'd never understood that before now."

"I'll make sure sharing my embarrassing prom night is at the top of the list." He rolled his eyes, but was smiling at the two of them.

"Don't give my new friend sass or else I'll ground you." Rebecca linked her arm with Nia's.

"I'm a little too old to get grounded Mom," Elijah shook his head.

"Don't sass your mother, it's not good for your health." Nia added, which made Rebecca smile.

"I like her. I think we'll be good friends. I do wish I had met you Nia back when you two were in college." Rebecca's hands pressed into hers. "You seem like a good influence on my Elijah." Nia could feel Elijah's eyes bouncing between the two of them. She'd instantly liked Rebecca, and wished she had known her sooner herself.

Maddison came over and asked them to start loading up into production vehicles so they could travel to the next location. Nia had wanted to ride with Elijah and his mother, but somehow Warren had drawn Nia away from them, and was asking her random questions while Isaac steered Elijah and his mother to a different van. It was only a little odd - normally they rode together - but she figured they'd catch up at the next location.

ELIJAH

Elijah was glad Nia had gotten along so well with his mother, who was usually reticent with people she didn't know. But they'd been chatting like old friends, which had made him smile when he'd seen the two of them together. She'd known about his and Nia's relationship back in college and was curious to see how Nia was in person, especially now knowing that Elijah still had feelings for her.

They were headed to Echo Park, to meet April and her family at the lake. The day was shaping up to be gorgeous, with only a few clouds dotting the sky. Hopping out the van, Elijah saw that Nia was a little ways down, chatting with Kerry as they looked out over the lake. The sunlight caught her, highlighting the gold tints in her brown skin, and the sparkle in her eyes as she caught him looking at her. His heart skipped a beat as he grinned back at her.

"Looks like you've got it bad, kiddo." Rebecca said, watching her son watch Nia. "I see why you don't want to tell her anything."

"Should I wait, then?"

"Absolutely not. The longer you wait, the harder it is. For the both of yoi."

Elijah was stopped from responding by a sudden shriek in the air. April, of course. She was heading his way...sprinting, actually, while waving happily as her mothers trailed behind her. As soon as April was close enough, she leapt into his arms, wrapping her legs around his waist. "Elijah, I missed you so much!" She planted a kiss on his mouth, and he had a small feeling that she'd left lipstick all over his face.

It's been two days. "It feels like we're in a whole new era," is what he actually said. Elijah tried to subtly wipe his lips and found a bit of her makeup on them. His mother kindly provided him a wipe from her bag.

Nia ambled over, a twinkle in her eye as cameras followed her. "Aww, look at the love birds reuniting. How does it feel to be in LA, April?"

April threw her arms around Nia, to her obvious surprise. "Oh, I've missed you Nia! And everyone! The island felt like a whole new era, as Elijah put it. But April loves being here in LA, and exploring the city with my mom!" April smiled prettily at the camera.

"LA is always amazing. And you're from Texas, is that right?"

"Hell yeah, straight out of Austin!"

"Now, if you two are our final couple, how does that work out? Would you move your life to Texas, Elijah, or would you come to the city of Angels, April?"

"We haven't talked about that yet. But I'd love to live in LA, I think they could handle a little April out here." Elijah rolled his eyes but couldn't help smiling at her exuberance. He could definitely see April on her own television show.

Nia smiled and directed a question solely at him. "And what about you Elijah? I've heard so much from April, I'm curious what you think."

"We haven't discussed it, but I'm honored that April would be all right with uprooting her life to come to Los Angeles."

"Who wouldn't? This is the city of dreams." And April actually twirled in a circle as she said that, to Nia's delight.

A few more questions and then Elijah, April, and her two moms were loaded up into a swan boat, where they were toured around the lake. It was funny to watch the follow boat with a few cameras gliding behind them, two swans dancing around the lake. As the boat only seated four, Rebecca let Elijah ride with April and her moms, deciding to sit this one out. He tried to keep his attention on April, but smiled when he saw Nia pedaling out with his mother and Kerry. They looked as if they were getting along well, and he wondered if he could steer the boat close enough to hear what they were talking about. As it was, Elijah had to give most of his attention to April and her moms, Angie and Jamie, who asked a lot of in depth questions.

Eventually, they made their way back around to the docks, where he was able to wrap up their conversation. They dismounted, and after saying their good byes, packed up into the vans. "That was so much fun!" Rebecca smiled, falling in step next to Nia and Elijah as they headed to the vans.

"I love how they trick you into exercising with all that pedaling." Nia shook her head. "At least I don't have to go to the gym tonight."

"Nia, can I borrow you for a moment?" Isaac interrupted their conversation, getting in the way of Nia's path to the van. Elijah frowned - he'd noticed a solid attempt to keep him and Nia apart today. If it wasn't Kerry distracting Nia, it was Isaac.

Just as he was about to say something, his mother beat him to the punch.

"You aren't going to steal my buddy away now, are you? We have so much to talk about." Rebecca smiled sweetly at Isaac, linking her arm with Nia's. Elijah had to smother a smile at Isaac's face, who looked torn for a moment.

"Of course not." Isaac eventually managed, before allowing them to load into the same van. Rebecca threw a wink at Elijah before she climbed in. Elijah slipped in next to Nia, before the door was shut behind them.

As the van pulled out Nia wiggled in her seat, excited. "I haven't been to the Observatory in such a long time! It was always one of my favorite places growing up."

"What do you like about it?" Elijah asked, his leg pressing up against hers. He felt her lean slightly into him, the smell of mango drifting to his nose.

"Just that…space is so vast and interesting. I love learning about it."

Elijah smiled. "My mom loves the Observatory. Actually, most museums. I think her favorite is the Getty."

Rebecca smiled. "I love it when people can enrich their minds past top forty hits and whatever is on television. A museum is the perfect place to explore and get a little more culture in your life."

"I can't say that I've ever been to the Getty, now that I think of it." Nia paused thoughtfully.

"We'll have to fix that. Let me know when you're ready and we'll go together, make a girl's trip of it."

It warmed Elijah's heart to see his mom getting along so well with Nia. They got along better than he could have anticipated, and it made him a little frustrated with his current situation. In a perfect world, they'd be dating openly, and he could wrap his arm around Nia's shoulder like he wanted to. Instead, he settled for reaching for her hand, lacing their fingers together as the van bumped along the road. It wasn't enough, but it was all he had for the moment.

NIA

They arrived at the top of the hill, the domed top of Griffith Observatory catching the sunset rays of light. Filing out of the van, Nia stretched her cramped legs as she took in the curious gazes of a few tourists who were wandering the grounds. A few even snapped photos once they saw Elijah, who waved to them before being bustled inside. Following their tour guide, the made it to the Edge of Space exhibit they'd had closed off for the last date with Lily.

The lower level was nice and cool and romantically dark, the lights and vivid colors popping as their eyes adjusted to the dimness. Nia could see Lily standing by one of the exhibits, her family close by. Elijah went to speak with her, while the cameras followed him over. Nia tried not to obviously watch the two of them together.

Even she had to admit that they looked good, like a matched set.

"She's pretty." Rebecca commented, looking over at Elijah and Lily. "Seems like the only one we've met today with some sense about her."

"Lily is one of the few contestants that I actually like." Nia admitted, despite herself. "She's genuinely a good person."

"That's good to hear." Rebecca was watching Nia closer than she'd like. "The jury's out on whether or not she'll be good for my Eli though."

Nia couldn't help feeling a little jealous, even though she knew that Elijah had said that he wasn't picking anyone. And it was hard not to like Lily, as kind as she was. Thankfully, Kerry came over, wanting to get started right away which helped distract Nia from her thoughts.

Elijah and Lily were positioned in front of one of the galaxies, and Nia tried to put her professional cloak on. "Lily, good to see you as always."

Lily smiled, offering a sincere smile and hug to Nia before stepping back. "It's great to see you too."

"This has been a wild ride, but we're so close to the end. Hopefully, you and Elijah are coming out of this with a better understanding of each other, and how you'll fit together in the real world. What would the first year of marriage would look like for you two ideally?"

Elijah paused, looking at Nia before over at Lily, before responding. "I've always thought the first year is your foundation year. It can be tough, merging two lives together, but would set the tone for the rest of our time together. I'd want someone who's up for the ride, all the ups and downs, highs and lows. Someone who's willing to put in the work."

"I hadn't thought of it that way, but it makes perfect sense." Lily chimed in. "Marriage is two people blending their lives together, and the start can be tricky. But if you're doing it with the right person? It makes it worth it in the end."

Nia could see the surprise on Elijah's face. He hadn't been expecting such a poetic answer from Lily. She hadn't either, honestly, and yet she agreed with the both of them. The right person would make it all worth it in the end.

Elijah spoke with Lily and her family for another hour before they called it a night while Nia wandered the exhibits, lost in her own thoughts. She wanted to think she was doing the right thing, picking Elijah despite everything that told her she was being a fool. But her heart was set on him, and Nia didn't want to risk missing out on a good thing with him. *Right now*, she thought, *it was enough*.

Once filming wrapped up for the evening, Nia and Rebecca made their way to the van as Elijah spoke to Isaac and Kerry off to the side. "You know, Mulholland drive has some of the best views of the city, especially if you go at night. It really makes you realize how big this city is and how small we really are." Rebecca mentioned as they looked down at the city lights below them.

"I love that drive. I used to go there all the time growing up." Nia let Rebecca hop in the van before her.

"It was Eli's favorite as a child. Maybe you two should go together." Rebecca sent a knowing look in Nia's direction that made her want to blush for some reason.

"I don't know. We'll have to see what happens after the ring ceremony." Nia shrugged, trying to downplay anything. The driver hopped out the van for a moment, running to the bathroom and leaving the two of them alone.

"I'll put a bug in his ear." Rebecca said. After a moment, she added, "He really likes you."

That caught Nia off guard. "Why do you say that?"

"I've seen the way you two look at each other, only a fool wouldn't notice it. But he also cares about you. He didn't date for a long time after the two of you separated in college."

"Really? I didn't know that."

"I have to apologize to you," Rebecca's eyes met Nia's. "I told him not to say anything about the abuse - I was angry and embarrassed. But I didn't know for a while how it had affected him. Elijah was angry, and didn't talk to anyone for a while. He took it very hard that he hadn't been there to help me. The only reason he took that job was because we had a lot of debt afterwards, and the advance they offered was too good to pass up. He used all that money for my medical bills." Rebecca teared up a little, and Nia couldn't help reaching out for her hand to hold it.

"Wow…"

"And somehow he'd gotten it in his thick skull that he shouldn't be happy if his mother wasn't happy. When I found out he broke up with you, I told the idiot to go and get you back, but it was too late. And then his career was taking off, and he wanted to make a name for himself. But he was always planning on coming back to you when he'd proved himself."

Nia was stunned. Elijah was planning on coming back to her?

"I know he's doing this stupid contest, but my boy has always had his heart set on you. I just hope he does the right thing." Rebecca saw Elijah headed their way. "Besides, you're the girl I really liked meeting most today." With a small smile, she deftly changed topics as Elijah climbed into the van with them, sitting next to his mother.

Nia looked at Elijah from a whole new standpoint now. He wasn't the ass she'd thought he was - he was a wonderful, stupid man that had somehow managed to steal her heart. And she was glad he had it. Her phone buzzed as the door shut.

ELIJAH: DINNER?"

She looked up to see him smiling back at her. Of course he was texting her from the same car.

NIA: I'D LOVE THAT.

The Final Ceremony

NIA

Finally, the night of the final Ring Ceremony was here. Nia had woken up that morning completely excited. *I get to be with Elijah, for real, today.* It had been so long since she'd felt such a good mood. Goldie was excited as well, smiling at Nia's exuberance. "You're glowing babe! It's adorable." Goldie had laughed as Nia floated through their yoga class.

"A girl can be happy." Nia grinned. That happiness bled into the rest of her day, growing as she drove over to the Hollywood Hills mansion where they would film the ceremony. She didn't even have her usual road rage, making it to a parking spot just as the sun was starting to set. Maddison met Nia outside, leading her to her dressing room where she would dress and do hair and makeup.

"I'm so glad this is almost over," Nia commented, as Pom worked on her face. Kerry bustled around behind her, reading papers and responding to text messages. Nia wasn't entirely sure Kerry was fully paying attention to her, but it was nice to have her there still.

"Totally," Kerry replied, absentmindedly. *Definitely not listening,* Nia smiled. She smoothed down the jewel green dress she wore, loving the way the silky fabric caught the light. Elijah had mentioned before that he loved her in green, so when she picked out her final ceremony dresses, this one came to mind. It was fitted to every curve, with a halter top that showed off her shoulders and a hemline that just kissed the floor when she slipped her heels on. She felt gorgeous, like this was her own fairytale, and she couldn't help the thread of anticipation that snaked its way through her body at the thought of Elijah taking it off of her later.

Tonight was the night they could finally stop hiding their relationship in the shadows. Nia had wanted to know what exactly Elijah was going to say to her, but he had been pretty close mouthed about it. She figured that it'd be better that she didn't know, so she could act surprised as well. There was a little tingle of satisfaction that Elijah was picking her - it was what she wanted most at the moment.

The door creaked open, and Maddison poked her head in. Nia overheard something about Isaac and Warren needing her in five. After the door shut, Kerry shook her head and finally took a seat, still scrolling through her phone.

"She sits! You were making me dizzy watching you." Nia laughed, as the Pom finally stepped away from her.

"I feel dizzy myself. I just can't wait for filming to be over." Kerry sighed, dropping her phone. "But then we're prepping for the first few episodes to start airing on Netflix, and I hope to God it's well received – "

"The show is going to do amazing." Nia offered, thinking about all the crazy times they'd had that she'd seen, and she hadn't even seen all of filming. "People love love."

"I know I'm excited to watch." Pom smiled, as she cleaned her brushes.

"It better. Warren has been so stressed ever since he found out that Lily has to win, so this whole editing process has been about making her look good – "

It took a minute for Nia to understand the words that Kerry was saying. "Wait, what do you mean Lily has to win?"

Pom set down her brushes, surprised. "Spoiler alert! Ah well, they're cute together. I think I won the betting pool though!"

Kerry froze, eyes on Nia. "Shit. I'm so sorry, I wasn't supposed to say anything."

"Lily has to win?" It was like every good thought came grinding to a halt.

"I'm so sorry Nia. One of the big wigs, Chris Parker, came in with a last-minute call that he wanted his niece to win, for the publicity. She's a budding actress as well, you know."

Thoughts were racing through Nia's head. She was trying to remember if Elijah had mentioned anything, but he hadn't. It felt like a lead bar was sinking in her stomach. Had he never planned on actually picking Nia? Again?

Pom, confused, looked back and forth between Nia and Kerry. "Did I miss something?"

"What does that mean for Elijah?" Nia wondered, dreading the answer.

"Well, it's at least a year commitment to her, so we can milk the press junkets and social media. The world is going to love the two of them together."

"And he's going to do it?" Nia whispered, dreading the answer.

"He's supposed to. I heard he got offered a huge project if he does." Kerry bit her lip, watching the play of emotions on Nia's face. "I hate this. I don't agree with it at all."

Nia tuned Kerry out, though she kept talking.

Elijah had lied to her.

Again.

What had happened in college was repeating itself, except Nia was older, and yet somehow not wiser. She felt like she'd been played. It was a nasty feeling, worming its way through her body, whispering insecurities that she'd thought she'd killed, making its home back into her mind. It all boiled down to one thing – she wasn't good enough. It had been clear to her back in college, and she'd been a big enough idiot to believe she'd actually meant more to him this time around.

"Nia? Are you ok?" She looked up to see Kerry's worried eyes on her.

There was another knock on the door, saving her from having to answer. They were ready on set for filming to start. Nia stood, smoothing out her dress, glad she looked stunning even though she didn't feel particularly great at the moment.

"Everything is exactly right. Let's do this."

The mansion was beautiful, the perfect romantic setting. It was dark out, leaving the twinkling lights of the city shining below, tiny bright things in the night. Filming was taking place in the back yard, a wide, space with a sharp drop off. It had been decorated with palm trees, roses, and other flowers, almost reminiscent of the Banyan house in Oahu, minus the banyan trees. Candles were strategically placed, along with hidden lights that made it a romantic, cozy scene. Nia noticed all of this with a bitter heart. A slight breeze teased the air, chilling the skin that was revealed on Nia's arms, but it was no colder than her heart was feeling at the moment.

Crew members bustled around, adjusting lights, cameras, and Nia was shown her place in it all. Warren was full of energy, more so than usual, and was barking orders at people and making last minute adjustments. "Why are these miniature candles? They were supposed to be full sized!" He shook his head at one of the plants. "This plant is too green, this one isn't green enough, fix it please!" Seeing Nia, he spared a look in her direction, before snapping at a poor production assistant who brought his coffee that was a shade too hot.

"Places people! Filming starts in two minutes!"

Nia took a few calming breaths, trying to ease the racing in her mind. She had to focus on her work, and nothing and no one would get in her way. Some little voice of hope said that he could still be picking her, and just hadn't told anyone yet. Nia wanted to trust Elijah, wanted to know that it hadn't been misplaced. There was still time for him to do what he said he would. Nia clung to that bit of hope, convincing herself that she heard wrong and that he was still going to pick her.

But, where was he? She finally spotted Elijah, speaking to Warren in hushed tones, a little hidden behind some of the foliage. She tried to sneak over to hear what they were talking about, but their conversation broke before she made it there. Warren brushed past her, yelling "Are cameras ready yet?"

Elijah looked tense, lost in thought. He didn't notice Nia coming up, until she laid a hand on his arm. "Is everything fine?"

"Just perfect." He hadn't looked at her yet. He *wouldn't* look at her, actually. The lead in her stomach sank a bit more.

"Places people!" Finally, he looked up, and what she saw there made the bubble of hope burst. There was an apology in his eyes, as well as regret. She knew what it meant. Later, Nia could dwell on it. For now, she went over to her mark. Someone yelled action, and Nia snapped into business mode.

"Here we are at the final Ring Ceremony, where perpetual bachelor Elijah James will meet one last time with the lucky ladies vying for his heart. But who will he choose? Feisty Danielle, lovable April, or charming Lily?"

As Nia called out their names, each entered to stand at a prearranged spot. Danielle was in a fiery red gown, April wore a dainty blue number, and Lily was pretty in a blush pink. "That's the question on everyone's minds, and tonight, we will find out. Here comes our bachelor now."

Nia turned to watch Elijah enter, looking pensive and tense. He stopped by a small stand that held a heart shaped box, and stared at it for a moment before his eyes connected with hers briefly. Cold, Nia deliberately turned back to her camera. "Let's see what happens next."

ELIJAH

Elijah took a deep breath before he looked up at the ladies. He and Warren had argued earlier about his choice, but he knew what he had to do. This wasn't just about him, but it was killing him when all he wanted to do was sweep Nia off her feet and run away. She'd looked stunning in her green dress, but he had kept his mouth shut, not feeling like he deserved to compliment her when he was about to do something that would shatter her. There was still time, he reasoned, but as the women started filing out, he realized he was trapped in. He'd almost missed his cue to head out, and made it only because someone had tapped him on his shoulder.

He looked up at the three women, all nice in their own ways, but not the one he wanted to be with. "This has been a wild ride, and I wanted to start by thanking all of you for coming along with me."

Stepping up to Danielle, Elijah took her hand. "Dani, you are such a firecracker, and the energy you bring with you everywhere you go lets people know you are here, makes you feel alive. Life with you would never be dull."

Danielle's hand tightened around his. "I really think we can make something beautiful between the two of us Elijah. Not just as the next big power couple, but I love how much of a gentleman you are. My parents loved you, and that's saying a lot."

Elijah chuckled briefly before moving on to April. "There's such a sweetness in you that I love seeing. You approach life with such joy, that any man would be proud to experience life with you."

April grabbed both his hands with hers and pressed them to her ample chest. Nia could practically see Danielle practically seething that she didn't think to do that. "Elijah, you bring out the good in me. Together, I've felt things that were downright magical, and I would love to be the one you choose forever with."

He tried to gently wrestle his hands back away from April's grasp. "Thank you." He moved onto Lily, the last woman left.

She looked up at him with stars in her eyes, and Elijah hated that he couldn't put an end to this right now. "Lily, what can I say about you? You have such a soothing presence, but you're one of the strongest, nicest people I have had the pleasure to meet in a long time. And when I think of you, I can't help but to see my future." The words didn't mean much to Elijah, besides the fact that he *had* to pick her, to make sure his future was set. But he realized they could mean a lot once he saw the way her eyes lit up at him.

Elijah glanced up to look at Nia, who had a carefully blank expression on her face. He could see Warren behind her, watching him intently to make sure he did the right thing. Taking a deep breath, Elijah turned to the stand next to him, picking up the lone ring box sitting on the silk cushion. Picking it up, he turned the box carefully in his hands. His stomach churned at what he had to do.

"You all have meant something to me, and I would never trade our time together for anything else. I have learned so much about myself, and what I'm looking for in a partner, and I'm glad to say that I've found it during this time on the island. But that means two of you will go home disappointed."

Silence reigned in area, as the crew collectively held their breaths, waiting to hear who he picked. His eyes found Nia's, glistening with unshed tears as she listened. "The woman I am choosing…is…Lily." He approached her with the ring, and she threw her arms around him, planting a kiss on his lips that Elijah had to remember to reciprocate for the cameras.

But his heart was breaking, knowing what he'd just done to the woman he actually loved.

He couldn't look at Nia, because he knew he'd see nothing but betrayal in her eyes when she looked at him. Around him, April and Danielle gave their own well wishes before being discretely ushered away. Lily held him close, smiling with tears in her own eyes as he slipped the ring over her finger, sealing his fate.

Somewhere in the distance was yelled cut, and he broke apart, unable to keep up the act up. There was so much commotion, so much noise compared to the utter silence during filming. A few crew members were trying to offer Elijah their well wishes, but he couldn't focus on that. His eyes were looking for Nia, who had disappeared in the crowd. Lily was happily showing off the ring, and Warren was drawing her away to do a post ceremony interview.

Kerry stopped him as he was moving, trying to steer him back to the fold. "Wait, where are you going? We still have to do your interview together – "

"I need a minute, Kerry." He barely spared her a glance as he searched for Nia.

A splash of green caught his eye, and Elijah darted after it, seeing Nia disappear into a green room. He just made it to her before the door closed, slipping in behind her and shutting it behind him. She stood looking out a window, arms crossed against her middle, back rigid. Elijah took a step forward, wanting to hold her in his arms. "Nia…"

She wouldn't look at him.

"I'm so sorry. Can I explain?"

"Explain what, Elijah? That you lied to me? That doesn't need an explanation, it's pretty straightforward."

He stepped closer, placing a hand on her shoulder but she jerked away from him, finally turning to face him. It was like a blow to the gut to see her reddened eyes, and the hurt on her face. "Nia, I swear to you that I honestly meant it when I'd said I wouldn't pick anyone, but things changed."

"What changed?" Her arms were crossed protectively over her torso, and he wanted nothing more than to hold her right now.

Elijah ran a hand through his hair. "Warren pulled me aside and told me that her uncle, one of the executives, wanted me to pick Lily, because she's polling well and they wanted her career to take off. They thought throwing in a huge job would sweeten the deal." He paused, not wanting her to know what they had of her on camera. Picking Lily meant keeping Nia's reputation safe. And if that meant he looked like an ass…so be it.

Nia's eyes were hard as she looked at him. "Why didn't you tell me about it?"

"I wanted to, but it never seemed like the right time, and we were having so much fun that I didn't want to ruin it. And then after you left, Warren basically threatened everything if I screwed this up."

"You did this for a job?" Nia laughed bitterly. "I shouldn't have been surprised.

This is almost like what you did in college."

"Why do you keep circling back to college? We were different people back then!"

"But here you are, doing the exact same things as a grown ass man."

"That's unfair, and you know it. Things are different now, the stakes are higher!"

"And yet you couldn't have a simple conversation about it with me? You chose to hide it instead."

"But I still want to be with you!" Elijah tried to grab her hands, but she jerked the away. "At most, I'm committed to her for what, a year? And then I can call it off, saying we have our differences and then we can pick right back up."

"You can't be serious."

"I am." Elijah was pleading with her at this point. "We can still do us behind the scenes, and I'd just have to do promotional stuff with her for a while, but it could work."

"Are you serious right now? We can't pick right back up, Elijah!" Nia exploded. "You can't expect me to wait around for someone who won't even pick me first! How would that make me look? Desperate and lacking self-esteem and I'm not that girl anymore. But apparently you're the same guy I know."

Her words hit him, gutting him. He wanted to tell her she was wrong, but was she? Elijah took a hard look at Nia, seeing the anger in her eyes and the sadness right behind it. "Nia…"

Someone knocked at the door, interrupting. It was Maddison, who peeked her head in the room, obviously noticing the "Elijah? We need you back on set for your interview."

"One second!" He yelled at the door. "Look, Nia, I'm not the same person – "

"But aren't you?" She rubbed her eyes, sinking down onto the arm of the couch. "What hurts the most is that I almost believed you when you said you loved me. Almost. But now, I'm just realizing you're an even better actor than I suspected."

"I'm so, so sorry Nia. Let me fix this."

"You can't Elijah. The damage is done." Her lips twisted as a tear fell down her face. "Just leave."

"I swear to you, I'm going to fix this somehow – "

Someone knocked at the door again. Warren's voice came through. "Eli, man, we need you out here."

He was torn, looking between the door and Nia. She shook her head. "Go ahead. Work is calling."

"Can we talk later? Please?"

"I can't promise that. I think we should stop whatever this was. I would say we're done, but we were never a thing."

"Don't say that." Elijah felt his own heart breaking.

"I wish you and Lily the best. And good luck in your career."

There was nothing he could say to her that would change what happened. He knew that look she had on her face. With one last look at her, Elijah stood and slowly left the room.

He wasn't there to see her face crumple, and the tears that she'd blocked finally come falling down.

The Heartbreak

NIA

Somehow after all of that, Nia managed to escape the mansion, and made her way back home. She just wanted to go lie in her bed with a bottle (or several) of wine and ice cream and forget that she ever knew Elijah James. But she'd forgotten about Goldie, who was lounging in the living room, doing a face mask and waxing her legs when Nia walked in. She practically jumped in the air when Nia walked in.

"I thought you were staying over at boo thing's house tonight?" The words died on her lips once she got a good look at Nia's face. "I'll go fight him right now." Nia let out a soft snort, looking Goldie up and down. She was a little terrifying, with the mask, head wrap and wax hanging off her body. But then Nia felt her face crumple and she flopped down on the couch, burying her face in her hands.

"I would tell you to go for it, except he's definitely not worth it." She'd thought she'd cried everything out in the car, but apparently not.

"No one is worth making my bestie cry. Hang on, let me get you some wine."

Nia tried to control her tears as Goldie rummaged around in the kitchen, bringing back another bottle of wine, a second glass, and a tub of butter pecan ice cream. "Want to tell me where he fucked up?" the soft glug of wine being poured and the click of the wine glass being set next to her punctuated the silence.

"Not right now." She couldn't rehash it all right not. It was too soon. Goldie, bless her, made it her mission to help Nia focus on other things, telling her all about the horrible men she went on dates with, and turned on reruns of Nia's favorite office themed television show.

Nia just couldn't believe that it was over. Her thoughts were all over the place, but the loudest ones were fussing at her for opening up her heart to someone and trusting that she wouldn't make the same mistake twice. That was the kicker, to know that she shared herself with Elijah, shared her fears and insecurities, and he still picked himself over her first. And Nia was tired of coming in second place, tired of people trying to make decisions in her life for her.

Goldie's hand covering hers interrupted her thoughts. "Just know that whatever happened, that I'm here for you. And my offer stands to make a eunuch out of him. I've got my shears ready."

"Thanks Goldie." Nia sighed and curled up into herself on the couch.

Over the next week, Nia tried to ignore the hollow feeling in her chest, going on her second audition as well as a few more, and shooting a commercial. If she wasn't working, she was at her new Improv class in Hollywood, helping Goldie out at her shop, or working out, determined to blast any and all fat from her body. In other words, she was avoiding feeling anything. It didn't help that Elijah called her several times a day at first, and when he realized she wasn't answering, he switched to daily text messages. It crushed her bit by bit each day that she saw his good morning and good night text messages, messages from him asking to give him another chance. Nia ignored those. Mostly. In actuality, she read them, cried, started to delete the messages but couldn't let go of even that tiny part of them. Not yet.

Lexi and Yaya came over for a girl's night a few days after the breakup, and tried not to comment on the hyper-focus activity Nia was on. Yaya couldn't help trying to lighten the atmosphere "I'd forgotten you get like this. I wish you would come and help me organize everything." Nia tried to smile at the joke, but it felt impossible to do even that.

In her usual breakup angst, Nia had rearranged and reorganized everything, and hers and Goldie's apartment now looked like some sort of catalogue. "I'm going to grab the cheese plate." Nia said, disappearing from the living room.

In the kitchen, she could hear them talking in low voices. "I haven't seen her this bad in forever. She's like a little robot, not expressing any emotion whatsoever."

Yaya nodded, sipping her wine. "Yeah, she's always been like this. It how she copes with things. I really hate that he did a number on her."

"He doesn't deserve her. Of all the high-handed things he could've done, I can't believe he expected her to wait for him while he's in a relationship with someone else." Lexi rolled her eyes from her perch on the couch. "As soon as she's ready I'm introducing her to all of my single male friends."

It was kind of them, but not necessary. Nia had sworn off dating for the next ten years. Hopefully by then her heart would be healed.

"You don't have to do that Lex." Nia said, coming back with an elaborate fruit and cheese tray that might have come from the store. "I'll be fine. I know I have weird coping mechanisms, but I'm processing it still I guess."

"Take all the time you need. We're here for you," Goldie smiled at Nia, wrapping an arm around her.

"And it's ok to hurt. I know you are, but you'll get past it." Lexi added. "

"But what if I don't?" Nia asked, staring into her glass of wine. "I thought I wasn't going to get past it in college, and I was hung up on him for years. I can't go through that again."

"You're not alone, you know. There's three sets of shoulders here for you to lean on when you're ready." Yaya leaned on Nia's leg from the floor. "You don't have to be strong all the time."

Rationally, Nia knew this, but it was almost too much to let those feelings in. As if reading her mind, Lexi added, "It's ok to hurt sometimes. It helps you appreciate the good moments for what they are. Just know that it only lasts as long as you want it to."

Nia sniffled. "Thanks, you guys." She didn't know how long it would take this time for her to get over Elijah. She didn't know if she would find someone who'd understood her as well as he did. But Nia did know that she had a group of people there for her, ready for whatever.

She finally let her tears fall, and her friends were right there with her.

A few weeks later, Nia got the call she'd been waiting for. She was at Let's Chakra Bout It, helping re-sort the stones that had been knocked over by an errant purse when her phone rang. Stepping out for a moment, she answered the unknown number.

"Hi Nia, it's Jennifer with Direct Casting calling about the role of Cassidy for the untitled pilot?"

"Yes, hello." She held her breath, waiting to hear what Jennifer said.

"That role has been filled, unfortunately." Nia's breath let out in a whoosh. She'd thought she'd had it in the bag, but it was always hard to tell.

"But that's because the director loved you so much, he wanted to cast you as Ava."

Nia's brain was slow to catch up. "I thought I didn't fit that casting bill?" More specifically, the initial casting had been looking for a white or white passing woman for the leading lady role of Ava, which Nia obviously didn't fit. Instead, she'd gone out for the role of one of her friends.

"True, but he's decided to go another way. They're all really excited to see where you take this character. You've got the role, Nia. Congratulations!"

So many thoughts whirled through her head, but Nia managed to eek out a professional thank you and hang up before she let out a whoop of joy. A few tourists passing by jumped, looking at her sideways before continuing on but Nia barely noticed them. The joy of landing this job finally pierced the grey veil that she'd felt had descended over her life. Something good had finally happened. She'd landed her first big role, which had a great chance of going to series. Even though her love life was in the dumps, her work life was stepping up nicely.

Making her way back inside, she could see Goldie looking at her curiously but with the start of a smile on her face. "Can I assume that the crazy lady shrieks in front of my shop were due to good news?"

"You absolutely can! You're looking at not the black best friend, but the leading freaking lady of a major network pilot!" Nia did a little happy dance, a huge grin on her face as she was brought in for a huge hug from Goldie.

"Leading lady? That's what I'm talking about! I'm so happy for you!" Goldie finally released Nia when she realized she was smothering her.

"I just can't believe it. I keep thinking they're going to call back and say they made a mistake." Nia leaned on the counter, a smile still lingering on her lips.

"You better nix the negativity sis! You absolutely deserve this. I've watched you bust ass these last few years, and it's paying off like it should."

Goldie was right. Not to toot her own horn, but Nia had been working diligently to make this happen. So many nights of networking, so many free and underpaid projects, shelling out a crap ton of money for acting classes had finally, *finally,* paid off.

"You're right, I'm going to own this now. I need to tell my family." Nia couldn't wait to see the smiles on her mom and sister's faces. If she was being completely honest, she couldn't wait to see her dad eat his words. She'd made it.

"This is cause for celebration. I'll close up early and we'll grab a drink tonight."

"Are you sure?" Truthfully, Nia could use a drink. It was cause for celebration. Her first leading role. On top of that, *With This Ring* was set to air tomorrow - not that Nia was planning on watching it. Everything was too fresh still.

"Absolutely. It's a Thursday, which is the new Friday anyway. I'll call Yaya and Lexi. Feel like that one spot in East Hollywood?"

"The Virgil? Perfect. I feel like dancing."

ELIJAH

Elijah was in a hell of his own making. He was stuck doing photoshoot after photoshoot and endless interviews with Lily, having to act like the blissfully happy couple for people he didn't care to impress. He wanted Nia, and he was kicking himself for not choosing her and damning the consequences. Never had he missed anyone more than he had missed Nia. It had gotten to the point that Lily had figured out something was up, though she kept up appearances on her side even as she tried to figure out what was going on with Elijah. Warren was on his ass all the time, constantly reminding him that it was for his career and a bunch of other bullshit he didn't want to hear.

The day before *With this Ring* was set to drop on Netflix was one photoshoot where Elijah had finally had enough. He was posing with Lily in a damned uncomfortable suit, and the photographer had had the idea to have them sitting in a sand pit of all things. And of course, he had sand in his pants.

"Give me something to work with! Yass Lily, you are absolutely crushing this." The photographer, a character who went by the name Big Red but dressed only in shades of orange, pranced around them snapping away. "Elijah, I need more from you! You love this woman, remember?"

Elijah's thoughts turned to Nia, latching onto how he'd fucked up with her, yet again.

"Whatever you're thinking of, don't please." Big Red stopped, letting his camera hang around his neck. "That was such a...sad, miserable face. Not at all what

I'm looking for."

Elijah's hands curled into fists, and Warren scooted in to diffuse the situation. "Let's take a quick breather, yeah? Elijah can I talk with you."

It wasn't a question. Elijah followed Warren out the stage to a patio out back. The sun was unfairly bright, doing nothing but reminding Elijah of his bleak mood.

"What the hell is wrong with you? Are you trying to tank this before we even get off the ground?" Warren demanded, pacing the short area.

"I did what you asked me to, what else do you want from me?" His words were calmer than he was feeling.

"I want you to act like you want to be here – "

"I don't though." Elijah crossed his arms. "You strong armed me into a decision that I didn't want to do, and now my life is not my own for the next year while I have to promote a show I didn't want to do in the first place."

"Is this about Nia again? Look man, she's a nobody. There's a dime a dozen out there like her, and you can do way better."

Elijah saw red for a moment and barely managed to control himself when he wanted to launch his fist at Warren's face. "Fuck off Warren."

He prowled back into the office and managed to finish the shoot with some semblance of dignity. When they were finally finished, Elijah was trying to leave as fast as possible, but Lily stopped him before he could reach the door. "I wanted to know if you wanted to grab a drink with me? I don't think I can watch the first episodes just yet." Her words trailed off, and Elijah finally looked at her. Lily's face was earnest, but he could see confusion and hurt in her eyes as well as she twisted the engagement ring on her finger. He immediately felt bad. She didn't ask to be caught up in his drama, but he couldn't bring it to himself to fake a relationship on his off time. But the first few episodes of the show were to be released tonight, and he just wanted to go home and crash.

"Raincheck? I'm just not up to it today." As much as he felt bad, he'd feel even worse leading her on with hopes of a relationship that would never happen.

"Sure thing." Lily tried to sound upbeat, but he could tell she was upset. Even though this relationship was fake to him, it wasn't to her. As she started to walk away, he called out to her.

"Lily? I could go for one drink."

Which is how he found himself in a dark East Hollywood bar on a Thursday night sharing a drink with the woman he was technically 'engaged' with. The bar was moody and quirky, with a few people hidden away in the shadows. It was split into two sides, the other half housing a dance floor that promised to fill up later in the evening. He and Lily slid into a table after grabbing their drinks, but Elijah was at a loss for words. He stared into his Old Fashioned, wondering how soon could he get out of here without it being rude.

"So, what's the deal?"

He looked up, startled to see surprisingly pragmatic eyes coming from Lily.

"What's that?"

"What gives?" She took a sip of her Sidecar. "Obviously I'm not your choice for who you actually wanted to get engaged to, and I'm just trying to figure it out."

Elijah scrambled to find an answer. "It's not you, it's me."

Lily snorted into her drink. "That's highly lame. You can do better than that."

He couldn't help the chuckle that escaped. "I know it's the corniest thing ever, but it honestly is the truth." There was no way he was telling Lily that he'd had to pick her, that he'd been planning to not pick anyone of the women from the island in favor of Nia. He wasn't drunk enough yet to open up like that.

"What's with all the bull?"

Sighing, he took a swig of his drink. "It's none of your business."

"It is when I'm trying to make us look happy together and you're hell bent on sabotaging it for whatever reason." Lily sat back in her chair, watching Elijah over the rim of her drink. "I wonder how Nia's doing?"

It was almost shocking to hear Nia's name come up.

Lily took another sip, watching the emotions play across his face. "Let's just get through the rest of filming, and see how we're doing after that." Her hand covered his, and he looked down at it.

"Sounds like a plan." He rubbed his neck feeling goosebumps. Elijah took a look around the room, where he saw Nia surrounded by her group of friends. Their eyes connected, even in the dim room, and Elijah could see that his hand was still covered by Lily's. She registered it, before making eye contact with Elijah one more time. Hurt, confusion and a hint of anger warred for prominence for Nia. He tried to pull his hand from underneath Lily, but Nia conferred with her friends before they disappear right back out the doors. "Nia, wait." He tried to get them to stop, but the music had ramped up and the once quiet bar was now starting to feel a little packed with new waves of people coming in. Following her out was hard thanks to the crowd of people who were starting to recognize him despite the dim interior of the bar.

"Interesting." Elijah had forgotten about Lily, who had followed behind him. "I think I'm starting to see now." All he saw was the disappearing tail lights of the car that took Nia away from him, again.

The Premiere

NIA

"Of all the places in LA, he had to be there?" Nia asked as they were spirited away in their Uber. "This city is not that small."

"That is a wild coincidence. I wonder what your chart has been saying for today?" Goldie murmured, pulling out her phone.

"We're not going to let him ruin your night of celebration." Yaya's face was lit from passing streetlights. "We are going to party it up, ignore the release of the show, and find some hot guys to go home with."

"That's my kind of plan!" Lexi cheered, helping to keep the mood light.

"Let's do it! Fuck him anyway." Nia added, determined to not let him ruin her night. She was going to have some fun, and not think about one Elijah James or the show that she was desperately curious to watch, but definitely not ready to relive just yet.

Which is why, when she woke up the next day, Nia had a raging hangover and a mouth full of cotton. The sun was ruthlessly bright, shining through the sheer curtains Nia had just had to have for her room, swearing it made everything look better. Groaning, she slowly made her way into a mostly upright position, and eventually out to the living room where she found Goldie on the couch, a cooling mask over her eyes.

"Why did we think that was a good idea?" Nia asked, settling beside her and propping her feet on the table.

"Because YOLO, obviously." Goldie barely moved.

"No one says that anymore." Nia groaned. "Should we eat something?" The thought of food was repulsive, but Nia couldn't think of anything else to do.

"Nope." Goldie turned a shade of green underneath the mask. "No food."

"Good idea." Before they got too comfortable, someone's phone began to ring, the sound piercing through their fog and causing them to groan.

"Make it stop." Goldie buried her head under a pillow while Nia stood on shaky legs and looked for wherever her phone landed after last night. Finding it in the kitchen of all places, she managed to silence it. But it started ringing again just a few minutes later. Blearily, she wondered what she had done to warrant this sort of torture.

Looking at the screen, she saw it was Lexi calling. "How are you not hungover, witch woman?" Nia croaked into the phone.

"Because I drink water between every alcoholic beverage." Lily's voice came through, void of any sort of lingering iciness from last night's drinking. "But you might want to sit down."

"Why?" Nia rubbed her temples, trying to soothe the headache. She wondered if it was bad to make a drink this early in the morning? It might help the hangover...

"It's about *With This Ring*. The first six episodes are up."

"Yeah, I know. What, people hate it or something?" She wouldn't be surprised if it had mixed reviews - it wasn't like they'd set out to make Emmy material.

"Nia - they've showed you and Elijah. Together."

"Of course, we're together, I'm the host - "

"Not like that. I mean, together, together."

The pieces finally aligned in Nia's muffled brain. She leaned against the counter as a wave of nausea passed over her. "You can't be serious."

"Unfortunately I am serious."

Oh god, this can't be happening. Nia's mind was racing, trying to remember all the times she was with Elijah. What exactly they could have used? Her mind went to their time in the cabana and she felt a hot wave of embarrassment wash over her.

"How bad?"

"You're trending on twitter. #HornyHostess."

"Stop it." Nia couldn't even spare a laugh for the god-awful hashtag they'd used. "Should I watch it?"

"I...it's up to you." Lexi's answer was vague, which made Nia all the more determined to see just how bad it really is.

"I'm watching it." Hanging up, she grabbed a bottle of vodka, forgoing a glass and headed back into the living room where Goldie had finally uncovered her eyes.

"What's going on?" She asked, catching sight of Nia's face as well as the vodka in her hand.

"I'm about to find out." Grabbing the remote, she turned on Netflix and found the show.

The first bit of it was harmless, really. But then after the second date, they showed Nia and Elijah and the kiss he laid on her their first night, taken way out of context.

"Damn girl, that's a kiss." Goldie was glued to the screen. "I didn't know you had it in you."

"Oh god." Why did it have to be her? Why wasn't she stronger at avoiding Elijah? Nia wanted to crawl back into bed and pretend this hadn't happened, but for some terrible reason she couldn't stop watching.

Everything after that went downhill. In between date and activities, Nia was shown to be lusting after Elijah, and not in a good way. She was being made to look like she was star thirsty, and it didn't help that their moonlight talks on their balcony were recorded, to her dismay. Nia couldn't help but watch it all, the sordid, vulnerability she'd felt taken all out of context. It was a literal waking nightmare, and there was nothing she could do about it.

"Did they mention they were recording all of this?" Goldie asked, as they watched Nia and Elijah flirting off camera before the pool volleyball action.

"Technically, they said they were filming everything, but I didn't think they literally meant everything. I definitely didn't know they had cameras in my room too." That was not told to her, and Nia hadn't asked as she definitely wasn't under the impression that they were going to use her in the show in that way.

"Wow, I mean…this is a lot." Goldie sighed, as they kept watching.

A lot was underselling it. She felt exposed, and lied to; Nia thought of Kerry and Isaac, and wondered if they knew and were in on it the whole time. The thought sickened her, especially since Nia had talked to Kerry about her past with Elijah, had thought she was confiding in a friend. Her gut didn't want to believe they would do such a thing, but it was getting harder and harder to know who to trust. Now, she didn't know what to think.

The very last available episode included a piece of her and Elijah getting caught in the rain in the gazebo. Watery footage was shown of their admissions to each other and kiss, before fading to black suggestively.

Goldie's hands pressed to her head, mouth wide open. "Don't hate me, but this is good. Like, I know they're showing you in a terrible way, but I'm also weirdly invested in it?"

Nia fell back on the couch, hiding under a throw blanket. "I can't show my face now. I'm going to be nothing more than #HornyHostess for the next year, minimum." A thought occurred to her. "What if this hurts my show?" Her heart was racing. All that work, down the drain. They would be well within their rights to recast for someone with less drama attached to them.

"If that ever happened, which I hope it won't, we'll sue their asses for defamation, causing you to lose out on work, everything." Goldie was adamant, looking scarier than Nia had ever seen her.

As Goldie continued to fuss about lawsuits and astrological charts, Nia was at a loss. She didn't want to go on social media and see all the negative comments that were sure to be there, but she didn't want to go outside and see if anyone recognized her on the streets either. She felt well and truly trapped.

ELIJAH

Never had Elijah been more pissed than he had been watching the show. Before he'd even made it past the second episode, Elijah was dialing Warren's number.

"Elijah! We did it!"

"Warren – "

"The show's a hit! It's already been viewed over two million times and counting! Your star meter is through the roof!" Warren's chipper voice filled Elijah's ear as he paced the floors of his apartment.

"Warren – "

"They are lining up to interview you and Lily, and we might even have you do one with Nia, that'd be amazing – "

"*Warren.*" The severity of Elijah's voice finally cut through Warren's fog. "What the actual fuck were you thinking, using me and Nia like that?"

"What do you mean? Everything was fair game, we told you that – "

"No, you definitely did not. You promised if I did this you wouldn't use that footage."

"Seriously man, what are you, twelve? You signed up for a reality TV show, and this is what happens. That footage was *gold.*"

"This is not just *what happens,* and you know it." The guilty silence stretched on the phone line as Elijah tried to rein in his temper, and then refusing. Fuck that, he could be as pissed as he wanted to. "What happened to just airing the dates with the actual women who showed up to date me?"

He could practically feel Warren shrugging. "Look, I wanted to give you a heads up, but the studio accidentally got a hold of the two of you and wanted to use it.

"And how exactly did they get ahold of that footage?"

The guilty silence told enough. Elijah tried to hold back a groan, clenching it in his hand to keep from throwing the phone around like a deranged maniac. He was pissed, and there was nothing he could do about it. Elijah wanted to rip someone a new hole, but he didn't know where to start with. His thoughts were on Nia, who might have heard it without any warning, and his heart clenched. He'd already tried calling her several times that morning, but her phone was going directly to voicemail. Wherever she was, Elijah just wanted to know she was safe.

"All you did, Warren, was make me look like an idiot for trusting you."

"Come on, man, it's just one show – "

"This is my life, man. And you've been playing god since day one, and it's over. That was the last time I'm working with you."

"You can't be serious. For some chick?"

"I'm very serious." Elijah said, calmer now.

"We've got interviews, showings – you signed a contract. You can't just quit."

Elijah knew he was legally bound to them for a while longer, though he'd have his lawyers try and figure out a way around it. "I'll do the scheduled interviews. Anything beyond that, you need to figure out." Elijah was a man of his word, and he would finish what he'd started. But he'd be dammed if he kept working with someone who cared so little for his personal life. That wasn't the sort of person he wanted to be around.

"What about the role – "

"Goodbye Warren." Elijah hung up despite Warren still talking. His fist pounded the counter, wanting to do damage to something. *Think*. This couldn't be where it all ended. He had to figure out some way to make this right. But how?

The Infamy

NIA

Notoriety was something Nia had figured she'd slowly deal with, if ever a time came when she was starting to become more visible in the world. But what was happening now was something she wasn't prepared for. Her social media had blown up. As in, she'd had a maybe a couple thousand followers the night before the party, and her count had skyrocketed up to eighty-thousand followers overnight. Nia had had to turn off her notifications due to her phone overheating thanks to all the alerts.

Her parents were concerned; Yolanda didn't want her daughter to be in any danger, saying, "Look what they did to princess Di!" Her father wanted her to stop by the restaurant when she had the time from all of 'this' press nonsense. Yaya on the other hand had been unaccountably thrilled that she had a sister who was making the news. She'd called Nia, telling her to get in an elevator fight with Elijah with her in it so she could channel her inner Solange. Nia had rolled her eyes and ignored that.

Thankfully, her parents weren't making a big deal out of the whole thing with Elijah, and Nia couldn't help but think her mother had a hand in that. Her dad had been unusually silent on the whole matter, making Nia wonder what he was really thinking. She promised to stop by the restaurant as soon as she could figure out how to deal with the paparazzi.

And the paparazzi. Determined, sneaky individuals who had made it their goal to get scandalous pictures of the woman trying to sneak Elijah James away from the 'legitimate' women, and had taken to camping outside her apartment in order to get it. What exactly did they think they were going to see? Nia tripping on the sidewalk or ducking into her car? It all made zero sense to her. Nia hadn't left her apartment in over a week, and was going to fight someone if she couldn't get out soon. Thankfully, Goldie had stepped up and helped out, grabbing groceries and bottles of alcohol to help her in her isolation.

Coming back from one such run, Goldie plopped the bags on the counter, eyes animated. "You know Ms. Augusta a few doors down? You should have seen her giving this one pap a piece of her mind for daring to step on the grass in front of the building. It was freaking amazing."

"I wish I could have seen it." Nia sighed. It was frustrating to be locked up in her own damn apartment, trapped by people who had nothing better to do. *I'm BORING. Go home already.*

"You know, you can always just go out there and own it." Goldie said as she unloaded groceries. "Don't let the people get you down."

"But they're waiting for me." The thought of paparazzi hounding her made Nia a little light headed.

"Yes, but I figure the longer you wait, the more desperate they get to find something of you. Might as well get it over with, you know?"

Though she wanted to protest, Nia knew Goldie was right. The longer she delayed the inevitable, the longer her own personal hell went on.

"Maybe you're right. I shouldn't let them keep me down."

"Hell yeah. What you're going to do is put on a bomb ass outfit, do something to your face and hair, and then strut yourself out to show the world that you are here honey." Goldie ended her speech by pointing the top of a wine bottle at Nia. "Also, you can give me a ride to work."

"I can do this." Nia stood, smoothing down her hair. She would do this.

"You absolutely can do this."

Heading back to her bedroom, Nia took a shower, shaving, exfoliating, and buffing to make sure she was looked good, even if she didn't feel it. She then put on one of her favorite outfits, a fitted light wash jean skirt with a graphic tee knotted just above her belly button, with a pair of Doc Martins to complete the look.

Nia felt ready on the outside at least, but was she ready on the inside? She knew the paparazzi would write whatever they wanted to write about her, but being honest with herself, she wanted it to be positive. Was that asking for too much?

Probably. Actually, yeah, it definitely was asking for too much.

Sighing, she grabbed her purse and went out to living room where Goldie was flipping through channels. "I'm heading out there. Let's do this."

Goldie jumped up, grabbing her purse. "You got it boss. Kill it out there."

With that vote of confidence, Nia stepped outside, placing a pair of sunglasses over her face. She felt marginally shielded, and popped out the gate to meet her makers. It was comforting to know Goldie was with her, in case any of the paparazzi got out of hand. A few of them tried to get her to look in their direction, but Nia kept her cool, heading down to the street where she'd left her car.

"How does it feel being a home wrecker?"

"Are you upset that Elijah James picked Lily over you in the finale?"

"Are you still sleeping with Elijah James?"

The questions were relentless, and Nia just wanted to get to her car and drive away. Maybe it was time to upgrade and just pay the fee for the extra parking space. At least she wouldn't have to deal with paparazzi on the roads. Reaching her car, she slid in, shutting the door to their questions with a sigh. That wasn't so bad. They were still taking pictures, but she'd made it. Starting her engine, Nia pulled away from the curb, leaving the photographers behind.

After dropping Goldie off, Nia took the scenic route to her her parent's house. For awhile she just enjoyed driving around the city and being out and about.

Summer had finally hit, the cloudy gray skies of May finally clearing to leave Los Angeles in a sunny, vibrant glow. She loved summer in LA, despite the mass influx of tourists taking, but it was part of the environment like the perpetual presence of smog. Stopping through a drive through to grab a cup of coffee and a pastry, Nia fiddled with the radio while in the line, tired of hearing the commercials. But she couldn't help but stop when she heard her name being talked about on one of the stations.

"Hashtag Horny Hostess, aka Nia Austin, is all people are talking about after watching *With This Ring* it seems, but honestly, can you blame her?"

"Girl I do not blame her at all. If you'd put me on an island with a shirtless Elijah James, you bet your ass I'm shooting my shot!"

"I'd do the same damn thing. If anything, Nia Austin represents women going after what they want, and I am always here for that."

"Do you think she was wrong for hiding their relationship ?"

"What else was she supposed to do? Honestly, love is love. We can't control who we like and when it happens. And I'm disappointed in the people who are tearing her down - it does take two to tango, if you know what I mean."

"Preach! Give the girl a break already. But what do the listeners think? Call in and tell, after this song."

A pop song faded in as Nia took in the radio personality's words. Maybe it wouldn't be as bad as she thought; it was good to see that at least some people were on her side in this whole thing.

Her day looking up a little more, Nia changed directions and finally began making her way over to her parent's place. While heading there, her phone rang.

"Remember how we were unsure how this whole Horny Hostess thing would affect your career?" Lexi asked as Nia pulled into her parent's driveway.

"Oh god, please tell me something good." Nia put her car in park and killed the engine, waiting for whatever bad news Lexi had to give her.

"It's better than good – everyone wants to talk to you! I've got requests for talk shows, magazine articles, not to mention more auditions than you can probably handle."

Nia could not believe what she was hearing. "Are you serious?"

"Very serious. This is the momentum we've been looking for! We need to take it and run."

So many emotions were running through Nia as she listened to Lexi detail everything that she had in the pipelines for Nia. It was all happening. She felt a sense of relief, to be sure, but she also couldn't help but wonder if it was worth it. It had been four months since they were on Hawaii, and she still missed him as if he'd just left. If that wasn't annoying, she didn't know what was. Despite him being a complete asshat…Nia still cared for him.

"Are you even listening Nia? There's so much to do!" Lexi's voice cut through the thoughts Nia was having.

"Yes, I am. I'm just processing it all." Shaking off her Elijah thoughts, Nia saw the front door opening, and her mom come out on the front, with a questioning look on her face as if to ask why in the world was she still sitting in the car. Nia waved, before continuing. "I've got to go though, I'm at my parents. But we'll definitely talk more about everything, ok?"

Hanging up, she got out her car, stretching after having sat for so long. Yolanda waited at the front door as Nia made her way over. "I was going to call the cops before I realized that it was my daughter sitting in my driveway."

Leaning in for a hug, Nia couldn't help but laugh. "You'd call the cops on another black person?"

"I didn't, that's all that matters," Yolanda said with a roll of her eyes.

"Is that Nia?" A loud thumping down the stairs announced the arrival of Yaya, who slid to a stop in front of Nia. It was hard to remember Yaya was only three years than Nia's twenty-nine, but Yaya had always had a youthful personality.

"No, it's the pizza delivery guy."

"Hey, I'd be just as happy to see Rob too." Leave it to Yaya to be on a first name basis with the delivery guy.

"Is the fame going to your head yet?" Yolanda asked, as they made their way into the kitchen.

"I wouldn't call this my version of fame, Mom. They're raking me over." Nia sighed, leaning on the counter.

"That's because the world is full of sheep, and you dared to be something other." Nigel announced, surprising Nia. He was flouring the counter, a ball of dough in a bowl beside him. Her dad always made the best pizza, though it wasn't something on the menu at his restaurants. "Come chop up these onions Nia."

The onions always made her cry, and he knew it. She washed her hands and got to work while Yaya prepped garlic bread ingredients. The chopping soothed her, even though her eyes were slowly beginning to water from the first dice, but Nia powered though it.

"You're on TMZ!" Yaya squealed, bringing her tablet over for the family to see. They already had up photos of Nia and Goldie leaving her apartment that morning, speculating on her destination. "My sister is famous."

"More like notorious." Nia kept up the steady chopping motion.

"I just hope that it dies down eventually so you can get back to normal." Yolanda sighed, spreading pats of butter on a fluffy loaf of Italian bread.

"There are a few good things about all of this 'fame'," Nia commented. "Apparently this is helping my social profile, to an extent. Everyone wants me to go on all these talk shows, and do interviews. My social media following has been increasing steadily too."

"Does that mean more work?" Yolanda asked, wiping her hands clean.

"Potentially - I've got my pilot to shoot in a few months, and Lexi says it's been a ton of requests for me to come audition for various parts."

"Doing the reality show turned out to be a good thing?"

"Despite all the headache, yeah, it did." A few months ago, Nia would not have admitted that. But now, it seemed like things could be picking up.

"So…does that mean you're kind of a success now?" Yaya asked slyly.

"Well…" Nia looked at her dad, unsure of his reaction. He'd be unusually kind today, but she wasn't sure how long that would last.

"About that." Nigel was layering sauce and cheese on the dough, but stopped to look at Nia. "I should have never doubted you. I've realized recently - "

"With my help." Yolanda interjected, pouring a glass of wine.

"Of course. I've realized that you are an adult, that your mother and I successfully raised, and that you know what you want your life to look like. And even though I would love for you to have chosen to come work with me, I know that whatever you choose, you're going to succeed, because that's the daughter we raised."

The onions had to be abnormally strong because Nia was tearing up more than usual. She looked at her dad, and saw the sincerity in his eyes. This was a whole new Nigel, and Nia was glad he finally understood. Smiling, Nia gave him a watery smile. "Thanks dad."

Yolanda patted Nia's hand as she passed behind her. "What your father didn't mention is that whenever you get invited to a red carpet, we want to be your plus twos."

"What about me?" Yaya asked, sneaking a slice of pepperoni.

"Get in line." Nigel chuckled, sliding the pizza into the oven. "We've got seniority."

"I hate to hear you talk about yourself like you're one foot in the grave, Daddio."
Yaya said, sneaking one last slice of pepperoni.

"What I want to know is when one of you are going to give me grandchildren? You're not getting any younger." Yolanda asked, swatting Yaya's hand away from the pepperoni.

"Ma, we'll get there when we get there. Well, I will. Nia, what's your excuse?"

"When the good lord sees fit is when you'll have grandkids mom." Nia smiled, setting Yolanda off on a tangent about how back in her day, she'd already had kids by their age. Her family moved around the kitchen, seamless and easily. It was good to know that she had them in her court, even when things seemed like they were down in the dumps. She'd always known her dad loved her, but this was even better – the undeniable knowledge that they supported her, even when things got tough. It felt like a weight had been lifted, and it would be easier to get through these next few weeks with her head held high.

"They want to do what with me?" Nia wasn't sure if she'd heard Lexi correctly. It had been a few weeks since the show had premiered, none of the excitement having faded yet. Actually, it was growing, as more and more people watched the show. Nia was back at Goldie's shop, helping her out behind the counter while she went to a doctor's appointment. It was unusually busy – word had gotten out about her working there occasionally - and now people were flocking in from everywhere to spy on her.

"A post show interview. They want you to come in with the other contestants and give your feedback on how life has been since the airing of the show."

One girl was trying to take a photo of Nia, barely trying to be discreet. "So, the people who sneakily went and showed some budding relationship between me and Elijah without telling us, want me to come and remark on what happened?" *Is Elijah going to be there?* Nia threw that thought out the window before it could take up more space in her brain.

"Basically. You'd be compensated; I negotiated a pretty penny if you do decide to take it up."

Unbelievable. Nia hadn't even gotten an explanation when she'd called them; Kerry hadn't known Warren was using that footage until it was too late to say anything. Warren didn't feel bad about it, saying she knew the risks when taking on a reality show. Nia had questioned their integrity as producers, which had put Warren off. Since then, she hadn't spoken with them, preferring to leave it alone and hope it would die off eventually.

"While I'd like to think I'm emotionally mature enough to handle that, I don't know right now Lex." And that was on being honest.

A middle-aged customer came up to Nia, holding a few stones in her hands. "Which one of these is good for my sex life?"

Nia pointed to two of the stones in her hand. "The rose quartz and the carnelian."

"What's that?" Lexi asked, confused.

"Sorry, this store is super busy today." Nia added, as another woman came up to the counter to ask for her autograph. "With a purchase, you can get an autograph." *Might as well help Goldie's business if they're going to be here.*

Lexie's voice huffed through the phone. "Got it. I know you're not particularly fond of this group of people at the moment -"

"That's putting it mildly."

"But this could be your chance to go and set the record straight. Let the world know that you're human, and don't deserve the way they portrayed you on the show."

Nia sighed, looking at the mass of people who were in Let's Chakra About It just to witness the Horny Hostess Home Wrecker. Her social media was still growing, but so was the amount of people who were leaving negative comments on her photos, casting judgement on everything about her based on that one show.

If she was being honest with herself, she would love the chance to set the record straight. But that meant she'd have to face Elijah again, and she didn't know if she was ready to face him, especially now that everyone knew their business.

Her thoughts were interrupted by a girl who looked barely out of college. "Do y'all sell Yoni Eggs?"

"No – those are actually really bad for you."

"Oh. Right." Nervous, she went back to browsing. Nia turned her attention back to Lexi, still on the phone. "Let me think about it, ok? When do I have to let you know by?"

"End of day. They want to shoot the interview on Thursday."

That was only in two days. Nia sighed, wondering what in the world she should do. "I'll let you know."

Hanging up, she sighed, leaning against the counter and watching people trying not to be obvious about watching her. This whole thing was ridiculous. In a way, she wanted her regular civilian life back, but that wasn't happening. But she wouldn't be so silly not to recognize that she'd been on more auditions in the last month than she'd thought possible. And she was booking them too. Now, she had guest appearances, commercials, small film roles lined up and it was thanks to the stupid show and one very stupid man.

Nia noticed when the tittering got even louder in the store, and wondered what was happening. Did she have something on her face? Looking around, she heard the bell above the door twinkle, and turned to see none other than Lily walking into the store with a few friends. *Just perfect.*

The people who were already trying to be subtle about taking pictures weren't even trying now, whipping out their phones and snapping away. Lily was dressed casually, in fitted jeans and the requisite California crop top now that it was full blown summer. Nia felt underwhelming in her shorts and blouse, but there was nothing she could do about it.

As Lily approached, Nia was unsure of what reaction to give. She wasn't actually mad at her - it wasn't her fault (exactly) that Elijah had to pick her (unless she'd asked her family to win? She really needed more details on all of this). But still, Nia had liked Lily during filming, who had been one of her few friends on the island. She hated now that media had portrayed them as mortal enemies, as it would have been nice to grow their friendship. But whenever Lily mentioned in the tabloids that

Nia wasn't all that bad, they just made Lily out to look like a saint, and Nia the lucky one to be forgiven. It was a lose-lose situation for her either way.

Lily too looked a little nervous, a small smile tentatively breaking on her face. "Long time no see."

"I've seen you on the news." *That sounded harsher than she'd wanted.* "But yeah, it's been a while. How've you been?"

They both knew that she'd been living the life with Elijah, parties, interviews, and the like. It was all over social media.

"It's been a whirlwind." Lily said, crossing then uncrossing her arms. "I wanted to ask - would you be willing to grab a cup of coffee? I feel like there's some catching up to do."

An olive branch. Nia wanted to say no, but was hyper aware of the crowd of people watching them.

"Uh, sure, I guess. I'm waiting for my friend to get back, but I could get something in an hour or so."

Lily's face brightened, and she let out a breath she'd been holding. "Great. I'll text you a spot, and just let me know when you're heading there."

"You have my number?" Nia frowned, wondering when she'd given it to her.

Lily looked bashful. "I may have taken it from Elijah."

Nia tried not to let the sound of his name affect her any more than it should. It was a normal name, held no meaning to her anymore. Right.

Lily's friend came up, holding a few stones and incense she wanted to buy. Nia rang them up, and watched as they left, wondering what Lily could want to say to her.

Nia wasn't sure how it had happened, but she was going to get coffee with the woman who was engaged to her not really an ex. *Is this what adulting felt like?* Nia dryly mused to herself.

Once Goldie finally came back, Nia ducked out the shop, relieved to be free of the counter and eyes watching her. That was such a strange feeling, to know there were eyes always on her. It was almost like…filming a reality television show. Nia laughed at her bad joke. Her phone buzzed with Lily's text, asking to meet her at a coffee shop in Venice. It had been a while since Nia had actually driven out to the beach. Maybe she'd grab some dinner there before heading back to Hollywood.

The traffic was surprisingly light, given that it was a Monday, and Nia cruised down the highway, enjoying the breeze coming through her open windows. It was a gorgeous LA day, the sun bright, the weather hot, and Nia couldn't wait to set eyes on the water. There was something about the ocean that always calmed her, and she couldn't wait to sink her toes in the sand. It was a pain finding parking, but Nia finally found a street meter, shelling out a few coins to fill it up.

She made her way to a little shop called Menotti's, running into Lily who was waiting by the door. "Thanks for coming." Lily smiled, opening the door to let

Nia in ahead of her.

"No problem. Was there something you wanted to talk about?" The sooner they talked about whatever Lily wanted, the sooner she could get away.

"Yes, do you want to grab coffee first? I figure we could take it and walk along the beach?"

Seeing no fault with that plan, they ordered their coffee - an Americano for Lily and an iced Mocha for Nia. Once they had their drinks, they set off for the beach, dodging tourists and bicyclists alike.

Taking a sip, Nia fell in love with her coffee right away. "Oh my god, this is the best mocha I've had. Ever."

Lily smiled. "I love it. I haven't had one bad cup of coffee there. It's all amazing."

"I wish I didn't live in East Hollywood, I'd be there all the time."

"There is a Hollywood location, if I'm not wrong."

"Stop it. I'm there." Nia took another sip. "What's up?"

Lily took a sip of her coffee, looking for the words. "I hate the way it all ended. The show, I mean. Like, I knew that they wanted me to do well, but I wasn't going in expecting to win the competition, you know what I mean?" She looked at Nia, earnest.

And for whatever reason, Nia knew she was being real. "I get that. If it helps, you're one of the few who could have actually won. Those women weren't exactly the cream of the crop."

"Ugh, that Danielle still tries to talk to me as if we're best friends." Lily rolled her eyes. "But anyway, I'd had a sort of idea that maybe you and Elijah had a thing going on? Like, I'd see him talking to you, and think he never looked at any of us contestants like that."

Nia hadn't realized that. She wondered if anyone else had noticed. "Like what?"

"Like you were his world."

There was a pause, just the sound of the sand crunching underneath their feet as Nia thought about that. Had it really been that obvious?

"And then it just always seemed as if you two were always together, for it to be a dating show. Some of the girls just thought you were just good friends, but maybe the romantic in me saw something more."

Nia didn't have anything to add to that, so she just took another sip of her coffee.

"And when we were back in LA, I knew we were supposed to be falling in love, we each had a part to play, but when he disappeared after announcing me as the winner, it wasn't like I was convinced that he actually loved me, you know?" Lily took a sip of her coffee, figuring out her next words. Nia was focused, wanting to know what happened. "And when we ran into you at the Virgil, when he saw you, it all clicked."

"What clicked?" Nia asked, somewhat breathless.

"That he loves you. Still does." Lily paused looking out at the ocean, before adding. "Elijah only picked me because he'd found out that Warren had video of you two together."

"What do you mean?" Nia frowned.

"Warren told Elijah that if he picked me like they'd wanted, they wouldn't use the footage of you two together. He didn't want them to mess up your reputation. It didn't matter though, Warren still used it anyway as a ratings boost, and Elijah lost out on you."

They stopped on the beach, watching the waves crash on the shore. Nia couldn't believe what she was hearing. Elijah had done it to protect her? She wondered why he hadn't said anything, and just let her think the worst of him?

"I haven't talked to him since we finished filming." But she thought of the flowers he'd send her every other week, the phone calls and texts she'd left unanswered. And felt like an ass for not even hearing him out.

"It's been eating him alive. He's stuck in this stupid contract that has us together for the next few months, but I can tell all Elijah thinks about you."

Nia was blown away. She'd figured Elijah had moved on, especially since anytime she saw him in the media, he'd looked mostly happy with Lily. He had to be an even better actor than she realized if he was miserable.

"I don't know what happened between the two of you, but I wanted to let you know that for him, he's still thinking of you. And as soon as we figure out a way out of this contract, he'll come straight back to you."

"Thank you for telling me this." Nia ran a hand through her hair, feeling like her world had tipped over. "I know you didn't have to."

"I just wanted you to know that even though he's been with me, technically, he hasn't been 'with me' at all. And that I really hope you come to do the reunion filming. I want you to be able to voice your side of things."

"I don't know if I want to put myself out there like that for the show to twist my words and actions again." But more than that, Nia wanted to see Elijah again, and really listen to him this time.

"Understandable. But you do deserve the closure either way."

It was a lot to take in, and it boiled down to one thing in Nia's mind - he had picked her first. She knew it in her heart that he'd sacrificed his own personal happiness to make sure she wasn't hurt in the crossfire. Sure, it had all blown up anyway, but Nia knew that he was trying to protect her. And that meant so much to her. "Maybe…maybe it'll be good to get in and share my side. Stop hiding."

"Yes. I love it." Lily smiled as they started making their way back towards the boardwalk.

Bumping Lily's shoulder gently, Nia smiled at her. "You know, you are pretty awesome for going out your way to tell me this."

"Of course I did. That's what friends are for. At least, I hope we can call ourselves friends?" Lily smiled hopefully at Nia.

Nia grinned. "Definitely friends." It was not the conversation Nia had been expecting, but she was glad she met with Lily. Her stomach felt like it was filled with butterflies, thinking about the fact that Elijah had still be thinking of her, all these months later. She couldn't wait to see him. Nia had a phone call to make.

The Reunion

ELIJAH

He'd made it. It had been two days since he'd learned that Nia was going to do the reunion episode. Two days for him to figure out what he was going to say when he finally saw her. Two days for him to freak out if she'd even talk to him. Elijah knew what he had to do, what he should have done to start with.

Elijah would give it all up, if it meant being with Nia. The last few months without her had been the longest days of his life. He'd barely been a functioning human being. Elijah showed up, turned on the charm, then went home and wallowed, wishing Nia was there with him. Rebecca had had enough of the wallowing. She'd called him when he'd missed their Sunday dinner, and chewed him out for not doing the right thing in the first place. "You screwed up - now it's time to fix it. Time to put on your big boy pants and make a decision and stop acting like you have no damn sense. And then give me some grand babies."

She had been right, of course. Not about the kids, but how it was time to fix things. Elijah had to figure out how to fix it. And he'd finally figured it out. Well, almost.

His friends tried to get him to come out the night before the reunion episode taping, but Elijah brushed them all off. He didn't want to speak with anyone, not until he had a solid plan to win Nia back. Elijah was going through his speech one more time when a relentless pounding started up on his door. That could only be one person.

Carter, his most annoying friend, stood outside holding a case of beer and a bag of what smelled like tacos. He grinned, pushing his way in past Elijah and making himself comfortable on his couch.

"Sure, come on in, make yourself at home." Elijah closed the door, rubbing his temple. "Every time you bang on my door, Ms. Castello calls the office with a complaint."

Carter shrugged, pulling tacos and chips from the bag. "I brought food, you can't kick me out."

Elijah's stomach rumbled. "I'll kick you out after I eat." He flopped down on the couch, grabbing a carnitas tacos and downing it in two bites.

"So are you completely whipped now?" Carter asked around the mass of food in his mouth.

Elijah shrugged "I don't know what you're talking about."

"Whipped." Carter dug into the guacamole. "What are you going to say to her?"

"Haven't figured that out yet." Elijah had tossed so many ideas around it was laughable.

Carter cracked open a beer, taking a swig. "You should have never asked her to wait." Then ducked as Elijah threw a pillow at his face.

"You told me to ask her that!" Elijah threw another pillow for good measure.

"I was just saying shit! I didn't think you'd actually do something as dumb as that."

Groaning, Elijah let his head drop in his hands. He didn't want to mess this up. Carter slid a beer down the table to him. "Look man, if I know one thing, just be honest with her. It doesn't have to be some pretty, Hollywood line. Just tell her how you feel."

"And that's supposed to work?" Elijah asked, twisting the can in his hands.

"If it's meant to be, it will." Carter dug around the bag for another taco.

Elijah knew that Carter might be right. He'd just go in there, tell Nia that he loved her and pray for the best. Because he knew he loved that woman, and would do whatever it took to get her back.

The next day, Elijah hummed with tension. He was more tightly wound than he'd ever been before - he'd finally get to see Nia today. Currently he was camped out in a green room, waiting for filming to start. He paced back and forth, before heading out of the room. He wanted to see if Nia as there yet. As he searched the stage, he saw a few familiar faces; Alex, the camera operator was back, as well as Maddison, their PA in Hawaii. "Hey man! The show's a hit!" Alex said, slapping Elijah on the back as he drew him into a hug. "How've you been?"

As much as Elijah wanted to find Nia, he didn't want to be rude either. "I've been alright, just working, getting shit done."

They made a few more minutes of banal conversation before Alex was called away to help rig his camera up. Elijah kept up his search for Nia, looking around as casually as possible. Maybe she'd changed her mind? But even if she didn't show up, what he had to say today would change everything. He just knew that he couldn't keep this up much longer, damn whatever else anyone wanted him to say or do. He was done making decisions that kept him away from the woman he saw his future with.

Elijah was checking another room when Maddison found him, asking him to head to set since filming would start soon. Sighing, he followed her back toward the stage where crew was bustling around. Quickly, hair and makeup checked him out for last looks, which he tolerated for a few minutes before shooing them away. He took up a place in the corner, watching as Lily came in with a group of women from the island, smiling and catching up like old friends. If he was doing his job right, he'd be over there with her, making nice and acting like they had a good relationship. But he was done with that. His eyes were still scanning the room for Nia.

"I've been looking for you." His heart jumped, before he realized it wasn't Nia's warm voice speaking to him, but Kerry's. Turning fully to her, he took her in with Isaac right beside her. She was as put together as ever, but there was an air of nervousness surrounding her.

"Hi Kerry."

"Hey. We just had a few things we wanted to say before we started filming."

"We?" Elijah looked around, to see Warren coming towards them. "Oh. Fun."

He hadn't spoken to Warren since he'd ripped him a new one a month ago. Warren was also sporting an apologetic look on his face, something Elijah had rarely seen.

"Elijah, I am sorry your story was manipulated the way it was. It seemed like a good idea at the time, something that could take the show to the next level," Warren said, looking truly remorseful.

Kerry shot a look at Warren before adding, "The idea wasn't the best one, and we should have built the show around the initial story we'd set. I should have been better about giving you and Nia a heads up." Kerry grimaced, rubbing a hand on the back of her neck.

Elijah sighed. He was mad at them, but they were good people. And sometimes good people got caught up doing things they weren't necessarily proud of. "I guess I can say I get it? But I don't like being blindsided, or being told I have to choose a job over a political necessity."

"You're right, we should have never held that over you." Isaac added. "I just hope you can find it in your heart to forgive us."

"As long as you know that I'm done holding up this end of the farce." Elijah said, looking the three of them over. "I might have lost out on the best thing that's happened to me, and I'm not going to keep stringing Lily along. Understood?"

Kerry and Warren looked over at each other before back at Elijah.

Kerry smiled at him, squeezing his hand. "You do what you need to, we'll support you however we can."

Debating, Elijah looked Warren up and down, determining if he was being sincere. The man certainly looked it, and Elijah barely had it in him to be the bigger man. He clasped Warren's hand in his own, signaling their truce.

"Thank you." It wasn't perfect - and seemed too little to late, especially since the damage was done. But Elijah also didn't like holding onto unnecessary grudges. As long as he had the opportunity to break free and do what he needed to have Nia back in his life, that was enough for him.

"Can we go film an episode now?" Warren asked, breaking away, but the huge smile remaining on his face.

"Yes please. It smells like old moths in here." Kerry's nose wrinkled, as she led Elijah over to the stage. Now if he could only get the girl. But filming was about to start, and he still didn't have eyes on her. Elijah held out hope still; his gut had the feeling that Nia would be here.

NIA

Nia was a nervous wreck. She finally pulled into the lot after being stuck in horrific traffic, as trying to get to the studio in Playa del Rey from Burbank, where she'd come from yet another audition, was a mess. She'd dressed in a pink two piece jumpsuit hoping the bright color would give hearth pop of confidence she needed to get through today. After her talk with Lily, Nia hadn't been able to focus on much as she called Lexi to let her know she'd do the show. Knowing that he had been pining away for her despite their months apart did funny things to her stomach. And she'd finally realized what she'd been trying to hide for so long - that she was still in love with Elijah, and wanted him back in whatever way she could get.

Spying the yellow sign for their production, Nia made her way into the correct building, where Maddison found her and showed her to hair and makeup. "I'm sorry I'm late. Has filming started yet?" Nia asked as the makeup artist draped a cape around her.

"Just about. We'll get you hair and makeup ready, and then fold you in after."

With a smile, Maddison left Nia to her hair and makeup team, who bustled around making small adjustments to what Nia came in with here and there. It was over before she knew it, and they sent her on her way. But she ended up having to wait to go inside the stage since filming had started, which only gave her more time to really wonder what the hell was she doing here. Just as she was seriously considering leaving, she heard someone come up behind her, and turned to see Kerry, who had a small smile on her face.

"Nia, I'm so glad you could make it."

"There's still time for me to run," Nia was only half joking.

"Can I at least get out an apology first?" When Nia slowly nodded, Kerry continued. "I am so sorry that we didn't tell you everything, especially when you confided in me that you and Elijah had history. And then when that footage made it into the final cut, I should have given you a heads up so you wouldn't have been completely blindsided."

Nia was surprised. She hadn't been expecting an apology from Kerry. "A heads up would have been nice," She said wryly.

"I - we - just got so caught up on making a hit show that everyone was up for fair game, and did something we're not proud of. I hope we can start over."

The red light turned off, and a buzzer sounded, letting them know they could head inside. Nia turned Kerry's words over, thinking on it. "I should be more mad at you all. But I'm trying this thing where I'm more vocal and set my expectations. So, yes, we can start over. But if this interview is twisted in any way – "

Kerry shook her head, adamant. "This interview is our way of letting you all get the truth out there. We won't mess it up."

"Well then, let's shoot this thing." They shared a smile before heading into the stage.

Letting their eyes adjust to the darkness around them, Kerry showed Nia around to the side of the set, stepping over cables and waving to crew as cameras adjust slightly before gearing to roll again. Nia could see the cast on stage, the ladies from the island seated between a few couches on the ground and chairs on risers behind them. Straining to see around crew and equipment, Nia finally saw her first glance of Elijah, who was seated in the middle of a large couch, with Lily next to him. A new host was seated on another couch, with Danielle and April next to her.

Elijah was as gorgeous as ever, in a button down black top and jeans, his skin glowing in the camera lights. He hadn't seen Nia yet, and she was able to simply look at him, hoping that by the end of this, they'd both have what they wanted. Somewhere in the distance, a voice called for quiet on set, and they started rolling again.

ELIJAH

They'd already started filming and Elijah still hadn't seen Nia. He tried not to get antsy, having to consciously remember to not tap his leg while on camera. *What if she changed her mind?* An icy wave washed over Elijah. He would not like that. What he had to say, he would rather say to her, but maybe that wasn't in his cards.

Before he got too lost in his thoughts, they were yelling rolling and the cameras were back on his every move. Victoria, their hostess for the evening, was the sort of woman who always seemed to have a smile on her face. Young and feisty, she had the sort of focus that made Elijah feel a little too seen, like she was tracking his every move.

She'd introduced herself to him before they'd started filming, letting him know that she was Team Nia all the way. It was something that had been happening for some time now, random people coming up and letting him know whether they were Team Nia or Team Lily. Not that he cared what random people thought, but it was fascinating to see how people were divided.

Victoria smiled for the cameras, big and white, before turning and addressing the group. "We've seen the drama, we've seen the fights, and we've seen the love on season one of *With This Ring*. Now, let's hear from the contestants themselves. How's everyone doing?"

The women responded with varying degrees of excitement. Nicole broke over the rest of the voices, determined to be heard. "You know Victoria, things have been fantastic since the show aired. It was so hard keeping everything a secret."

"Tell me about it." Roxy laughed. "But it was so worth it all."

Tiffany jumped into the mix. "I know! My social media grew like crazy. I get paid to endorse diet teas now!"

"Are those actually good for you?" Camille and Sam shared a look with each other. They looked even more like twins than usual, now that their hair was about the same length. Elijah had to do a double take to make sure he got their names right.

Victoria reigned everyone back in. "Can you all believe it's been three months since your time on the island? Tell me, what was it like living on a resort for a few months?"

Beside her, Danielle spoke, taking attention to her. "It was amazing, one of the best times I can say I've had filming."

"I'd have to agree with Danielle," Sam added. "It was so much fun to have a little slice of island life, and I'd love to go back some day."

April added, "But like, we couldn't have our phones. No internet, no magazines - it was like focus on falling in love. I don't know about y'all, but focus ain't exactly April's strong suit."

"We know." Danielle added, rolling her eyes. She and Nicole giggled together. Elijah was glad he'd dodged those bullets. He didn't know what he'd do if he'd had to pick one of them to win.

Victoria had picked up on Danielle and Nicole's chatter, and zeroed in. "Now, there was a little tension between some of you ladies on the island." Victoria said, with a pointed look at Danielle and Nicole. "Was that for the cameras or were some of the girls actually bitches in real life?"

Sam laughed, shaking her blonde head. "There was some tension for sure. You put thirteen women together and told them to fight over a man. Of course there's going be drama."

"But some girls took it farther than they should have." Cristal threw a look at Danielle and Nicole. "I know we were competing against each other, but that didn't mean we couldn't be kind to each other."

"I don't know what everyone keeps looking at us when they talk about drama." Danielle rolled her eyes. Elijah had a vague wish that they'd get stuck like that.

"Because you were one of the nastiest girls on the island!" Camille stopped beating around the bush.

"Don't blame me because you can't handle a real woman."

"Let's see how real you are after I yank those fake blonde clip-ins out your head." Elijah shook his head as the girls argued. He was never doing a reality show again.

NIA

While the girls argued and called each other out on their level of bitchiness and Victoria did her best to mediate (and stoke it a little, she noticed), Nia just got more and more restless. Her hands were cold, almost shaking. She wanted to get out there and get it over with. It was weird, she didn't normally get stage fright anymore more, but she was definitely nervous today. She still didn't think this was a good idea, but she was stuck here now.

Beside her Kerry watched the group, occasionally sharing quiet whispers with Warren and a few others, who were watching the drama unfold. Just as Nia was getting ready to ask for the third time when she was going on, she heard Victoria bring up her name.

"Now, let's talk about the curve ball that is Nia Austin. Did anyone expect to see that in the series?"

The women shared looks with each other. Cristal spoke up, nibbling on her lip. "I can't say that I knew anything about the two of them, but can you blame her? It was the perfect romantic setting. And she always seemed like the type to go get what she wants."

Camille nodded. "I hate that her character was so twisted on the show. Nia was like, seriously the best and it was always great to have her around."

Touched, Nia listened as the ladies continued to stand up for her. "But like, if she wanted to have a shot at Elijah, why not just audition to be on the show? It just made it harder for the rest of us." This came from none other than Danielle, who was of course, less than thrilled with Nia taking away attention from her.

"You can't help who you have feelings for. I'm just glad she wasn't scared to go for it." This came from April, who had a dreamy look on her face. "Sorry Lily, I know Elijah picked you but Nia is something of a personal hero of mine."

Lily smiled, shaking her head. "It's fine! I absolutely love Nia. I just wish I'd known about how she'd felt sooner."

Victoria pounced on this. "And why is that, Lily?"

"Because I wouldn't have gotten in her way."

There was a pronounced silence, as this statement was digested. Nia watched as Elijah's head whipped to Lily, a questioning look in his eyes. His voice came out hoarse. "I'm sorry, what?"

The look on Lily's face was earnest. "I wouldn't have. From what I saw, she and Elijah have this connection that I felt, even before I knew that they were together."

"Is that something you'd like to tell Nia?" Victoria asked, leaning forward in her seat. Nia got a tap on her shoulder, from Kerry who was motioning for her to take her cue. Her stomach dropped. She couldn't do this.

On stage, Lily was nodding vigorously. "I would love the chance to tell her that."

"And what about you Elijah? Can you tell us your side of things with Nia?"

Elijah nodded, leaning forward. "What a lot of people don't know is that Nia and I were together back in college. I wasn't the best to her then if I'm being honest, but I never forgotten about her. She was the standard that I compared every other woman to after that."

"College? Wow, so you've known each other for a long time."

"Exactly. And when I saw her again during casting, I knew that I wanted another chance. I just didn't know how that would happen, considering I was literally about to do a dating show."

"Do you mean you didn't start out with the intent to make your feelings known?"

A somewhat sheepish laugh escaped Elijah. "I can't say that. I just knew I wanted any way to be with her."

In the wings of the set, Nia felt a smile break through. There were warm, fuzzy things happening in her stomach, her eyes locked on Elijah.

Victoria turned a megawatt smile at the camera."Wow, this is all really romantic. Do you have any brother? No? Well luckily, we have Nia in the building - let's bring her out so you can tell her yourself!"

With a prod, Nia started her walk out, the bright lights blinding for a moment, a brief pocket of silence as she made her way towards him. Elijah's eyes locked with hers, and she couldn't help the smile that came across her lips. Surprisingly, she felt calmer, looking at him, making her way to the couches, where Lily and April stood, excited to see her. Nia was wrapped in a huge hug from April, who could barely contain herself. "Nia! I had no idea you were coming! Girl, you look divine!"

"Let her breathe! There are others who want to say hello," Lily had a sly look on her face, watching Elijah who had stood to greet her.

"Nia…" she watched as his throat worked, his eyes traveling up and down her form as he took in his first good look in a while.

"Woo, is it hot in here or is it just me?" Roxy fanned herself, dissolving into giggles with Camille and Samantha.

"Sit next to me." Lily pulled Nia down to the couch, deftly placing her next to Elijah, was still standing. He was like a deer in headlights, and Nia had to hold back her laugh.

Victoria looked up at him, amusement on her face. "Elijah, it is safe to sit down." He sat down, his thigh brushing Nia's, making her extra aware of the muscles that lay underneath his smooth pant legs.

"This is great," Victoria wiggled in her own seat. "Elijah, Lily, is this the first time you've seen Nia since the island?"

Elijah cleared his throat, managing to look at Victoria and not Nia. For two point five seconds. "Yes, well, we ran into each other once, but didn't get to speak."

"I saw Nia a few days ago, at her friend's shop in Hollywood." Lily smiled as if she and Nia were old buddies.

"How did you feel, Nia, after the show premiered and you saw that your secret relationship with Elijah was revealed for the world to see?"

Nia straightened her shoulders, putting on a brave face. "Honestly, I was shocked. I hadn't known any of that was being recorded, or that they had planned on using it in the actual series. It wasn't what I signed up for."

Victoria nodded, focused on her. "I can imagine anyone would have felt betrayed. How has life been since then?"

"Bumpy for a while," Nia thought of all the comments, looks, gossip she'd dealt with since the show aired. "I was called a home wrecker, the side chick, baby momma - I think twitter used the hashtag Horny Hostess? That was fun."

"Speaking of the wedding, Lily, care to tell us when is that happening? If it's happening…? I hear the date hasn't been set yet." Victoria went in for the meat of it.

Nia saw Elijah open his mouth to speak, but Lily cut him off. "I haven't spoken about this with Elijah, but it ties into what I wanted to tell Nia." Lily turned, facing Nia and laying a hand over hers. "I'm calling it off."

In the background, Nia could hear small exclamations from the women, but it took her a moment to really understand what Lily was saying. There wouldn't be a wedding. Nia's eyes cut to Elijah, wondering about his big project that was tied with his relationship with Lily.

Elijah tried to cut in but Lily kept going. "Elijah has been wonderful, but it doesn't sit right with me that I'm keeping two people from each other."

"Lily, you don't have to do this." Elijah face registered his surprise that she was calling it off. Nia felt her eyebrows raise. It seemed as if he hadn't known that Lily was going to make this particular announcement.

"I do though. I want you two to have a chance with each other. So, make it work," Lily playfully knocked Nia's shoulder.

"Just to make sure I am hearing this astounding news correctly - Lily, you are calling off the wedding?"

"Correct." Lily nodded once, firm in her choice.

Victoria looked like a kid in candy shop, a litany of questions on her face and an eagerness in deciding which to pick first. "What an astounding change of events! Elijah, how do you feel about this?"

Looking up at Elijah, Nia met his eyes, seeing a warmth in those green orbs. She smiled, spurring him into action. "Well, a little relieved honestly. No offense to Lily who is an amazing woman, but with Nia there always been something there, that I want to see grow into something more. I want to make things right with her, if she'll give me the chance." Beside her, Nia felt Elijah take her hand, lacing their fingers together.

"If she doesn't want him, can I have him?" April sighed, helping the tension break on the set. Nia laughed at that, as she searched his eyes, and saw a wealth of emotions running through them - hope, sincerity, a little bit of fear? And she knew what her answer would be.

Victoria's words broke through their connection. "Nia, this is a lot to take in, but what are you feeling right now?"

Whatever Nia had expected this dialogue to be coming into this interview, it wasn't this. Her hand came to her face, double checking that her jaw wasn't hanging down. "Um, wow. Definitely surprised. It's a lot to take in."

"You weren't expecting any of this today, were you?"

"Not entirely. I always knew going into this that Elijah would have to pick someone to win the show, and it couldn't be me. But it was hard to stay away, believe me, I tried to fight it. But now…" Nia became extremely aware of many sets of eyes on her, and tried to carefully choose her words.

"Now what?" Victoria was holding her breath.

"Now, I want to see if we have a chance. If we can make things work." Nia looked up to see Elijah gazing down at her, a huge smile on his face. He lifted their hands, bringing them up to place a kiss on her knuckles.

Elijah leaned over, pressing a kiss to her temple. His voice low, just for the two of them, he whispered in her ear, "You have no idea how much I want that."

Victoria sighed, smiling at the two of them. This was going to be a great reunion episode. "I haven't seen it all, ladies and gentlemen, but this is simply touching. A wedding cancelled, lovers reunited. Season one of *With This Ring* has been a whirlwind, and I can't wait to see what happens next."

    Nia couldn't agree more.

The Reconciliation

ELIJAH

Once filming was finally over, all Elijah wanted to do was sneak away with Nia so he could have a heart to heart with her. But everyone wanted to talk to them after they'd wrapped, sharing well wishes and encouragements. As a compromise, Elijah didn't let go of Nia's hand. He just had her back, and wasn't ready to let her go. And from what he could tell, Nia felt the same. Most of the girls swore to use their new social media fame in support of Elijah and Nia. Lily had found the two of them, pulling them to the side while Nia was getting her microphone taken off. "Sorry I kind of stole your thunder out there. I just didn't want you to take the brunt of it."

"The brunt of what?" Elijah was curious, though his eyes were mostly on Nia.

"I overheard you and Warren talking about how your next job was tied to you having to pick me as the winner. I hated that my uncle did that, and maybe sort of ripped him a new one and made it clear that he was still giving you the job no matter what."

Elijah didn't know Lily had it in her, but had a newfound respect for her. "Wow, thank you. I really appreciate it."

Lily laughed, and shooed the two of them away. "Go ahead and skip out of here. I promise to keep everyone else at bay."

Nia wrapped Lily in a hug, before she disappeared down the hallway with Elijah.

Outside, the sun was starting to set, a cool breeze drifting across the air that was a nice reprieve from the day's heat. They drifted over to her car, hands still linked together.

"Where's your car?" Nia wondered as she found her keys, losing her hold on Elijah for the moment.

Elijah shrugged, sheepishly rubbing a hand through his hair. "I didn't drive today."

Laughing, Nia shook her head. "Just like your car really wasn't in the shop when I interviewed for all of this?"

Elijah's hands ran down her arms, until his hands met hers. "I just didn't want you to slip away again."

"I wasn't going far." The soft admission filled the air between them. Elijah drew her into a hug, wrapping his arms around her. This was what he'd been missing. Nia fit like the missing puzzle piece, and it felt like he could finally take a breath of fresh air now that he was back.

"I missed you. So damn much." His lips pressed a gentle kiss on her forehead, his arms tightening around her. "Can we talk? About everything?"

She nodded yes. "I'd love that."

A burst of laughter came from behind them, and they turned to see a few crew members filing out of the building.

"We should go somewhere quieter." Nia breathed, but made no move to release her arms from around him.

"My place is close."

"Let's go there."

They drove in relative silence, Elijah holding Nia's free hand, his thumb making smooth strokes over her skin. So much needed to be said, but for the moment, they simply enjoyed being back in one another's company.

Nia

Once Nia parked, Elijah led her up to his apartment. Opening the door, he let her precede him inside, before following her in and shutting the door behind him. Suddenly unsure of what to do with herself, Nia perched on the arm of his couch, watching him flip on lights as he came to her.

"Can I say how I royally screwed up?" Elijah knelt before her like some knight in a movie, which caused an unladylike snort from her.

"What are you doing? Get up here." He reluctantly stood as she pulled him back up to his feet.

"I was making a grand gesture. I thought you'd like it, since Lily kind of stole my thunder on the show." His hands traced patterns on her thighs, causing Nia to shiver a little.

"She did, didn't she?" Nia smiled at that. "Are you glad you can keep the job?"

He shrugged, unbothered by it at this point. "I can, but that is literally the least of my concerns right now." Elijah took a step closer, breaking into her personal space. "I just wanted to be with you." He suddenly turned, sitting on the couch and pulling her down with him. Nia giggled as he settled her on his lap. This was comfortable, the two of them together. Nia had a flash of their future, of them sitting together on couches, as the world changed around them. That was what she wanted - a future with Elijah. And now, thanks to some amazing people and a turn of events, she just might have that.

"Nia, I am so, so sorry for fucking up. I won't ever let a job come between us again. These last few months without you have been miserable."

"Lily may have mentioned that to me." Nia smiled, thinking how hard Lily had worked to make sure she and Elijah were together.

"Remind me to get her something nice from us." He wrapped his arms around Nia, holding her close.

She murmured, feelings heart beat in his chest."I like the way that sounds."

"What's that?" Elijah asked.

"Us. It has a nice ring to it." Nia smiled up at him. "You know, we both made mistakes Eli. I pushed you too hard; honestly, I was scared of repeating the same mistakes I did back in college, and was punishing you for it. I had some growing to do myself." She laced her fingers with his, loving the way his hands felt connected to hers.

"I should have never gone against what we discussed. You deserved better than that."

"Let's promise to be better to each other in the future."

They sat together on his couch, looking down at their linked hands in the moonlight and appreciated being together now.

Nia looked up, watching the light from outside play against his strong features. "Tell me what you want, Eli."

"I want to work this out between us." Elijah whispered, looking straight into Nia's eyes. "I want us to be together. When we were apart for so long, it felt like I was missing my hand or something."

"I know," she whispered back to him. "That time apart made me realize something, Eli." His hands drew up her thighs, leaving little trails of fire behind.

"What's that?" He was close, his breath warm on her ear as he trailed little kiss along her face. One on her forehead, one on her cheek, another on her nose.

"That I love you. Is it too early to say that right? Never mind, because I'm not taking it back and you'll just have to deal with it."

She laughed at the expression on his face before he was kissing her. His lips came down over hers, kissing her with a passion that hadn't be let out in far too long. Strong hands came up to cup her face, gently holding her as if she were the most precious thing in the world to him. Nia's hands drifted, sliding around his neck to pull him closer. She felt the gaps between them closing, scars mending, and couldn't help the smile that kept breaking through.

Elijah broke the kiss, his voice rough. "I won't let you. I love you too much to let you go again. It would break me."

"You're stuck with me." Nia's breath hitched as he hitched one leg over his hip, bringing them closer together, allowing her to feel what she did to him.

"Perfect."

Elijah kissed her again, deeper this time, pouring everything he felt into it. Nia gave back as good as she got, running a hand underneath his shirt with the need to feel his warm skin on hers. "I need to get you to my bedroom."

"Yes, you do," Nia managed to say between kisses.

They stumbled back to his room, shedding layers of clothes together until they tumbled into his bed, warm smooth bodies pressed together. His hands glided up her sides, causing a little giggle to escape. "I missed this." Nia hooked her legs around him, drawing him directly to where she needed him. He looked into her eyes, as he positioned himself at her entrance. "I love you so much."

Nia let out a moan as he pushed himself in, sliding into her easily. As he moved, she gasped, feeling the way their bodies perfectly fit together. "Say it again." She pulled him in for a kiss before he could, and he laughed, before he rotated his hips, making her moan.

"I love you, Nia Martine Austin." He dropped another kiss on her lips.

"Elijah, you are the love of my life."

Later when they were spent, Elijah holding her close as they drifted to sleep, Nia's last waking thought was how lucky she felt to be given another chance with the love of her life.

Nia woke sometime in the middle of the night, feeling Elijah leaving the bed. Sleepily, she tried to stop him, reaching out for him as he turned, dropping a kiss on her forehead. "I'm coming right back."

She fought back sleep as she waited for him to return, wanting his heat back next to her. Elijah came back in the room, holding something in the palm of his hand. She couldn't see exactly what it was, but he slid underneath the sheets, bringing his warmth back with him.

"I have something for you." He pressed something smooth into her hand.

"What's this?" Holding it up to the moonlight, Nia saw he'd pressed a wishing stone, set into a necklace, into her hand. Surprised she looked up at Elijah, who was smiling ruefully down at her. "Your wishing stone?"

"You'd told us that we had to give it away in order for our wish to work. But you are the only person I can give this to in order for my wish to work."

Nia could barely breathe. She couldn't believe he had kept it this long. A lone tear made its way down her cheek.

"Can I ask what your wish was?"

"I wished for a partner, a lover, my heart's desire. And I know who I want to trust this with." His hand covered hers, taking the stone from her hand and clasping the necklace around her neck where it settled right below the hollow in her throat. It caught the moonlight, picking up small sparkles that made it look like it had its own inner glow.

"That is the sweetest thing anyone has ever done for me." Happy tears began falling, and Elijah was quick to hold her close, dropping kisses and words of love along her face.

Nia's heart was full. She literally did not know how she would keep all of this joy inside. To be able to be with the man that had occupied her thoughts and dreams for so long was now officially hers.

Elijah pressed another kiss to her lips, drawing her back down to the sheets and into his arms. "Can I take a picture of us?"

Nia nodded, and he reached over for his phone on the nightstand. He drew Nia right up to him, and they smiled, taking one perfect picture.

That picture would later gather so many likes and comments, becoming one of the most liked photos on Instagram. Romantics would swoon over the simple caption under the photo, which just said, "Mine."

The Happily Ever After

ONE YEAR LATER

"You may now kiss the bride."

Nia watched from her place a few steps behind Kerry as Isaac bent down to kiss her smack on the lips. The small crowd cheered, Nia joining in, happy to see the two of them finally sealing the deal. They were back on Oahu, but this time for Kerry and Isaac's beach wedding getaway. She'd managed to patch things up with both of them, and had formed a solid friendship. When Kerry had asked if Nia would stand up with her as one of her bridesmaids, Nia had immediately agreed.

Now, she watched as Isaac deepened the kiss, before they broke away, both blissfully happy. They couldn't have asked for a more perfect day to hold a beach wedding, the warm air not scorching, an easy breeze ticking hemlines and providing some relief.

Nia couldn't help but feel…satisfied. It seemed as if so much had changed since the last time they were on the island. As they began their small processional back up the beach and to the reception, Nia beamed when she saw her gorgeous hunk of man. Across from her, Elijah had his arm out ready to escort her back up to an open-air area where the reception would be held, close to the resort they were staying at.

He was unfairly handsome in his crisp, white shirt, open at the neck, with tan pants held up by a pair of suspenders. Nia had never truly appreciated suspenders until she'd seen them on Elijah, and she had plans for them that evening.

Her arm slid into his, and he ducked down, pressing a soft kiss to her lips. "They already did the kiss, you know," she smiled up at him.

"I didn't get to kiss you." His hand laced with hers, keeping them close together.

"Come on you two lovebirds! Time for pictures!" Kerry yelled back at them, eliciting laughs from the crowd and bridal party.

Once they'd been positioned and staged in countless ways, they finally made their way back to the reception area, where Kerry and Isaac were announced as the new Mr. and Mrs. just as the sun was beginning to set, it's fiery rays casting everything in a beautiful glow. They ate, danced, celebrated well into the night, raising toasts one after the other to the success and happiness of the new couple.

Kerry came up, throwing her arms around Nia in a huge hug. "Have I mentioned how you are just an amazing human being? Thank you so much for standing up with me today!"

Nia laughed, returning her hug. "I'm just so happy for you two! The ultimate power couple."

"That goes to you and Elijah! Didn't you two just make some big shot all-time list?" Nia laughed, remembering that she and Elijah had in fact been voted Fashion Magazine's most favorite couple, which had included a nice spread in the magazine. "Me and Warren, we're just happy in our obscurity." She watched as Kerry smiled over at her new husband, who was dancing in the middle of the floor with a few of his family members.

Obscurity is not something that she and Elijah were able to enjoy, Nia mused as she found him dancing with Warren. After the reunion episode came out, there was a wave of shock as people realized that Elijah and Lily had called off the wedding. It was only a little scandalous, especially since he'd posted the picture of him and Nia before it came out. But they made it clear that despite the naysayers who still wanted to believe Nia a home wrecker, that they were happy together. Lily had even become one of Nia's friends, folding into the group easily, and hitting it off as if she'd been part of the group for a while. Lily also made a mean Moscow mule, that Goldie loved so much she refused to drink anyone else's but hers on Girls Nights.

Nia's show, *Leagues of Hope*, had become a hit, already green lit for a second season even before the first was finished airing. Critics couldn't get enough of Nia's performance, calling her refreshing and dynamic, a rising start to watch. There was even talk of a few breakout awards for her once awards season rolled around, but that wasn't something she was *too* worried about. Lexi was all over it, making sure her schedule was full of work.

Elijah's career was as hot as ever, a few movies he'd film coming out to be wildly successful, solidifying him as the next Hollywood leading man, up there with the likes of Chris Evans and Michael B. Jordan. On top of that, early reviews of his new super hero film were positive, suggesting that more was still to come. Seeing Nia watching him from across the floor, Elijah gave her a slow smile that promised more to come for that evening.

Her parents were happy, especially Nigel, who told anyone and everyone who came into the restaurant that one of his daughters had an amazing show. He'd even started taking off Thursday nights when it aired to tape the shows at home, saving every piece of his daughter's success. Nia was happy that he was embracing it with open arms. Nigel had even begun taking Yaya's help more seriously, and the two of them were happily working together at his restaurants. Yaya had had so many great ideas, and it was always fun to see her pushing back at Nigel, who'd grumble, but eventually realize that she had a point.

Elijah started making his way to her, drawn as always to Nia's side no matter where she was.

"Seems like things are going well for you two." Kerry smiled, loving the chemistry that sparked between her two friends.

"Things are fantastic." She couldn't have asked for anything better suited for what she'd needed all this time. They moved in together a few months after dating, and though Nia was sad to leave Goldie, she had been ready to take that step with Elijah. They were growing, blending their lives together and figuring out what it all looked like.

Rebecca had been thrilled to have them together, and they'd started doing the occasional family dinners. She had become fast friends with Yolanda, and the two of them had ganged up on Nia and Elijah, demanding grand babies soon. Nia had laughed them off, but the idea of children with Elijah was tempting. Very tempting actually. Their relationship wasn't without it's bumps, but they'd always managed to come out stronger than before.

Stopping in front of them, Elijah smiled, taking Nia's hand in his. "Mind if I steal my favorite person away for a moment?" His eyes never left Nia's, and he dropped another kiss on her hand. He'd been doing it all day, taking her hand and leaving little trails of kisses along her knuckles and fingers.

"Don't mind me! Just bring her back in time for the bouquet toss." With a wink, Kerry made her way over to her husband, who swooped her up into his arms, bending her down into a dip before dancing with her around the dance floor.

As Elijah led her away, easily moving them through the crowd, Nia couldn't help the little sigh of happiness that escaped. They broke away, heading down towards the beach. "Where are you taking me?"

"I wanted to show you something." He was more cryptic than usual, stealing her further and further away from the crowd. "Come away with me, just for a little while."

They walked along the beach, their bare feet sifting through the cool sand. In the distance, Nia could see some sort of structure, dimly lit from within. It was a beach cabana, filled with decadent cushioned chairs that had rose petals strewn around and an ice bin that held a bottle of chilling champagne. Around the tent, small candles were lit, emitting a soft, romantic glow. Elijah drew her inside, a secretive smile on his face.

"What's all of this?" Her heart pounding, she accepted Elijah's help to sit in one of the chairs, before he settled next to her. He leaned down, pressing a soft kiss on her lips.

"If you'd asked me a few years ago if I'd thought I'd be happily with someone, I would have laughed. I wasn't ever expecting anything like this."

"That's reassuring." Nia said with a smile.

"But the reason why I wouldn't have expected it, is that I hadn't found anyone who was even close to how amazing and beautiful you are. I knew I hadn't appreciated it way back in college, but missing you, those first few years, made me realize just how unique and precious you are to me. And then to think, I almost went and messed it all up for something so trivial as a dating show."

"We're past that now," Nia said softly, taking his hands in hers.

"We are. And this past year with you has been one of the most happy years of my life."

Elijah got down to one knee, pulling a small box out of his pocket. "I can't see myself without you in my future. You're in everything I want to do, everywhere I want to go - you're part of me in a way that I never want to leave any doubt, for anyone, how I feel about you." He opened the box, revealing a pear-shaped diamond ring that caught and reflected back the dim light. She could feel small tears making their way down her face, so full to bursting with happiness that she couldn't contain.

"I love you so much, Nia, that the thought of living any life without you in it leaves me cold. And I wanted to know if you would take this step with me- "

"Yes, of course! Eli, I love you, adore you." She pulled him up to his feet, throwing her arms around his neck for a passionate kiss. "I'm sorry for interrupting your speech, it was beautiful, but I wanted to tell you yes as soon as possible." He laughed, wrapping his arms around her, spinning her around before setting her gently back on her feet.

"As long as you said yes, the rest of it doesn't matter."

"I'll keep saying yes, as long as I'm with you."

Elijah grinned on her lips, before pressing in for another deeper kiss, full of promise, signaling his devotion and care for her. He broke the kiss, to slide the ring on her finger. It sparkled, a perfect fit, and he lifted her hand again, kissing her fingers.

"Is that why you kept kissing my hand all day?" Nia wondered as their fingers laced together. "You were planning this?"

"I was picturing my ring there," Elijah said with a little grin. "I couldn't help myself."

"That is hot." Nia looked at him, then down at the benches, figuring they could take both of their body weight. Elijah caught her look and smiled, drawing her back into his arms.

"That will have to wait. I made a promise to have you back." He trailed kisses along her jawline, making Nia moan before pulling away.

"Fine. I'm going to jump you anyway once we're back in our room."

"I'd expect nothing less." He held her, and they watched the waves crash gently on the shore. Nia looked up at the man holding her, thrilled to think of what the future might hold for the two of them.

It had been a bumpy ride, but they were here now. And what a place it was to be.

THE END

About the Author

Courtney Mariah works in the not always glamorous side of film production, where she stares at doors and gets people coffee. A graduate of New York University, Courtney now lives in sunny Los Angeles, in her brick walled apartment with no air conditioning, a few healthy plants, and the coziest reading chair in existence.

Visit her online at www.writingsonthewalls.com and on Instagram at instagram.com/courtneyorcoco.

Made in the USA
Columbia, SC
27 November 2020